KINGDOM IN CHAINS

J.W. ZULAUF

KINGDOM IN CHAINS
Kingdom in Chains - Book 1

FIRST EDITION SOFTCOVER
ISBN: 1622533526
ISBN-13: 978-1-62253-352-7

Editor: Deb Hartwell
Interior Designer: Lane Diamond

www.EvolvedPub.com
Evolved Publishing LLC
Butler, Wisconsin, USA

Printed in Book Antiqua font.

INTRODUCTION

Thank you so much for picking up *Kingdom in Chains*, and welcome to the Kingdom of Kuldaire. I've been slowly piecing together this world for some time now, the story having been on my mind for nearly three and a half years. To see it come together is an incredible feeling for me.

To keep this brief, I'll leave you with a fun fact about the map, a thank you, and guide you to my website for more information about Kuldaire and all things JWZ.

I was born at Lake Tahoe. If you're not familiar with it, allow me to summarize and just say it's easily one of the most beautiful places in the world. That place holds a significant place in my heart. In fact, I'm certain my heart could be the very shape of it. This leads me to my fun fact.

I took a topographical map of Lake Tahoe, flipped it on its side, and used that as the outline for Kuldaire. I mapped everything out for perfect measure, and all the lakes and ponds surrounding this beautiful place have shifted to islands and other land masses. Point is, when you look at this piece of land—Kuldaire—know that it's so much more than a generic land mass. It was created with the love I feel for the very place I'm from.

If you visit my website (www.JWZulauf.com), I'll continue to update items and expand the world outside of this book.

Again, welcome to the Kingdom of Kuldaire, thank you for stopping by, and I hope to see you again soon!

JWZ
10 May 2017

THE KINGDOM OF

KULDAIRE

CAPE CRASHWATER
WHARF
LOTHIAN
LUVIAN
PROCTOR
BLACKWOOD FOREST
BLACKWOOD LAKE
MOLTEN EYE
WARSHIRE
MEZZOAH
WEMILAT
TRADER'S RUN
DESOLATION WASTELAND
SKELETON COAST

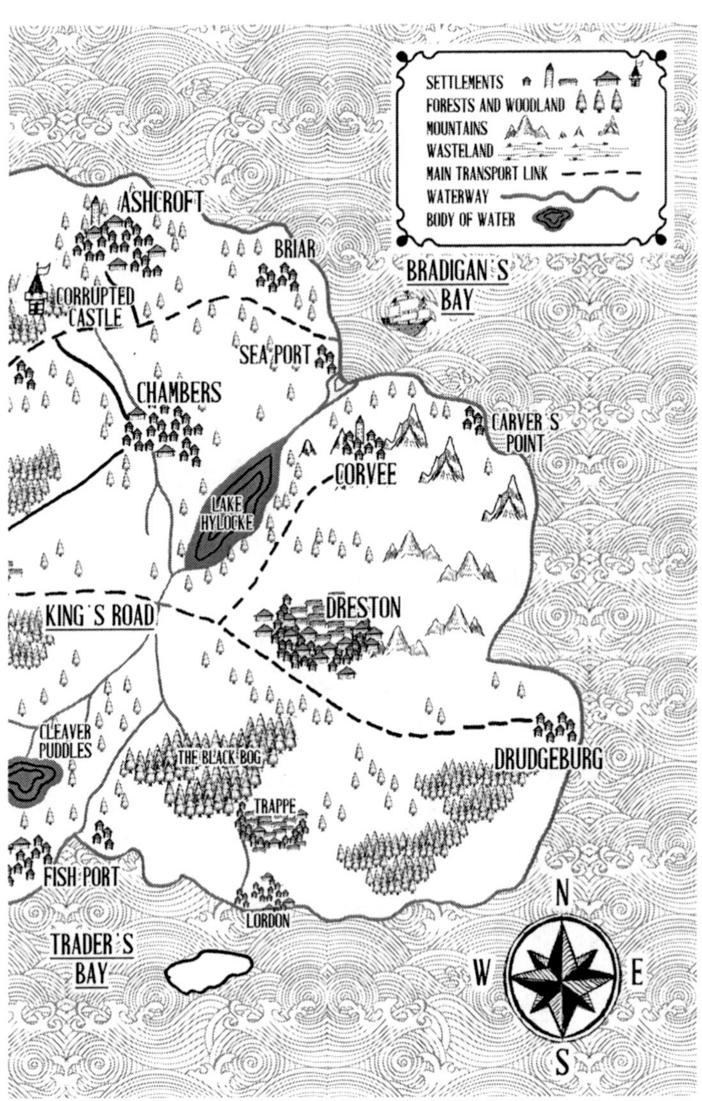
SETTLEMENTS
FORESTS AND WOODLAND
MOUNTAINS
WASTELAND
MAIN TRANSPORT LINK
WATERWAY
BODY OF WATER
ASHCROFT
BRIAR
BRADIGAN'S BAY
CORRUPTED CASTLE
SEA PORT
CHAMBERS
CARVER'S POINT
CORVEE
LAKE HYLOCKE
DRESTON
KING'S ROAD
CLEAVER PUDDLES
THE BLACK BOG
DRUDGEBURG
TRAPPE
FISH PORT
LORDON
TRADER'S BAY
N
W
E
S

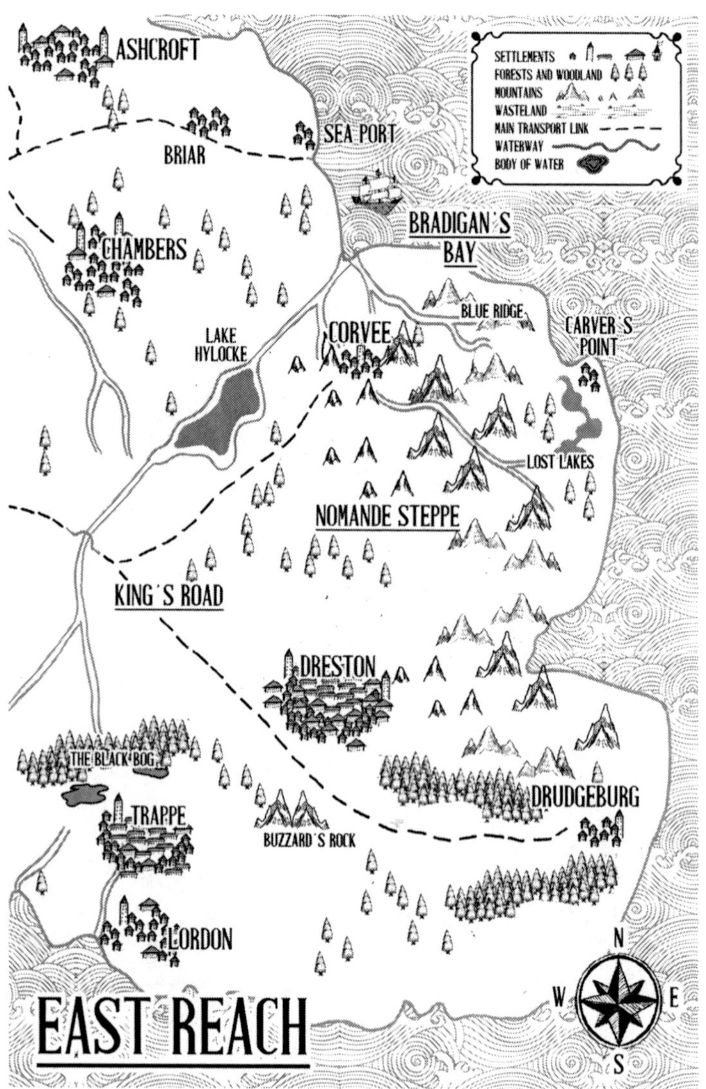
ASHCROFT
SETTLEMENTS
FORESTS AND WOODLAND
MOUNTAINS
WASTELAND
MAIN TRANSPORT LINK
WATERWAY
BODY OF WATER
SEA PORT
BRIAR
CHAMBERS
BRADIGAN'S BAY
BLUE RIDGE
CARVER'S POINT
CORVEE
LAKE HYLOCKE
LOST LAKES
NOMANDE STEPPE
KING'S ROAD
DRESTON
THE BLACK BOG
TRAPPE
BUZZARD'S ROCK
DRUDGEBURG
LORDON
N
W
E
S
EAST REACH

Chapter 1 – A New Set of Rules

Barloc and seven other slaves marched through the outer gatehouse of Drudgeburg, an old castle at the end of East Reach. The temperature chilled as they entered the castle grounds, and the familiar sense of dread washed over him at the thought of being sold to a new owner. They pulled a wooden palanquin barely large enough for the slaver sitting atop, the cart's chipped wheels wobbling with each rotation. Old rusted chains connected them in two rows of four, yielding only a yard of space between their shoulders. A handful of guards and another cart remained outside the keep.

A man in a green woolen cloak stepped in their path and signaled for them to stop. "Greetings!" His black hair hung to his shoulders in straight, sharp lines, and white peppered his dark beard. His gray eyes resembled storm clouds, and a mixture of scars and age lines traveled across his right cheek.

When he spoke, a row of surprisingly white teeth flashed in the sun. "And to whom do I owe the pleasure?"

The slaver's nasally voice carried over their shoulders as the reigns connecting their chains slackened. "Martin, my... lord.... *You* are Lord Harbor, leader of Drudgeburg?"

Barloc turned to better view the interaction. Martin eyed Lord Harbor from head to toe, and somehow Barloc knew what the slaver was thinking. Traditionally, lords adorned themselves in fancy armor or exotic garb, but this man wore a simple woolen cloak that floated an inch above the ground. His hands, covered with black leather gloves, rested on his crossed arms.

"The one and only." Lord Harbor bowed, not removing his eyes from the slaver.

Martin scoffed and glanced from Lord Harbor to his surroundings.

Barloc used the brief distraction to accomplish the same. The keep stood tall before him, the walls fusing with the sky. The courtyard stretched away on both sides. Six thatched, windowless buildings lined the curtainwall, three on each side of the front gatehouse. Dozens of slaves worked on various tasks around the yard: two men laid hay along one of the rooftops; more than a handful tended a small square of crops; and a tall man in a leather apron beat a hammer against a piece of glowing steel atop an anvil. Guards dressed in all black paced back and forth, surveying the labor, ignoring the arrival of Martin and his cargo.

Lord Harbor smiled and cleared his throat, drawing the attention back to him. "How fares your travels?"

"As well as one could hope, I suppose," Martin said, his jowls wiggling as he spoke. "We were caught in a storm. It didn't bother me much, but this filthy rabble seemed miserable holding the tarp above us." The slaver smiled, revealing crooked and yellowing teeth. "How about you, my lord? How have these days been treating you?"

"Oh, normal, for all that matters. It's tough to keep an eye on so many." Lord Harbor lifted his arms. "Say, you wouldn't want to sell me one of your vanguard?" He leaned forward slightly, looking past Slaver Martin to the guards outside the castle.

Martin's smile fell into a straight line. He wiped sweat from his lip. "I don't sell *free* men, my lord."

"Of course not." Lord Harbor waved the conversation away and stepped toward Barloc, the first of the eight slaves. "I would never think you so inhumane. I was merely commenting on my lack of trusting hands." Lord Harbor moved between them, ducking under their chains, inspecting the manacles. "Whose markings are these, Slaver Martin?"

"You don't have to style me Slaver. Martin will do fine, and it's a mixed bag. Some were Lord Rhotec Helory's. He needed coin to repair winter damages. Some were picked up from the dungeons, and others were traded as we went... and then the story was told." The slaver spread his hands out as if that phrase explained it all.

Lord Harbor lifted his hand to his chin. "The thing is, you *are* a slaver, and your name *is* Martin, so, therefore, you *are* Slaver Martin, is this not so? Also, you don't have the right to address me in any tone you please, for you're on my land, and I'm the man purchasing the king's merchandise. Yes?"

Martin's jaw dropped.

The slaves drew a collective breath and held it.

Barloc's muscles tightened, waiting for the snap of the whip, but it never came. *Only King Sclavus has the authority to speak to a slaver with such indignation, especially some upstart noble at the edge of civilization.* Barloc watched Lord Harbor closely. *The road must have stolen the slaver's vigor,* he thought. *More like drained his purse.*

Martin cleared his throat. "My apologies, my lord. It's been a long journey, as you can imagine."

"I can hardly imagine. I don't travel. I get to live here in the comfort of my castle while men like you do all the hard work." Lord Harbor smiled again and moved to the front of the slaves, his cloak fluttering with each step. "But it's said that slavers are the backbone of the kingdom, which is why you're paid so well.... Speaking of which, what *is* the price for these men?"

"These *slaves,*" Martin emphasized the word, "are fifteen gold coins for the lot."

Lord Harbor glanced between the first two.

Barloc met his eyes and quickly looked down.

"Fifteen is high. Is the king inflating the cost for good labor?"

"I can't do anything about that, now can I?"

"No, I suppose not, but let's say the king only requested twelve for the lot, the same price it's been for three moons, and you added a few to further your own pockets. Surely he sent orders with these fine slaves, and I don't doubt for a moment that you can read, Slaver Martin, but I must insist." Lord Harbor's open palm materialized in front of him, inches from Barloc's chest.

The certainty that Martin's whip would graze his ear on its journey to split open Lord Harbor's skin kept Barloc's muscles and shoulders tight, but when it didn't, he chanced another glance back.

Martin's cheeks flushed as he wiped his lips with his arm and opened a worn purse strapped to the side of the carriage. He withdrew two rolled parchments, both with the king's seal: red wax with two intertwined manacles. After inspection, he clapped his hands and laughed. "Look at that. I seem to have mixed up my orders. Yours is, in fact, twelve gold coins."

Lord Harbor smiled. "Of course, and your ability to read through a sealed and rolled parchment is impressive."

Martin withdrew his whip and snapped it forward, striking the closest slave's back. Blood misted the air. "What are you waiting for, scum?"

The parchment traveled down the row of slaves until it passed to Lord Harbor's hand, where it vanished inside his cloak.

"And my coin?" Martin now held his palm out before him.

Lord Harbor produced a small sack, opened it, and counted out twelve coins. He closed the bag and sent it floating hand to hand until it dropped into Martin's grasp.

The slaver tucked the coins into his purse. "Let this filth attach me to the other sleigh outside, and I will be on my way." He lazily lifted a hand and waved. A moment later, three armored men guided the other cart and its eight slaves down the bridge and into position.

Martin gripped his whip and pulled back, ready to strike the slaves, but before he could, Lord Harbor had withdrawn his own and sent it flying between the two rows. The whip wrapped around Martin's wrist and pulled taught.

The slaves spread apart as far as their chains would allow, gasping.

Blood crawled down Martin's arm. He reached out with his free hand and uncoiled the snakelike whip, watching it slither away. "You dare attack a servant of the king?"

Lord Harbor flipped his cloak back, revealing black leather armor, and clipped the whip to his side. "You dare come on my land and presume to speak to me any way you please, lie about the king's cost, then attempt to assault *my* slaves?" He crossed his arms. "Release them and leave, Slaver Martin. The need to endure your presence has expired."

Martin rubbed his wrist, then wiped blood on his pants.

Two more guards rode into the castle, hands on their steel. They stopped next to Martin and the other three men. "You'll find my guards are very cautious."

Lord Harbor slipped two fingers in his mouth and whistled. Feet shuffled all around the entrance where guards appeared, pointing their bows down at Martin and his men. "I'll also find that your guards favor their lives over your coin."

Sweat leaked profusely down Slaver Martin's face and into his eyes. "With slavers vanishing this far east, and this blatant disrespect, you'll never see me return."

"I wouldn't be too sure of that, Slaver Martin. In fact, you can't be sure about much these days."

Martin pursed his lips and shook his head, beads of sweat dripping into his lap. "I will tell the king of this. Now, what are you waiting for? Turn this cart around, and let's be off!"

No one moved. The slaver's guards held their positions. The slaves all watched, and Lord Harbor stood with his arms crossed.

Martin slammed his fists down on either side of him. "Now! Get this swine off my cart, connect me to the other sleigh, and let's move!"

Martin's guards dismounted at once, and within seconds, they unhinged the sold slaves, dropped the chains to the ground, and connected the two palanquins. The carts jolted forward as the slaves pulled onward, and the guards remounted and fell into the march.

Lord Harbor stepped into the center of the entrance and waved his hand. The portcullis lowered shut, but before it did, he faced the slaves and considered each one, walking slowly in front of them.

Two hooded figures emerged from the inner gatehouse and made their way toward the new arrivals.

Lord Harbor waved to one of the nearby guards, a bearded man in a green cloak, and pointed at the slaves. "Remove that chain linking them together so they can line up properly."

Barloc couldn't help but notice the change in Lord Harbor's accent. He had spoken proper and clean when dealing with the slaver, but now, the southern drawl of the inlands tacked onto the ends of his words.

The guard quietly removed the chain linking them together, and once they slipped free, Barloc fell in line with the other seven slaves.

Lord Harbor paced, his arms hidden inside his green cloak. "Things will work differently here. There is a new set of rules. You'll address me as Lord Harbor or my lord." He stopped suddenly and raised his voice, "How can you possibly see me if you're staring at your feet?"

The two hooded figures arrived, taking their places on either side of Lord Harbor. He nodded at them. "Now, where was I? Ah, yes. You'll address me as Lord Harbor. This large brute to my right is Sir Vigoronious, styled Sir Vigor. Address him as Sir Vigor only. He hates the title Master and Vigoronious is an awful job on the tongue."

Sir Vigor stood a foot taller than Lord Harbor, and even under the large, green cloak, he was as thick as both Harbor and the unnamed figure together. He drew back his hood with gloved hands, revealing a shaved head and oily, black skin. Two thick eyebrows lined his wide eyes, and a goatee faded into a design of three lines progressing up each cheek. A scar crept from under his facial hair, explaining the unique pattern. The damaged skin prevented the growth of hair and the opposite cheek was groomed to match. A hooped earring hung from his right ear, and two small flaps dangled where one used to be in his left.

"And this is Madam Constance." Lord Harbor directed his hand to his left.

Madam Constance drew back her hood.

Out of habit, Barloc glanced away but not because he wanted to. It wasn't often he'd seen a woman this close, and out of all the women it could have been, she was easily the fairest. Long, brown hair billowed past her shoulders, and she, too, wore the same black leather gloves as Lord Harbor.

Her soft, olive complexion blossomed from beneath her hood, revealing high cheekbones that ended just below two almond-shaped, green eyes.

She scanned the line of slaves, slowing enough to meet their gazes. When she arrived at Barloc, he stared at his feet, warmth climbing into his cheeks.

"These are two members of my council. First and foremost, you will respect them, hopefully without too much trouble. All of the Green Cloaks are masters in one sense or another, so mind yourselves around them." Lord Harbor moved to the first slave in the line. "What's your name?"

The slave blinked rapidly. "I'm sorry, my lord?"

"Your name, what is it?"

The man's eyebrows knitted together and he didn't respond.

"Did I confuse you? Don't you have a name?" Lord Harbor persisted.

Still, the man remained silent.

Lord Harbor pivoted around and returned to his place between Sir Vigor and Madam Constance. "Let's make this clear now. I'm not playing games with you, as some may have in the past. When I speak, I'm direct. My words are law. If I ask your name, don't fear retaliation. Simply answer the question. The only warrant for retaliation is insubordination.

"I'm a reasonable man. Now, down the line, I want your names. First and last if you have one." He pointed to the slave on the left end.

The man spoke, but his voice broke as if he hadn't used it for some time. "A-archer, my lord. My name's Archer Redkin."

"Next," Lord Harbor said.

Madam Constance held a piece of parchment where she scratched down each name.

Barloc did all he could to avoid dropping his attention to the ground, away from his new master's eyes. "Barloc, my lord."

"No last name?"

"Maghild, my lord. Barloc Maghild."

"Thank you." As the words left Lord Harbor's mouth, the slaves straightened up and cast subtle glances to one another.

Thank you? Barloc closed his eyes and lowered his head as if he were hit. He waited a moment before lifting his gaze.

Madam Constance scribbled down each name upon announcement until they had all been recorded, and the parchment vanished into her cloak.

Lord Harbor clapped. "Well, that will do it for records. You've come from all over the kingdom. The saying 'all is fair in trading bodies' has led you to be captured, disrespected, and treated like scum. You've been thrown from hand to hand like no more than a game of Stone Toss. The king's slavery doesn't target one, but all. Sclavus doesn't care what color your skin is, who your parents are, or where you were born. If you can't produce the coin to cover the king's tax, you lose your freedom.... But this can end here for you." He slipped his hands into his cloak. "If you follow my instructions, you can be free in thirty days. If you don't, you'll be here until you decide to follow orders."

Barloc scanned the row of slaves. All of them appeared to react in different manners: some opened their mouths in shock; some tightened their jaws wearing unbelieving looks; some held fear etched into their features.

"You've no reason to believe me. You should question everything I'm saying. If you've learned anything up to this point in your seemingly useless lives, it's that you can't trust a soul outside your own.

"Every day will be filled with labor. You'll be given a new quest each morning. Upon completion, you'll be rewarded and moved onto the next. Your wrist manacles will be removed after the completion of your tenth consecutive day, your legs on the twentieth, and your freedom comes on the thirtieth.

"If you can't complete the quest given to you, you'll be sent back to day one and start from the beginning. We currently have one man who refuses to make it past his thirty days. Maybe he's afraid of freedom after so many years of enslavement, maybe he's simply dumb as a stone.

"If you strike a guard, you'll be brought back to day one. If you run, you'll be made an example of, and that's not something you'll like. If you speak without being spoken to... well, you get the idea.

"You'll be given a new name, a loin cloth, sandals, and nothing more. As you complete your assigned tasks, you will earn more clothing."

Lord Harbor addressed his two counterparts. "Have I missed anything?"

Madam Constance and Sir Vigor shook their heads.

"Very well." Lord Harbor turned back to the slaves. "I don't care about your past. I don't care about the guilt of your old lives, your lost loves, or your families. Here, everyone starts fresh, and they work their way to freedom. Do you have any questions regarding my expectations? This will be the only time I'll ask, so speak now."

Silence filled the air between them until Barloc stepped forward. "Do you speak truly about freedom, my lord? If we complete your quests, we will be freed?"

Lord Harbor nodded. "I'm a man of my word. You just have to follow the rules."

Barloc lowered his head and returned to his spot in line.

"In that case, men. Welcome to Drudgeburg."

Chapter 2 – Initiation

Lord Harbor's voice crashed through Barloc's mind, followed by a wave of images: *I'm a man of my word.* He pictured home, though home had been destroyed, and talking with his father, though his father was dead.

He compared himself to the slaves standing down the line. They ranged in age, color, and health, and he hated that he'd just traveled across a kingdom alongside them yet knew nothing about their lives.

Barloc stood an average height compared to the other seven, and his skin held the same almond color as his eyes. His facial hair grew only on his lip and chin, and his scars and cuts from being whipped lined his back and arms.

"Follow me." Madam Constance interrupted his thoughts, stepping past the line of slaves.

Sir Vigor took the rear, and together they advanced toward the pavilions lining the inside wall of the outer bailey.

Chains scraped the gravel with each small step. The slaves moved in unison, a practiced march from tugging Slaver Martin across the kingdom.

Horses brayed from the stables across the yard while the steady banging of the blacksmith's hammer rang in the air. The murderous caw of blackbirds called down from the ramparts, and behind him, different colored flags poked up from the ground. Beyond those, in the dead center of the yard, stretched an old table with stools lining one side.

At the first pavilion, a patchwork of lumber, pieced together by various cloth and rope, stood a guard in black leather. He gripped a metal tool in his fist beside a waist-high barrel, and on the table behind him sat a small pile of manacles.

"Line up." Madam Constance withdrew a parchment from her cloak. "First order of business is replacing these manacles. Lord Harbor is kind. He has never been one to brand his slaves. After, I will assign your new names. This will be the only name used. I advise you to remember it. Failure will only hinder your progress here at Drudgeburg."

The slaves lined up while Madam Constance used the table to scribble on her parchment. She cleared her throat, drawing everyone's attention. "Because you were purchased on this fourth day of May, a red-letter day for the Nativity of Saint Mirillion Jace, you will be coded with the letters MJ, and then your number, one through eight."

The guard knelt in front of the first slave and removed his fetters with ease. After dropping the old chains into the barrel, he clasped the new manacles around the slave's ankles.

Madam Constance guided the slave toward Sir Vigor, who stood off to the side. As he walked by her, she announced his new name as MJ-1.

On his turn, Barloc watched the process, and by the end, he understood how the bindings functioned. First, the guard fixed a pointed pin atop the dowel and tapped it with a hammer. Once the pin sat secured, he placed a pair of wide-mouthed pliers around the manacle, and upon squeezing with both hands, the pin shot out of the bottom, breaking it free.

Madam Constance announced his name as he walked by. "MJ-7."

MJ-7. The name sounded empty, made up. His father brushed across his memory, and as he walked toward Sir Vigor, he vowed to never forget his name, no matter how hard they tried to take it away from him. His new chains allowed a better stride and the metal used was much lighter than his old ones.

When MJ-8 finished, he joined the rest of the slaves, followed by Madam Constance.

Sir Vigor leaned down so she could whisper in his ear. When he pulled back, he nodded and promptly departed.

Barloc watched him go—a tower with legs.

"Follow me." Madam Constance turned her back on the line of newly shackled slaves.

Barloc imagined one of the slaves racing up behind her and wrapping his hands around her throat. *Why would she turn her back on eight new slaves?*

How easy would it be to take her down and amass the others to rise against the masters? He braced himself, fearful that they may act, but shook the idea away once he saw that they all moved at the normal, broken pace. Guilt washed over him at even thinking such a thing, especially after all these promises of freedom, but he also knew that thoughts of hope were poisonous.

They arrived at the next pavilion where another guard, also clad in black leather, stood in front of a table with a stack of folded clothes and another of sandals. Next to him, a steel barrel blazed with a fire that licked up the sides and danced in the air. At their approach, the guard raised his arm and silently directed MJ-1 to the fire.

Madam Constance stepped to the table and scribbled without looking up from her parchment. "Remove your clothes and burn them."

The other slaves watched as the guard grabbed MJ-1's shoulder and forced him to face the fire. He took a blade from the table and carved off the slave's clothes until he stood naked. Cinders floated through the air like fireflies as his old clothes fell into the flames.

Barloc only felt so bad for him, knowing his turn was six slaves away.

The guard handed MJ-1 a dirty loincloth and worn-down sandals.

The slave lingered with the loincloth gripped in his fist, and as if a voice inside calmed him, his jaw slackened, and he slipped it on. When the guard motioned for the next slave, MJ-1 took his place beside Madam Constance, adjusting his new clothing.

Madam Constance watched indifferently as each slave went through the process, and on his turn, Barloc stepped in front of the fire, embarrassed.

He had never been naked in front of a woman outside of his mother, and that was when he was a small boy. When the guard handed him his new clothes, he shot a glance over at Madam Constance, who watched with still features. He looked away quickly and donned his loincloth and sandals before his old clothes caught fire.

After the final slave had been processed, Madam Constance turned away from the pavilion. "Follow me."

The slight comfort Barloc experienced when he received a longer chain and lighter fetters had deserted him alongside the weight of his old clothes. As dingy and worn as they were, they were his. Now he walked nearly naked and vulnerable.

They arrived at the next pavilion to find another guard holding a straight blade. One by one, the guard shaved the slaves' heads and faces.

Barloc's new masters had wasted no time in breaking them down. They made it a point to slap on new manacles, strip away their identities, and burn everything they owned. The words Lord Harbor had spoken about freedom faded fast.

At the next tent, the smell of food sent Barloc's stomach into somersaults. He approached two tables with four stools, and at each spot, a russet steel plate supported healthy portions of meat, potatoes, and vegetables. *Where are the eight guards waiting to eat the food in front of us, to add insult to injury?*

Madam Constance stood before the slaves, her face a mask. When she passed over Barloc, he caught and held her gaze. He didn't want to appear weak after having been stripped of everything, but in the end she won because his eyes turned back to the food.

She lifted her hand and waved it over the tables. "Your day is far from done. Eat, drink."

The slaves stared at one another as if waiting for someone else to move, to set off the trap.

Barloc tentatively took the first step, and when none of the guards rushed into the tent, he took another. By the third, the other slaves followed.

Madam Constance withdrew her parchment and sat down on a stool at the end of the first table, facing the slaves.

Barloc wolfed down his food, not taking the time to enjoy the flavor. The meat sloughed from the bone, and the potatoes had been softened with goat's milk, a taste reserved for free men. On the last bite, he allowed a moment to savor the juices.

One of the slaves whispered into Barloc's ear. "Meals like this? I'll never leave."

He quickly looked up at Madam Constance, who continued to watch silently from her stool.

The slave had taken the first step of his own, because full bellies made brave men, and the others began speaking to one another in soft voices.

Barloc watched Madam Constance scribble once more. He ignored the others and remained fixated on his plate, enjoying the warm food in his stomach.

A few minutes later, Sir Vigor emerged from the inner gatehouse, followed by three guards.

Madam Constance pointed behind Barloc. "Why didn't you finish your food, MJ-5? Surely you're hungry."

The slave shifted in his seat.

"Did you eat a big meal before arriving? Is that why you didn't touch your plate?"

He cleared his throat. "I... I don't feel much like eating after what you just did to me."

Madam Constance crossed her arms. "And what is it that I did to you?"

MJ-5 ran his hand over his freshly shaven head. "I loved my hair. That hair was all I had left, and you took it from me. So," he pushed the plate to the edge of the table, "I'm not hungry."

Madam Constance nodded, quickly removed her parchment, scribbled on it, and stowed it away. "Very well. Follow me." She turned her back once more and together they marched across the yard, arriving at a large square outlined by a low, wooden fence.

"Line up." Madam Constance took her spot next to Sir Vigor.

The slaves fell into formation on one side of the square with the three guards on the other.

Sir Vigor removed a haversack from his back and threw it in the center. On impact, the bag blew open, sending up a cloud of dust. When it settled, wooden training weapons scattered the ground.

Barloc scanned the pile, noting a staff, shield, sword, and many other weapon types he'd never seen before.

Madam Constance pointed at the first slave. "MJ-1, step into the battle square."

The slave hesitated but crossed the small barrier. His dark skin gleamed in the sunlight. Scars covered his torso and back, and an old slaver brand bubbled up from his right bicep. Tattoos in tribal designs danced around his shoulders. His muscles bulged with each movement, like thick cords underneath his skin.

The closest guard stepped into the square and moved to the weapons, grabbing the sword. Before MJ-1 could react, the guard struck the slave on the shoulder, knocking him off balance. The slave dove at the bag, seizing a mace, but the guard slammed his wooden sword across his back.

MJ-1 rolled, gasping in pain. When the guard pulled up the sword to attack again, the slave lunged at his ankles and brought him down. He gripped the mace and went to swing it at the guard's face, but before he could, another guard jumped into the square and removed it from his hand.

MJ-1 rolled to his knees and lifted his arms over his head.

The defeated guard stood and returned to his spot outside the arena.

"MJ-1, back of the line. MJ-2, enter the battle square."

The second guard remained, wielding the mace he had removed from the slave. MJ-2 didn't stand a chance. The guard wouldn't even let him near the weapons, and finally, when the slave tried to dive under him, it ended with the mace smashing into the back of his head.

MJ-2 fell hard, his face connecting with the dirt, blood splattering on impact. All three guards removed the motionless slave.

Fury burned inside Barloc. *First, they build our hopes up with the prospect of freedom and then tear it all down. Now they beat us into the dirt.*

The guards alternated each fight. MJ-3 and MJ-4 fell quickly. When MJ-5 stepped in, Barloc noticed that the man couldn't fight. His arms visibly shook, and his knees wobbled as the guard moved slowly around the square.

The guard noticed this, too, and allowed the slave to grab a weapon. MJ-5 made a feeble attempt that ended with one solid crack across the back of his skull.

MJ-6 landed a couple blows against the guard, but he fell to the same fate.

Barloc sighed and entered the square.

The next guard grabbed a quarterstaff. He moved as if he desired the skill but lacked the practice.

After watching six battles, Barloc could tell by the guards' blocky movements and poor posture that they weren't well trained. He remained still, waiting for the guard's advance, and when it finally came, he slid under his attacker and grabbed the shield from the pile. In one swift motion, he slipped his arm through the holds and parried a blow.

Five more attacks followed, and five times Barloc dodged or parried. A second guard entered the fight. Though much harder, Barloc managed to evade their blitzes. When he felt his energy wane, he ran to the opposite side of the square and dropped his shield, kneeled to the ground, and bowed his head.

Both guards approached on either side.

Stars bloomed across Barloc's vision and he leaned forward, barely catching himself. Another hit bashed against his back, but he remained kneeling. More blows followed, each striking harder than the previous, and after seven solid hits, he fell forward.

"Enough!" Sir Vigor's voice boomed like a cannon blast. The ground reverberated through Barloc's chest.

The guards immediately dropped their weapons and left the square.

Barloc pushed to his feet. Every bit of him wanted to glance at Sir Vigor and Madam Constance, but he fought the urge. Instead, he fell in line with the other defeated slaves.

MJ-8 entered the ring. He placed his hands behind his back, a symbol that he would not attack, but the guard still advanced, swinging his sword viciously. The slave managed to dodge three of the attacks, though the fourth caught him in the leg and brought him to his knees.

The guard slammed two solid blows onto MJ-8's back before tossing the weapon aside and exiting the square.

Finally, Barloc allowed himself to glance at Sir Vigor and Madam Constance.

After scribbling on her parchment, she stashed it back into her cloak and whispered into Sir Vigor's ear.

Sir Vigor pointed at the guards. "You two, take MJ-2 to the Healers, and you, gather the weapons." He led the three guards and MJ-2 toward a series of small cots, just past the stables, while Madam Constance directed the seven bruised slaves to what appeared to be the final tent.

As they marched across the bailey, the deep sound of a slave horn bellowed through the air, and with it, the slaves around the yard stopped working and lined up at each of the thatched buildings.

When they arrived at the final tent, Madam Constance withdrew her parchment and said to the guard, "Take those five." She identified everyone but Barloc and MJ-8.

Panic stormed his chest and mind. He knew he'd gone too far, and now he'd pay. Sweat formed across his forehead and palms.

Once the others left, only Barloc, MJ-8, and Madam Constance remained.

"MJ-7," she said. "Why didn't you fight in the battle square? Why did you let those guards beat you?"

"Lord Harbor said not to strike a guard, Madam."

Madam Constance smiled. To Barloc, it helped complete her beauty. Small creases lifted with her cheeks. "You *were* told this. Eight slaves were told the same thing. You and this sheep were the only two that listened." She pointed at MJ-8.

"MJ-7, you resisted nothing as we replaced your manacles. You moved quickly. You held your head high while your possessions were burned. You said nothing as we stripped you of everything. You didn't speak during the meal, and you didn't strike a guard in the battle square.

"This man kept his eyes on you. He saw you were quiet during the meal, so he, too, remained silent. He saw the beating you took and followed suit.... The point being that Lord Harbor gave all eight men the same, clear instructions. The first quest, which I thought obvious, was to make it through this day. Now those six will start over, and because we can't cut any more hair, burn their clothes, rename, or rebind them, they will spend tomorrow in the square until they learn what I consider to be quite obvious. You two move forward."

Chapter 3 – Becoming a Hero

The cot pressed hard against Barloc's back, and no matter which way he adjusted, the chains strapping his ankles to the top bunk bore into his bones. Each time he fell asleep, he woke from pains cutting across his back, legs, and arms. His muscles burned where the guards had struck him, and his head pulsed as if dehydrated.

He assumed his new master's plan was to make the slaves sore and tired, so when they finally received decent rest, they would feel thankful. This explained the beating they took in the battle square.

The slave horn bellowed, rattling the walls and bunks, jarring Barloc away from any chance of rest. The sound reminded him of Sir Vigor's voice.

As the horn's blare faded, two guards burst through the door and unlocked the slaves. Silently, everyone marched outside where they lined up in front of their bunkhouse.

Slaves and guards filled the courtyard. The sheer quantity of them overwhelmed Barloc. A long line of guards stood before the slaves, one for every three, each wearing the same black leather.

In the center of the courtyard, Madam Constance and Sir Vigor sat behind a long wooden table.

Sir Vigor bashed a mallet against a small gong. As the crash faded, the guards from the first bunkhouse led their slaves into a line in front of Sir Vigor. A second crash brought forth Barloc and the rest of the slaves from his bunkhouse. The others remained, waiting for their turn. As each slave approached the table, Sir Vigor and Madam Constance searched for their name on a parchment and assigned them their quests.

"Name?" Madam Constance asked, not raising her eyes.

"Ba... MJ-7, Madam."

Madam Constance flipped the parchment over. "Report to Master Sapper at the mine. Stand at the blue marker and wait for your escort."

Barloc walked around the table toward a series of markers poking up from the ground. Each slave around the blue marker wore different gear, a variation of tunics, sandals, pants, and gloves. Those with more gear also had slightly longer hair and scruff on their faces—signs that they'd progressed.

Another group of men formed around the green marker. Among them, Barloc noticed all the MJ slaves he'd entered Drudgeburg with. All except MJ-2, who had been injured in the battle square, and MJ-8, who had just joined him at the blue marker.

When Sir Vigor and Madam Constance finished processing the lines, the guards led their groups around the outer bailey. The blue group marched toward the portcullis, the exit.

Barloc surmised that his group consisted of twenty slaves with four guards on horseback, driving them forward. It wasn't until he stepped onto the gravel road that he noticed the weight of improper footwear. The jobs he would soon be forced to do in thin sandals worried him. If the small stones dug so deep while walking, how would the conditions of a mine fare?

They stopped before the gates of Drudgeburg. Slowly, the steel frame lifted, and when he passed through the barbican, he walked under two murder holes cut into the stone ceiling. Old oil stained the grates, and the thought that they had once been used sent a chill up his spine. He pictured being trapped in the small section while hot oil poured from above, burning him alive, melting his skin away.

The water in the moat lay stagnant with a green, oily film. Spikes made from thin trees poked out in every direction. Even climbing across them would prove difficult, and as he walked past, he noted the wood appeared freshly cut. Barloc thought it strange to have so many reinforcements at such a small keep. He'd seen at least thirty guards in the bailey that morning; to have such extravagant defenses made him wonder who they were trying to keep out. *Or in.*

"I'm Master Sapper!" a man standing at the end of the drawbridge bellowed, making his voice larger than it needed to be. His accent was almost as thick as he was, though he stood shorter than all the slaves. Something told Barloc that it wasn't fat underneath the green cloak.

The man's cheeks swallowed his beady, brown eyes, and when he spoke, black and yellow stains shared equal space across his teeth.

"Yer gonna load these carts with the stone blockin' a collapsed mine. Yer gonna work with a pickaxe and shovel." The man directed a hand to two large carts with a horse tethered to each. Beside them scattered more than twenty wheelbarrows, each with a shovel and a pickaxe resting inside. "We'll make one trip by noon, eat, and run the final load. Today *will* be hard."

Barloc suppressed a yawn and glimpsed back at the castle, the sleepless night weighing on him. Two towers stood tall like sentinels on both sides of the drawbridge. Arrow slits littered the walls, and the outer battlements ran tall and jagged like crooked teeth. Ivy meandered up a stone belfry, and though it had only been a day, he hadn't heard the bells and wondered if a vicar lived there. Another tower stood behind the belfry, higher than any other structure at the castle. Its thickness and spiraling windows suggested that rooms lined the inside walls.

Sapper climbed onto his horse. "Stay close." When he mounted, his cloak lifted just enough to reveal the bottom of his coiled whip. "For those who're new, ya may be back. As ya can see, we pull slaves from all over because work is work, and it needs to be done. The rules are a little different with me, ladies. If ya run, I'll kill ya. If ya fight, I'll kill ya. If ya do anything outside of transport stone, I might just kill ya. I don't have time to chase slaves. I have a hard job because I'm a hard man. Now, let's go!" Master Sapper led the way, followed by the caravan of slaves and the four mounted guards.

The sun beat down with a physical, hot weight, and between the pickaxe and the shovel, small blisters pushed through Barloc's calloused hands. Early on, one of the stones slipped from his grip and landed hard on his right foot. Blood seeped from underneath his big toenail.

Once the two carts were full, Master Sapper rushed the slaves to load stones into their wheelbarrows. He mounted his horse and rode in small circles around them. "Yer each responsible for yer own tools. If ya lose them, ya won't eat."

On the journey back to the castle, they moved sluggishly and in single file. Barloc spent his attention trying not to tip his wheelbarrow.

When they arrived, Master Sapper instructed the slaves to pile the stones on the left side of the moat. Dead-beaten grass circled the ground by Barloc's feet where he assumed old piles had recently been, and by the time the carts and barrows emptied, the stones stood taller than him. Once the last one had been placed, Sapper led the slaves to a large oak tree in front of the castle. After instructing them to sit, he sent one of the guards into Drudgeburg.

MJ-8 sat next to Barloc and cast him a tired look, which he ignored.

A few minutes later, the guard returned with a line of fully-clothed women slaves.

Barloc's mouth dropped open and his eyes grew wide. *Women in chains? Here?*

The women approached in a march of their own, their ankle fetters dancing across the ground, kicking up dust with each step. They wore what easily could have been a burlap potato sack turned into a dress of sorts, and filth covered their arms and cheeks. Their hair, too, had been cut short.

As they approached, Barloc clearly saw that their wrists were not bound. Proof of what Lord Harbor had promised walked toward him with trays of food in their hands.

Barloc's mouth watered at the sight of hot rice and vegetables. The moment the trays hit the slaves' hands, they devoured the food. When everyone finished, the guard guided the women back to the castle and Sapper commanded everyone to stand.

As they returned to the mines, Barloc thought on the women slaves. *How perfect was it that they showed up with food and without wrist manacles, right when we were so exhausted?*

These thoughts drove further into his mind when he began loading the carts a second time, and he decided it was just another piece in Lord Harbor's sick game. He wanted to break the slaves' hope and faith. He wanted them mindless, tired laborers.

They loaded the carts and wheelbarrows much slower the second time around, and Sapper made it clear how unhappy their progress made him. "I'll personally flog each of ya if we return after sundown!" He no longer sat under the tree. Instead, he rode on his horse, making his whip pop in their faces.

Barloc threw the final stone onto his wheelbarrow, and maybe because he knew it was the last, it seemed so much heavier than the rest; his legs quivered from fatigue.

The rest of the slaves topped off their piles as well, though while MJ-8 finished his, the unbalanced stack of stones toppled to the ground. With a loud bang, he lay half buried underneath the efforts of his labor. All around, the slaves stared, unmoving. Even Master Sapper remained still, watching with his arms across his lap, whip hanging by his side.

Barloc ran forward, adrenaline and concern erasing his fatigue. Grabbing at everything he could, he fought to clear the rubble from MJ-8. The heavy, jagged stones tore the nail from his pointer finger, but he pushed past the pain until he cleared enough to roll MJ-8 onto his back.

A soft clapping came from behind him. He faced Master Sapper, who remained on horseback. "Well, done, Hero. Ya saved another maggot's life!" He continued to clap. "Ya see this, ladies? We've got a hero." The slaves remained silent. "The only problem is... I never told ya to be a hero."

Master Sapper kicked over Barloc's cart. The rocks toppled with a loud crunch. "Ya may want to start fillin' those barrows." He smiled at Barloc. "If ya think ya don't like me now, see what happens when we return after sundown." He smiled again, showing every stained tooth in his mouth, and guided the horse back to the tree. "And if anyone helps them, may yer gods save ya."

Tears of frustration streamed down Barloc's face. His gaze shifted from MJ-8, who lay with his eyes moving back and forth behind closed lids, to the two scattered stone piles, and then the watching slaves. For only a moment, Barloc stared at Sapper, wishing for the strength to fight. Poisonous images barraged his mind. He caught his fists clenching as he pictured strangling Master Sapper with his own whip. Pains gained purchase as his adrenaline tapered. His fingers dug deep into his palms, pulling him from his trance.

Wasting no more time, Barloc flipped the wheelbarrows upright and loaded the rocks. He worked as fast as his failing strength allowed, though the sun descended with no regard for his duties.

Barloc placed the final stone on the cart once more and went to wake MJ-8. It wasn't until Barloc slapped him across his cheeks that he finally came to.

MJ-8 glanced at the row of watching slaves, to Sapper, the guards, and then the wheelbarrows before he understood what happened.

Barloc held a significant disdain toward the slave for not being stronger. He gripped the wheelbarrow's handles and waited for Sapper to mount.

The walk back proved to be long and relentless. Every hill or dip in the road acted as an obstacle, and the sun had long since fallen, which made it harder to guide the barrows.

After walking for a while, Sapper pulled his horse alongside Barloc. "Why did ya help the slave?"

Barloc ignored him.

Sapper cleared his throat and asked again, louder.

"What good would it have done leaving him under all that stone?"

Sapper considered the question and looped around the long line of slaves. "Ya won't make it ten days if ya play the hero. These people wouldn't spit in yer throat to keep ya alive. I could have ya back at day one, ya know?"

Barloc ignored his taunts and focused on the castle's towers looming ahead, his pace quickening at the sight.

Sapper shifted to Barloc's other side. "Do ya hear me? I can make it to where ya never succeed here. I bet I can have Lord Harbor make ya my personal servant."

Barloc slammed the wheelbarrow down and rounded on Sapper, who reached for his whip. The line of slaves and guards stopped, a few drawing in sharp breaths.

"What do you want from me?" Heat rose into Barloc's cheeks as he released all the rage he'd gathered since arriving at Drudgeburg. "What did I do wrong?"

Sapper began speaking, but Barloc cut him off. "Because I didn't watch a man die today, I'm being punished?"

Sapper moved his horse closer to Barloc, leaned down, and backhanded him, knocking him off his feet. "Yer being punished because ya think yer a hero, and yer not. Yer a slave and ya need to understand that." He leaned onto his elbows and peered into Barloc's eyes. "Why is it, out of twenty slaves, yer the problem?"

"He would've died!" As the words passed over his lips, he knew he'd gone too far. He stood, turned his back on Sapper, and lifted the wheelbarrow, figuring any damage was done. His punishment would now happen no matter what was said. When he took a step, he anticipated the burn from the whip.

Sapper rode down the line of slaves. "MJ-7 has given you all the honor of not eating a meal tonight. Ya can all thank the hero in yer own special ways." He rode back to the front of the line and stopped before Barloc. "This is going to be a rough journey for ya, MJ-7."

Barloc ignored him and focused on the castle, which appeared greatly different at night. An orange, effulgent glow surrounded the courtyard, and smaller ones lined the battlements, lighting it up like a beacon. Above Drudgeburg, the stars shined bright in the cloudless sky.

When they arrived, the slaves unloaded the stones into another pile. After, the group of slaves and guards silently followed Master Sapper, who hailed the gatehouse. The bridge lowered and they entered.

Sapper stopped and turned to Barloc. "This isn't over, Hero." He spoke to the guard inside. "Take them to their quarters. Make sure they don't eat, and if this one asks for a Healer," Sapper pointed to MJ-8, "send him directly to me."

The guards spread out, taking the different slaves to their respective bunkhouses. Barloc followed with MJ-8 by his side. *Now look what I've done.* He glanced over to MJ-8 who walked with his eyes on the ground. Cuts and scrapes lined his features and something terribly sad hid behind his eyes. *It's just not fair.*

The guard guided them to a different bunkhouse than the night before, and as he walked past the slaves already in their bunks, each one silently glared at Barloc and MJ-8, clenching their jaws in the dim torchlight. The men he'd arrived with stared at him, and what he saw in their eyes scared him more than anything Master Sapper could ever threaten him with. He saw broken men who resented MJ-8 and Barloc for making it one day closer to freedom while they took another long day of beating.

By the time the guard had clasped the manacles around his ankles, he'd realized that the unspoken bond between the slaves had broken, and all the MJ slaves he entered Drudgeburg with were now against him.

The guard double-checked his fetters and stopped for a moment. Their eyes connected, and he pumped his mouth open and closed repeatedly as if he had something to say, but after a moment, he only shook his head and walked away.

One final thought passed through Barloc's mind before exhaustion overcame him: *not just the masters... now the slaves, too.*

Chapter 4 – Another Day at the Mines

Master Sapper bore down on Barloc, snapping his whip, forcing him to run. A cacophony of chains rattled around him so loudly he attempted to jam his fingers into his ears and lost his balance, splitting his chin on the ground. When he looked up, faces floated in and out of the blanketing darkness: slaves he hadn't seen in years, each crying or screaming.

Barloc jumped to his feet and wiped the blood from his chin. The slaves approached him with their hands out, moaning like zombies. The whip cracked again, and at the same time, a blade appeared in his fist. He swung at the oncoming slaves, cutting each down into a pile before him. When he couldn't swing anymore, he lunged onto their backs and pushed as hard as he could, slipping on arms and legs and heads—anything to get away from Sapper.

A small ledge materialized above Barloc, and he knew it meant safety. The bodies shifted like broken ice on a pond, forcing him to lose his balance and drop his blade. Before he could jump, another figure appeared, its features bedimmed inside a green hood. Ignoring it, he lunged for the edge, but once he got to his feet, the clandestine figure grabbed Barloc and threw him back down the pile of bodies into Master Sapper's grasp. Sapper pulled him so close their noses touched, and when he opened his mouth, a deep and terrifying growl blasted out.

Barloc's eyes burst open, and he gasped, clawing at his chest where he was sure Sapper's hands had been only moments ago. The slave horn tapered off, and the weight from the manacles still wrapped around his ankles told him that it was just a dream. He rubbed his eyes, his muscles burning from the simple act of lifting his arms.

He still couldn't shake the images of Master Sapper while he waited in line at the sorting table. He focused on the ground, ignoring the leering glares from the surrounding MJ slaves.

"Name?" Sir Vigor asked.

"MJ-7, sir," Barloc's gaze shifted to Madam Constance while Sir Vigor searched the parchment. Sapper's last words danced in his mind: *this isn't over, Hero.* He somehow knew that he would be sent back to the battle square, back to day one.

Sir Vigor set the parchment down. "You're to report to the red marker, where you'll be fitted for new footwear."

Surely Sapper would've carried through with his threat. Barloc caught his mind trailing, quickly stepped from the table, and walked toward the red marker.

Five slaves huddled around the flag, each wearing a different amount of clothing, much like those from the mines on the previous day. One man with a dusting of a beard nodded at his approach. The others ignored him and rubbed their hands together, an attempt to keep warm against the morning chill.

MJ-8 joined the group and stood silently by Barloc, who now watched the lines. Sir Vigor and Madam Constance processed the slaves faster than the previous day, and before he knew it, the red group marched toward the tents.

The guard at the booth, a thick man with small scars covering his face, forced Barloc to sit on a stool while he performed his duty deftly, weaving cloth upon cloth, sewing, and stitching. In only a few minutes, Barloc's feet were covered in a type of cloth boot.

Barloc had always considered himself strong and tough, but it wasn't until then that he realized how feeble and soft feet could be.

As he waited for the red group to finish, Sir Vigor arrived and pointed at Barloc and MJ-8. "You two, come with me."

Barloc wasted no time and followed Sir Vigor across the yard, taking two steps for every one of his. When the giant finally stopped, he stared down at the two slaves for a quiet moment. "You've made quite the impression.... Master Sapper has requested you two personally."

Barloc's shoulders slumped, his face flushed, and he fought the urge to protest, to explain what had happened.

"Master Sapper's in front of the castle having the slaves break down and rebuild the stone piles. You'll find him there, waiting for you."

Barloc nodded.

Sir Vigor lifted a tree-trunk-sized hand, and a moment later, the portcullis clicked open.

Master Sapper paced back and forth on his horse, just beyond the drawbridge.

When Barloc started walking, Sir Vigor spoke, "Have you ever stepped on a hornet's nest?"

"No, sir."

"You have now." He nodded in the direction of Master Sapper. "And MJ-7, once you step on a nest, the damage is done. Try not to get stung too badly." He walked away.

The new footwear made a huge difference against the gravel, but walking toward Sapper dampened his spirits. No shoe in the world could protect him from that, and each step brought Master Sapper that much closer.

As they approached, Sapper began clapping. "Well done, Hero!"

Barloc's heart climbed up his throat at the sight of the other MJ slaves, though his attention rested on Sapper, where danger lurked in those brown, beady eyes.

"So good of ya to join us," Sapper said, crossing his arms. "Say, ladies, have ya seen the hero's new boots?"

Barloc scanned the slaves and found them all staring down at his new footwear, and he knew the hornets had started to swarm. Even one of the slaves from the previous day had returned with a scowl set into his face, and Barloc could only assume that it was because they hadn't eaten the night before.

Sapper laughed and clapped his hands. "I had them pointlessly moving these stones back and forth until ya arrived.... Now that yer here, we can march allllll the way to the mine, load the carts and come alllll the way back... Then we can do it again!" Sapper let his words wash over them. "Let's go!"

Barloc moved past the disgruntled slaves, avoiding eye contact.

MJ-8 stayed especially close by his side. Cuts lined his arms and legs, and when he walked he did so with a limp; the results from the stones collapsing on his feeble body.

Two more slaves stood by the wheelbarrows, both wearing long, filthy linens.

The first slave had the white hair of an old man with wrinkles deep around his blue eyes. His hands were covered with scars as though they'd been mauled by a dog, but even through all that, he gave off the presence of strength. He held his chest high and looked straight ahead, past the slaves, toward the mine.

The other slave was completely unforgettable. His right eye had been replaced with a milky white orb, and a deep, craggy scar cut above and below the socket. His hands shook slightly, jingling the chains around his wrists.

Sapper rounded the slaves up and led the way to the mine. Four guards surrounded the group, riding a slight distance from the slaves, two on either side. Once at the mine, Sapper instructed the slaves to load the carts. He remained on his horse and paced back and forth. Barloc kept his eyes on him, and he couldn't help noticing that Sapper seemed uneasy. Every few seconds, he cast his attention toward the tree line.

Barloc worked without incident from the MJ slaves, though he feared that they would take advantage of Sapper's divided attention. Out of his peripheral, Barloc caught them lifting their heads, both toward him and the guards. He knew it would only be a matter of time before they made their move.

How will they do it, though? Will they take turns or strike me all at once?

A wolf's howl ululated from the trees. The guards, Master Sapper, and all the slaves spun to the source. The howl came again, followed by five men stepping into the clearing. The moment Barloc laid eyes on them, he knew who they were: Howlers. The men carried long rifles strapped to their backs and wore a variety of filthy outfits. Armor hid among common clothes that were speckled by the silks of the wealthy, a clear sign that they geared themselves from their victims.

The lead man stepped forward, his outfit the only one out of the lot that held a consistent theme. He wore black leather, much like the guards at Drudgeburg, with blood-red lines cutting through in a design creating the illusion of burning coals.

Master Sapper moved closer to him. "Katiph!"

The man dipped his head, not taking his eyes from Sapper. "Running a bit heavy today, aren't you?" He straightened up and motioned to the slaves.

Katiph's voice came out in high, squeaky waves, reminding Barloc of a rat. His face pinched up, and his skin clung to his skull, a mask to the bones behind it. Thin facial hair dusted his cheeks, and hanging over one shoulder lay the long, braided strand of a rat tail.

Sapper shook his head. "Don't worry yerself about what I'm doing. Let's just get this over with." He lifted a hand and snapped it back down.

Sapper's foot guards grabbed the two unique slaves and directed them toward Katiph.

"Two? I came all this way for two?" Katiph shook his head and waved his hands in front of him. "That's not going to work."

Sapper's chest expanded and his hand twitched toward his whip, resting on the handle. "Yer gonna get what I give ya, and yer gonna like it!"

Katiph laughed. "The days where you tell me how things are going to be are coming to an end. I've become a man you don't want to mess with, Sapper. I've enough dirt on you to bury you in your own grave."

Sapper moved closer to Katiph, uncoiled his whip, and launched it at the strap attaching Katiph's gun. After a loud snap, the rifle fell to the ground, and before it landed, he lofted the whip forward again, breaking another one of the other Howler's guns free.

"Keep yer childish threats with yer toys, Katiph!"

The other three men finally grasped their guns and lifted them at Sapper.

"Why do ya prefer those useless scraps of metal? They can't pierce plate, ya can hardly aim true, and half the time they kill the man holding it!"

Katiph retrieved his weapon.

Barloc knew guns were few and far, more common with outlaws and Howlers. Though, Howlers *were* outlaws—King Sclavus's outlaws.

"This may be true for the inexperienced." Katiph smirked and pointed his rifle at the slaves. "Surely you can part with one more?"

"I had two prepared. What tale do I tell Lord Harbor when I return one short?"

Katiph shrugged and shook his head. "Tell him a slave ran away for all I care."

"What kind of master would I be if I let my slaves run free?"

"And what kind of mercenary would I be if I returned from such a long journey with so few?"

"I don't—" Sapper spoke, but Katiph cut him off with a wolf's howl.

From the trees, five more men, already gripping guns or bows, joined them.

"As I said, things are going to change around here." Katiph stepped through the slaves, observing each one. "Be lucky it's only one, Sapper."

Barloc's heart raced as Katiph neared, and when he felt the Howler's eyes dawdle on him, he coughed as hard as he could.

Katiph backed away. "You keeping the ill now?"

Barloc watched MJ-8, fearing he would copy his actions, but Katiph stopped in front of MJ-3.

"Tall... strong... looks healthy enough." Katiph lingered in front of the slave before sauntering back to his men. "Yes, I'll take these three."

Sapper glanced between the slave and the line of men before him, his grip tightened on the whip's handle, but after a moment, his fist relaxed. "How much?"

"Three gold coins."

Sapper lowered his head and rubbed his fingers into his temples. "Fine, but let's make this fast. I've other matters to tend to outside of ya, Katiph."

Katiph smiled. "Round them up."

Two Howlers grabbed the two prepared slaves while a third went for MJ-3.

MJ-3 shook the Howler off and broke into a run. His chains restricted how wide his stride would allow. "I won't go back with no Howler!"

Sapper mumbled and plowed by on horseback. As he advanced on MJ-3, he withdrew his whip and snapped it forward, wrapping it around the slave's leg. MJ-3 flopped down to the ground with a loud thump.

Dirt floated up, and before it could settle, Sapper was dragging him behind his horse, the whip cutting lines into the slave's leg.

Katiph clapped excitedly and produced three gold coins from a small sack, handing them to Sapper. After a long, exaggerated bow, the Howlers disappeared into the trees.

Sapper cantered past the slaves. "What are ya fleabags starin' at? Get back to work!" He moved to the tree by the mine and dismounted, pushing his back against the rough bark. He rolled one of the three gold coins across his knuckles.

The MJ slaves worked fast and hard, ignoring Barloc and MJ-8. Like tugging the slaver's palanquin across the kingdom, they moved as one unit. Seeing one of their own sold like fruit at a market altered the tension in the air, as if harder labor would exempt them from a future sale to the Howlers.

Questions assaulted Barloc. *Why would Sapper know a Howler so well? Does Lord Harbor know? Is he part of this?* The idea that Sapper had any part with the Howlers countered any progress he'd made in his mind about Lord Harbor and freedom. It now felt like a joke, like one misstep and he would be back in the Howlers' hands.

The castle had lost some of its previous nightly enchantment. It appeared rough, like a castle should, with long cracks cutting through the foundation like veins. Stone crumbled away at certain points, and the wood that lined the windows was old, as if washed ashore from the sea. He'd always known castles to be the strongholds of the kingdom, forts that stood up against battles and protected the people within.

Drudgeburg was built in a unique location, wedged in a valley between two tall mountains. A creek ran along the base of the left side, snaking in and out of the hardwoods until it disappeared behind the castle. Large trees lined the castle walls down both sides, also vanishing from view.

One road exited the castle and climbed up a hill, past the oak tree where they'd eaten the day before. Overgrown fields stretched both sides of the road to the forest line.

After the slaves finished unloading the stones, the same set of women returned holding a replica meal of hot rice and vegetables. With their bellies full, the slaves soon returned to the mine and loaded the carts a second time. Once again, their progress slowed as the day descended toward night.

On the return journey, Barloc focused on the woodlands lining the fields on both sides of the rutted road. Off in the distance, deer disappeared into the thick trees, and he remembered how the Howlers materialized out of nowhere. He felt like anyone could be watching them.

As they unloaded the stones, Barloc contemplated the four huge stacks. He wondered why they needed so many, but the way things were shaping up around Drudgeburg, it wouldn't surprise him if Sapper made them return each rock back to the mine, piece by piece.

Once done, Sapper led them into the courtyard and left them with a group of guards at the stables. Although Barloc's muscles twitched from exhaustion, he instantly felt relief with Sapper's departure.

A line of slaves stood before Barloc, and four at a time they stepped forward, where guards dipped brushes into buckets and scrubbed them from head to toe.

By Barloc's turn, the water swirled thick with dirt, and each swipe with the rough brush scratched his skin. After the last man, the horn called the slaves back to their bunkhouses, where the guards locked them in without a meal for the second night in a row.

Chapter 5 – The Funeral

The nightmare replayed, but this time, Katiph's wolfish howl crashed through the air while Barloc ran from Master Sapper. The slaves sold to the Howlers joined the army of zombies chasing him. He still lost his blade, climbed up the pile of bodies, and attempted to jump to the ledge, but the moment he tried, the faceless figure hurled him backward. Barloc's eyes flipped open before the deafening bellow erupted from Sapper's gaping mouth.

He wiped sweat from his lip and listened to his heartbeat pulse through his ears like a drum. The slave horn hadn't permeated the quiet, but outside padded footfalls moved around the yard.

The process repeated itself from the previous mornings: the horn blew, the guards and slaves lined up, Sir Vigor and Madam Constance assigned their quests, and they stood at their designated markers.

Madam Constance instructed Barloc to return to Master Sapper, but he would receive gloves first. As he waited at the red flag once more, he noticed that all the MJ slaves stood with him, except MJ-2, who now stood at the green marker, awaiting his day in the battle square, and MJ-3, who had been sold to the Howlers.

The lines depleted, and the slaves dispersed. The red group approached a tent where Barloc received used, brown leather gloves with patched fingers and dried blood across the palms.

Once the last slave collected his gear, a guard led them back to the red marker where Master Sapper waited with a parchment in his fist. As soon as the slaves were in earshot, he called out different names: "JF-3, JF-8, OM-11, DS-3, F-9, and JD-1, follow the guards. Yer gonna be dealin' with crops." He pointed at two guards standing to his left. "MJ-1, 4, 5, 6, 7, and 8, yer with me. Let's go!"

Sapper walked straight to the exit where he mounted his steed and waited for the gate to lift.

As the group of slaves moved toward the mine, Master Sapper called Barloc off to the side."Yer one smug slave, MJ-7. Ya come in here and do what ya please... like yer more than just a thrall. I bet ya think yer so cleaver for coughing like that in front of Katiph. In hindsight, I should've offered ya from the start."

Barloc remained silent.

"I bet ya think I can't break ya. Well, I can, and I will. If for no other reason, I'll do it simply to prove it." Sapper spurred his horse and rode to the front of the line, leaving Barloc to merge back with the group.

Barloc and MJ-8 worked as steadily as they could, side by side, and by the time everyone loaded their carts, gaps began showing in the collapsed entrance.

Much like the previous two days, they trekked back to the castle, ate, and revisited the mine for a second load.

On the return trip, Sapper pulled MJ-1 off to the side, out of earshot from the group.

When they arrived at the mine, the guards joined Sapper under the tree, leaving the slaves to their work.

Halfway through the load, a sharp pain stung the back of Barloc's head. A small rock bounced along the ground by his feet, and when he lifted his hand to his head, he pulled his fingers away wet with blood.

MJ-1 stood with his fists balled, glowering at Barloc.

Warmth flooded his cheeks as rage crashed through his body. Blood dripped down his bare back, and after a moment of uninterrupted staring, he turned to his wheelbarrow. When he bent down for his next piece of stone, another small rock buzzed past his cheek. Barloc spun around to confront MJ-1, instead meeting all four MJ slaves. He found the guards and Sapper staring at them with their arms across their chests.

MJ-8, who had been on Barloc's heels the entire time, now stood by the cave's entrance.

"You think you're better than us, Hero?" MJ-1 growled, and there it was: Sapper's words right out of the slave's mouth.

"We don't need to do this, Archer," Barloc said, remembering his name from the first day. Confusion glimmered across Archer's face at hearing his name, but Barloc pressed on. "Let's get back to work. Thirty days. We need to stick together."

Archer punched the air and breathed heavier, the muscles in his chest tightening then relaxing with each exhale. "Don't call me that, Hero. You don't know what you're talking about."

Barloc backed away one step only for the MJ slaves to take two forward. He pivoted to run, but the four men jumped on his back, smashing his face against the hard ground. Blood filled his mouth, and he curled up while they swarmed like hornets, jabbing their stingers into his sides, back, and legs.

His body shook from each hit. The onslaught hurt tremendously at first, but he quickly became numb. Barloc locked his arms in front of his face and waited for the slaves to tire or for the guards to intervene. He cried out for help between each strike against him, but he knew that no one would intervene. As a last effort, he called for MJ-8. A moment later, someone screamed and a deep thud echoed in the air. The kicking and punching tapered and then stopped completely.

The slaves backed away, and MJ-8 stood over Archer, holding a huge stone with a swatch of blood smeared across it.

Barloc's vision spun; he closed his eyes and rested his head. A bell rang faintly, like wind chimes in a morning breeze. The soothing sound calmed him, each bell ringing alongside his heartbeat.

A growl disrupted the oncoming tranquility. The ground shook around him, and the growl shifted into a bark. Faster, the bells and the bark alternated, the ground rumbled again, and something smacked his cheek. Weightlessness tricked him into feeling like he floated until a hard pressure nearly stole his breath, and finally, he opened his eyes.

"Grab MJ-1 and follow. Leave the carts and march back!" Sapper's voice rumbled louder than ever. "The bell means trouble; get back to the castle as fast as ya can. If I have any missing slaves, I'll make it my life's mission to personally kill each of ya. Understood?"

Barloc was flung over Sapper's horse like a sack of flour. He bobbed up and down as he stared at the filthy road. Each gyration sent a shockwave of agony through his chest. He tried to sit up until he felt himself slide and gripped onto the saddle. They rode hard, but before he knew it, they crossed Drudgeburg's drawbridge and stopped in the courtyard.

Sapper shoved Barloc off the horse.

Pain exploded across his entire body on impact. Using the horse for balance, Barloc managed to pull himself up to his feet. Once up, he leaned against the mount for support. The spectacle before him acted as a distraction from his own pain.

Lord Harbor ran across the bailey toward Sir Vigor, Madam Constance, and three other Green Cloaks. They circled around another man lying on the ground, covered in blood. Lord Harbor dropped to his knees beside him. "What happened?"

Sapper dismounted and joined the group.

One of the Green Cloaks greeted Sapper with a nod and spat out a small piece of grass.

Lord Harbor turned the dying man's face toward him. "Atticus, what happened?"

"M-m-my lord." The man's voice quivered and wheezed. "Scouts... by Buzzard's Rock." The man spat out a mouthful of blood.

Lord Harbor called back to Madam Constance, "Get the Healers. Now!"

She ran fast across the yard, her cloak billowing behind her like a cape.

Atticus coughed into his fist. "I was ranging along the mire... I found tracks. I figured it was just Katiph's men, but I followed them to make sure... all the way up to Buzzard's Rock where I found a camp."

"You're sure they were scouting us?"

"What else would they be scouting?" He spat again.

Lord Harbor gently wiped specks of blood from Atticus's face. "What happened to you?"

"I attempted a closer look, to see what their camp was about. How many there were and if they were a threat, but they discovered me." He fell into a fit of violent coughing. "One of them shot an arrow blindly into the woods and the bastard struck my shoulder."

Lord Harbor remained silent, kneeling by Atticus.

"I screamed when it hit me." He laughed a wet laugh that shifted into a fit of coughing. "Who the hell blindly shoots an arrow?"

"Scared men," Lord Harbor answered and added, "Fearful men."

"They came fast, but I hid behind a tree, broke the arrow and used it as a weapon to gouge the first face I saw." Atticus attempted to sit up but failed, landing hard on his back. "My left arm was no good, but I was still able to get my blade free." He wiped his mouth with the back of his hand. "I didn't want to, my lord, but I did what I had to... Not before I was smashed in the chest by a hammer, but I did what I had to do." His words trailed off as if he drifted into a memory. "Though, one got away. I couldn't catch him on foot. There was no way, so I had to backtrack to my horse, and by then he would have been long gone or hidden, so I returned to report."

Lord Harbor shifted on his knees and shook his head. "You did good. You're a brave man."

"T- t-thank you, my lord." Atticus rested his head on the hard ground, and that was when Barloc saw a pool of blood soaking into the dirt around him.

Madam Constance returned with two women wearing white dresses and long necklaces covered in vials. One older and one much younger.

"How confident are you in their numbers? Do you think there are more?"

The man spoke without opening his eyes. His words left his mouth lazily. "I can... guarantee... that there are." He coughed and tried to spit, but this time, it caught in his beard. "I'm sorry I failed."

The Healers lowered to Atticus's side.

Lord Harbor cleared away, giving the Healers room. "You keep that quiet, Atticus."

The Healers worked quickly and with few words. They cut and tore and untied as fast as their hands would allow, and by the time they removed Atticus's tunic, blood covered their long, white dresses. In the end, they stood and lowered their heads, crossing their blood-soaked hands in front of them.

Lord Harbor stared down at the lost man and shook his head.

Sun glared off the wetness on Madam Constance's cheeks, and seeing her crying surprised Barloc. She carried herself to be a callous woman, but to see her so vulnerable in front of so many people changed something in the way he viewed her. Every one of the Green Cloaks seemed deeply bothered, but not so much as she.

Lord Harbor pointed at two of the three masters but spoke to Madam Constance. "Take the body to the Vicar Farlen and tell him that we'll send Atticus off this evening."

Madam Constance nodded and wiped her eyes. Two of the Green Cloaks grabbed either side of Atticus and followed Madam Constance through the inner portcullis.

Lord Harbor addressed the Healers: "Thank you, ladies. You may return." He faced the remaining men. "I'll need council. Everyone meet in the castle. That includes you, Sapper." Lord Harbor bowed slightly and turned for the keep.

The scene captivated Barloc so much that he'd forgotten about the beating. He swayed, still bleeding from various wounds. Pains danced across his body, and he suddenly wondered how he stood at all.

Sapper barked orders at the surrounding guards, who ran for the stables.

Barloc pulled his hand away from the horse and stepped toward Sir Vigor. He dropped hard to his knees and attempted to stand again, this time falling face first into the dirt.

***

Glass tinkled followed by a woman's soft voice. "Hand me the hartshorn." After a small pop, a strong odor climbed into Barloc's nose. His throat tightened as if someone choked him, and all at once, his ears tingled, his nose burned, and tears forced their way out.

He gasped for breath and tried to sit up but couldn't move. Soft rope bound his arms to the sides of the cot. Barloc blinked until his vision cleared. To his right sat a young Healer, wearing a lacey, white dress that covered her body. Her sharp clavicles helped frame her shoulders, and her hair had been cut short. A necklace of tiny glass vials rested softly against her chest.

On his other side, a much older Healer hovered over him, holding an open vial in her hand. She passed it to the younger girl. When she spoke, she forced her words out as if she were new to the language, enunciating each syllable. "That should do it."

The younger Healer popped the vial back onto her necklace.

The older woman released the holds on his arms. "Can you stand, child? Only for a moment."

Barloc rubbed his wrists and stretched out his arms.

"You have to move. Everyone is required to bear witness at Drudgeburg." Both women pulled him up, and before long, he stood, his legs wavering. His fetters hung with an unreal weight, and his feet dragged along the ground, making it almost impossible to move.

"You need to follow, child."

Outside, every slave—more than he'd seen during the morning sorting—filled the outer bailey. He stood in front of a building just past the stables, tucked away in the corner. The position offered a view of the entire place without having to turn his head.

Lord Harbor paced up and down the path, just before a tall wooden funeral pyre where Atticus, the man who had died, lay atop. Ten Green Cloaks stood alongside five Healers. A young man in bright red robes stood in front of them all, his jet-black hair pulled back into a tight ponytail. A tribal tattoo climbed up his neck, stopping at his chin. In front of him, guards mixed in with the sea of slaves, standing so close their shoulders touched.

Lord Harbor stopped pacing and faced the mass of people. "As the sun sets on Drudgeburg, the sun sets on Master Atticus. I don't expect many of you to feel sorrow. Most of you haven't even met this man, and where a blind arrow has struck one of the many eyes of Drudgeburg, know that it made all the other eyes aware. Master Atticus... you will be hard to replace... Vicar Farlen, if you please." Lord Harbor knelt at the base of the wooden structure and lowered his head.

The man in red stepped forward and placed a hand on Lord Harbor's shoulder. Vicar Farlen turned back to the crowd. Even though wispy and cotton soft, his voice carried over the silent yard. "Death is serious. We live in a world under King Sclavus, a man who doesn't understand this. Death shouldn't be so quick. Too many of you have seen more than is suited for any one person. It's not fair, but it's the way of our world.

"A man's death has the weight of his life... Master Atticus lived a heavy life of sacrifice and hard work. When he placed someone before him, it wasn't as a shield, but to help that person forward, ahead of himself." Farlen faced the pyre. "Master Atticus, I hope your many sacrifices serve as payment from this life into the next. A moment of silence."

The vicar lowered his head, and when he lifted it back up, he said, "The fire will burn ten days in honor of Master Atticus. On the tenth, the ashes will be collected and mended back into the earth. Keep the fire burning!"

All of the vanguard, the Healers, Lord Harbor, and even some of the guards yelled back: "Keep the fire bright!"

Two guards handed Vicar Farlen and Lord Harbor lit torches, and together they approached the kindling below Master Atticus. At once it went up in flames. In only a few seconds, the popping and heavy breath of the fire overtook the awkward silence in the air.

"Come, child," the Healer said. "You need rest."

Barloc allowed her to guide him back the cot, and as he settled in, a thought dawned on him. "My lady."

The older of the two Healers stopped and spoke to him. "You may address me as Healer Haylan. This is Healer Altha."

"Healer Haylan, please don't keep me in here. I don't want to start back at day one."

Haylan considered him for a moment, searching his face. "I will be attending to you personally. You will remain here until I see it fit. Valerian." Haylan grabbed a vial from the younger Healer and leaned closer to Barloc. "This will help you sleep."

Haylan withdrew a dropper and dipped it into the vial. Once satisfied, she held it over his mouth. Two drops fell onto his tongue, and instantly the taste of sour cheese overtook his senses. He fought the urge to gag, and after multiple swallows, the taste finally faded.

"You need rest. Do not worry about day one or your other troubles. Worry about getting better so you can get through your time here. I will be back later." The Healers left the room, closing the door behind them.

Barloc's eyes felt heavy, and his mouth wouldn't stop salivating. Once again, Sapper's words managed to find a home in his head: *I can make it to where ya never progress at Drudgeburg.*

Chapter 6 – More than a Healer

Healer Haylan hovered over Barloc, her lips twisted in a grimace. "I hate watching people wake from hartshorn." She clipped a small vial onto her necklace. "But it is a necessary evil, I suppose."

Barloc coughed until his throat cleared and wiped tears from his cheeks. He sat up when a female slave entered with a plate of food and passed the meal to Haylan, who handed it to him.

Haylan watched the girl leave before facing him. "I am going to talk to you while you eat." She grabbed a leather-bound journal off the small table by the bed, removed the lid from an inkwell, and placed the tip of a worn quill on the parchment. "How old are you, MJ-7?"

Her sky-blue eyes pierced him with a warm kindness. Small, dark specks lined the borders of her irises, and her skin appeared almost translucent, as if she'd never stepped into the sunlight. Wrinkles fanned from the corners of her eyes, and her cheeks sagged with age, but she held a beauty he liked, a beauty that came with years of experience—eyes worthy of a memoir.

"I'm twenty."

She scribbled in her journal. "You appear older. You carry yourself well."

He remained silent. Compliments made him leery, especially from people he didn't know.

"How long have you been enslaved?"

"Since I was fourteen."

She nodded and wrote across the page. "And how did it happen?"

"Our family couldn't keep up with the king's tax. No one from town could."

She nodded again, continuing to write. "What town?"

Memories that couldn't possibly be his flashed through his mind, a compilation of stories he must have heard from other slaves... but he could still smell the fire from the burning buildings, and he remembered the autumn chill... and the look on his father's face.

Haylan cleared her throat, pulling Barloc back to the conversation.

"I'm sorry." He swallowed hard and shifted on the bed. "It just feels like a different life."

She rested a hand on his leg, a sign of comfort. "I understand. Do you remember what your hometown was called, child?"

"Chambers."

After jotting another note, she grabbed a flagon off the table and passed it to him. "Have some water."

Barloc drew two deep swallows and passed it back.

She waited until his head rested on the feather pillow. "Can you recall what happened the day you were captured?"

Barloc nodded and glanced at the wall, focusing on a white mark in the wood. "Howlers lit our homes on fire and waited for people to run into the streets."

"Can you tell me specifically what happened? I do not mean for you to relive old memories, but, well, let us say simply that this is a *hobby* I practice. If it is too much for you, especially in your condition, I understand."

Barloc quickly thought about his first day at Drudgeburg and how many people failed, simply by not complying with instructions. Healer Haylan fed him, kept him safe, and best of all, out of Sapper's reach. He wasn't about to upset her. Plus, the longer he captivated her, the longer he'd be away from the mines. He took a deep breath and summoned the memory from what felt like so many years ago.

"I was fishing with my friend, Alden. We were trying to catch dinner before evening fell. The river had run low with drought, and we'd almost fished it dry. We hadn't seen as much as a squirrel in weeks, and any meat we did get, we sold to help pay the tax.

"The last five families of Chambers met two times a day and pooled together all the food we could. No one family could survive without watching the others fail. But people grew desperate. They showed up with nothing and then ate their fair share. Hunger destroyed relationships, families. People accused one another of hoarding and fights broke out in the streets.

"Alden saw the smoke first. We left our gear at the river and ran, and by the time we got to the edge of town, the buildings were engulfed in flames." Goosebumps crept across his neck as he remembered the heat and how he could feel it from so far away. "Both Alden and I watched our lives burn."

Barloc wiped away a tear. "The hartshorn. It's still making my eyes water."

Haylan smiled and scribbled in her book, pausing briefly to dip the quill in the inkwell. When she finished, she rested the journal in her lap. "You do not need to finish unless you would like to."

Barloc shook his head. "I'm fine. It's just been a long time." He placed the plate next to him, realizing that he hadn't taken a bite, and pushed up higher on the bed. "Alden ran for the town. I wanted to stop him, to tell him to wait, but—"

"Why were you not just as concerned? Were your father and mother not there?"

"No, my mother was already dead. She died as everything started to unravel. She fell sick, and we didn't have the coin to travel to Luvian, the closest town with a Healer."

"I see."

"When I ran into Chambers, I could hardly see through the smoke. I charged blindly down the main road until I ran into a group of Howlers. They had rounded everyone up and tied them together in one big herd. When they captured Alden, I attempted to run toward the tree line, away from town. I ran as hard I could through the field, hoping to lose the Howler in pursuit." He spread his hands apart. "He caught me, and when he brought me back, my father slipped under the rope and ran for me, screaming my name.

The Howler holding me withdrew his gun and shot him in the chest."

Haylan placed her hand on his leg once more.

It dawned on him how odd the situation seemed. *Why is this Healer so interested in my past life?* Once again, Sapper invaded his mind with his promises of breaking him down. When he looked back at Haylan, he decided that he couldn't trust her. *All part of Sapper's plan.*

Haylan changed the conversation to his condition. "I would like to examine you. I am going to start with your toes. You tell me if anything hurts."

Barloc nodded and pulled his legs from underneath the blanket.

She started with his right foot and slowly squeezed each toe. Two of them sent pains up his leg on contact, and when she finished, she secured thin sticks up either side of the toes with twine. "Those two are broken. If you do not drop any more stones on them, they will heal fine, though it may be uncomfortable to walk." She pressed on his legs and bent his knees. "Anything?"

He shook his head.

She continued to apply pressure to his stomach, and each time she did, he hissed with pain. "Tighten your stomach for me."

Barloc squeezed his muscles as hard as he could, screaming with pain as he pulled his hands to his chest. After a few controlled breaths, he calmed down.

"How about your arms and fingers? I stitched up all the cuts. You had a nasty one on the back of your head."

Barloc flexed his hands. "No, I think I'm fine."

Without looking, Haylan lifted a hand and removed a vial from the many tinkling around her neck. "This will help with the pain. It is nothing to be alarmed of. All you need is rest. I do not think anything is broken outside of the toes. You may have a cracked rib, but there is nothing I can do for that. You simply need to rest."

She uncorked a vial of a swirling, silvery substance. A moment later, she held a dropper above him.

The metallic taste spread fast, warming his chest.

Haylan snapped the vial back into place and retrieved her journal. "I do not feel like going out there yet. Let us keep talking, shall we?"

Every part of Barloc wanted to protest, beg for sleep, and not dive further into the horrible memories, but he knew he couldn't. "I tried to run to my father, but the Howler wouldn't allow me, instead throwing me toward the rest of the group. I couldn't believe what I'd seen."

Barloc focused on the white mark again, noticing how different it seemed against the old wood and he wondered what it was that drew him to it. The urge to reach out and touch it caused his fingers to twitch, but he focused back on her question. "The man who shot my father yelled 'If anyone else wants to be a hero, act now.' No one moved, of course. Next thing we knew, the Howler whistled and all his cohorts separated the families—the old on one side, young on the other."

Haylan stopped scratching letters across the page, seemingly captivated. "What happened next?"

"The adults panicked, asking things like 'where are you taking us?' and 'why can't we be with our families?' It's amazing, but I can remember every word like it was yesterday." Barloc took another sip of water. "The Howler who had killed my father smashed the butt of his gun into an old man's face. 'We've no use for the old and feeble!' The Howler had laughed as though he enjoyed every moment. 'The young go to slavers, and your lot will be sold to the labor camp, Corvee.'

"We pleaded in every way we could to mend the gap between the old and the young, to bring our families back together, but in an instant, the Howlers herded us into a prison cart. That was the last time I saw my father, a huddled corpse on the ground in the center of a burning town."

Haylan wiped tears from her face. She didn't bother hiding how upset she'd become. She looked directly at him, sharing the pain as if she offered the opportunity for him to be weak. "You speak very well for being enslaved so young and coming from such a small town." As if an idea struck her, her eyes opened wider and she sat forward in her seat. "Do you know how to read and write?"

Barloc nodded, unsure if he should reveal this fact.

This inspired Haylan. She sat up straight and flipped to a blank page in her journal, dipped the feather in ink, and asked Barloc to write his name.

He stared at the parchment with the quill in hand and almost wrote Barloc, but that would leave written proof of him breaking one of the first rules given to him by Lord Harbor. After a moment of hovering over the parchment, Barloc wrote MJ-7.

She grabbed the journal and looked it over, smiled, and drew the book to her chest. "I am surprised that you are so educated, child. Education is usually only seen among the wealthy, which you were clearly not. Why is that?"

"My mother was. She was born into the Wemilat line, but my father was from some fisherman's town down south. I can't remember the name. My mother's family forbade her to see my father, but she refused, so they disowned her. She and my father moved to Chambers, where I was born."

Haylan's eyes narrowed and she seemed to speak to herself more than to Barloc. "Wemilat. I know that name. The Wemilat estate, west of Warshire, the king's castle. Very interesting.... That is ironic, you know?"

"What is?"

"That your mother came from one of wealthiest family lines throughout the kingdom, great contributors to King Sclavus, yet she passed away because she lacked coin."

Barloc couldn't find appreciation in the irony. He missed his mother and never understood why anyone should be allowed to die because they didn't have enough coin.

"She taught you?"

He nodded. "Also taught my father. She loved him. He was a good man, and it wasn't because of money or land or whatever else this kingdom deems more important than life, than love. She loved him because he was genuine and strong. She used to tell me that before bed. She said that she could teach me how to read and write or change my hair to gold, but it would mean nothing if I couldn't love properly."

"And wise words those are. Tough to live by, but a nice thought. MJ-7, are you able to recount, in writing, the events you just told me?"

He looked from the now cold plate of food to the vials around Haylan's neck and decided that he will likely never be this comfortable again. "Yes, I suppose I can manage."

"I am going to give you valerian and let you sleep. I will be back in the morning with another meal."

Haylan retrieved another a vial from her necklace. Barloc wondered how she kept track of so many. At least fifty different containers, of different shapes and sizes, hung there. Not only would she have to constantly keep them filled, but the weight of them alone seemed heavy enough to be a burden.

She dropped the liquid into his mouth, gathered her items, and left.

Barloc cleared his plate of cold food, forcing past the desire to simply set it down. He missed his father deeply, now more than ever, and for the first time since his death, he cried. He had promised himself that he wouldn't, to honor his father, to stay strong, but he continued to picture him running across the smoky road. He saw his father's shocked face as the bullet tore through his chest.

Barloc cried harder than he could ever remember. He cried for his mother, his father, and his friend, Alden. He cried for the innocent people who were taken to Corvee, and for the children that were spread across the kingdom.

Finally, he cried for himself. Long brays muffled by the feather pillow.

He closed his eyes and begged that he wouldn't wake, that Haylan had mixed up the vial with poison.

Chapter 7 – A Eulogy of Sorts

The slave horn rumbled the walls while Barloc cleared his plate, eyeing a new journal that had been left on his nightstand overnight. He picked it up and flipped through the pages. Not one word tarnished the book—a fresh start, a blank slate. The cover was crisp and new, as if bound that morning.

Barloc paused before writing, staring at the two inkwells, finding the task a bit ambitious. He pictured himself outside in line to be sorted. *What color marker would I have been sent to today? Would MJ-8 still be shadowing me?* He also wondered about Archer, remembering that MJ-8 had struck him hard enough to send him to the ground. The gong repeatedly crashed outside as the lines were processed, and when he heard people moving around the yard, he returned his focus back to the journal.

The valerian had taken Barloc to such a deep sleep that he hadn't dreamed, and for that he was thankful, though slightly groggy.

He pressed the tip of the quill against the parchment, considering a title. The ink pooled into a small circle while different ideas crossed his mind, and after a moment, he settled on his slave name and wrote it as clearly as possible, centered at the top of the first page. He began on the day the Howlers had arrived at Chambers. Each letter he scripted, he did with care and precision.

He took every opportunity to enrich the details for a stronger impact while keeping the facts as facts and attempting to recount everything as honestly as possible. Instead of writing that he ran through the grass, he noted how the blades whipped his skin, a precursor for his life to come. When describing the Howler who'd killed his father, he did so with such hatred, painting a bearded devil with skin as rough as tree bark. His blue eyes a slight, falsely casting a reflection of the heavens above. His hands one layer of skin away from being claws.

Weaving in and out of his memory, he carefully projected each event onto the parchment. When he finally finished recounting his father's murder, he understood why Haylan had left the additional ink. From the very first page, he'd wasted no space, placing each line as closely together as possible, and though writing down the memory had proved to be heart wrenching, he managed every word, to the very moment the prison cart pulled away from the ashes of his home.

Barloc reread the words carefully, and once satisfied, he flipped the page, dipped his quill, and began reliving the memory.

***

When the prison cart pulled away from Chambers, I didn't take my eyes off the pyre, not until the glow resembled the setting sun. The Howlers wouldn't travel at night, and the moon offered feeble light, for the roads held too many dips.

It wasn't until we stopped for camp that I realized the magnitude of my situation. Five Howlers held us captive, but I only managed to hear two of their names: Laufia, the square-jawed, bearded man who murdered my father, and Variegate, a long-haired man, clearly the youngest of the lot. Even though six others occupied the cart with me, I remained silent and kept my attention in my lap unless I thought it safe to steal a glance. I wanted to reach out and touch Alden's hand, to reassure him, but it wasn't worth the risk.

The Howlers took shifts keeping watch. They beat a stick on the bars every time one of us fell asleep. Though, when Variegate took over, he let us rest. Not once did he approach the cart, poke us, or hit the bars. He sat on a fallen log and whittled a piece of wood while chewing on a stem of grass.

I thought I knew hunger by the end of my time in Chambers, only eating two small meals a day, but I knew nothing. The first night of the journey to Warshire went by without so much as a sip of water or a crumb of food. The Howlers ate in front of us, flaunting what we couldn't have, and in the morning, I saw Eleanor, my neighbor's daughter, licking dew from the prison bars.

That morning began particularly rough for us. Elly, the blacksmith's daughter, rocked back and forth, crying. She couldn't control it. The mewling woke the Howlers, and Laufia didn't seem to think twice about his actions. Without a word, he jammed his key into the cage's rusty lock, reached past me, and grabbed the sobbing girl by her throat. In one swift motion, he threw her into the air. We all watched in horror as she floated, appearing suspended. The girl landed in the fire pit, sending up a cloud of ash and ember. Her cries turned to screams as her clothes caught fire.

Laufia slammed the cage shut and walked across camp. "Let's go!"

Before the girl could smother the flames, we'd left. I felt bad thinking it then, and maybe worse writing it now, but her absence offered a few more inches in the cart. Whenever I see a fire, I can still hear her screams.

Not one noise escaped our lips after what Laufia did.

Laufia had another victory when a traveler crossed his path on the King's Road. He made a game of the old man, circling him, poking him with his rifle, and by the end of the interaction, Laufia stripped him down, tied his wrists, and tethered him to the cart.

When the old man couldn't keep up, he fell, unable to stand again. The cart dragged him face down until Variegate cut the tethers and stopped next to the quivering body. Laufia confronted Variegate, though no words passed between them, and after a moment of building tension, Laufia rode to the front of the caravan, the other Howlers at his tail.

Variegate dismounted, withdrew his sword, and ran the man through. I've wondered for years why that old man was walking down the road alone. I imagine he'd come from a much safer time, but my father would've argued that the King's Road had never been safe.

When thunder rolled across the hills, Laufia assigned a Howler to scout for a campsite. When the Howler returned, the sun slipped behind dark clouds and soft rain misted my skin. He announced the discovery of an abandoned cottage off a small, overgrown path. "It's not big enough for the cart, but it's all I could find."

By the time we stopped, the cart smelled like an outhouse. A Howler removed the harness and guided the driving horse away. He secured the cart to two trees, blocking the path to their camp. Laufia rode ahead to check out the cottage, and when he returned, the Howlers lined up to follow, but when Variegate joined them, Laufia shook his head and pushed him back. "Where do you think you're going? You're staying here with this spume."

Variegate, clearly fuming, remained silent. Rain cast down his face, and the lightning flashes highlighted the circles under his eyes. The Howlers left him at the cart, taking the horses with them. Once out of earshot, Variegate cursed under his breath, paced back and forth, punching the air. He spat the piece of grass from his mouth and replaced it with another from his pocket.

Even though this man seemed to have some degree of compassion the previous night, his mounting anger scared me, scared all of us. The rain fell harder as the storm passed over, and Variegate found a seat on a rock and bundled himself tight.

A deluge of rain drenched us through the night. Each time I fell asleep, a chill pulled me back.

Variegate remained on that rock until the rain finally slowed, and when it did, he stood and stared at us before vanishing into the trees.

The girl next to me shivered so hard, she shook the cart.

"Move in closer," I whispered. "We need the body heat." I could barely get the words out, my teeth chattered so hard. I pushed up against her and everyone followed suit. I asked Alden if he was all right, but he didn't answer. He just stared at me with vacant eyes.

Variegate returned and approached the cart with his hands full. Without a word, he passed fruit and jerky through the bars. "Eat the cores. Leave nothing or I'll kill you all myself." He lingered a moment before returning to his spot on the rock.

I ate the apple as fast as I could, biting clear through the center. The bitter taste of the seeds almost made me gag, but I wasn't going to leave a trace, not after he risked feeding us. I mixed the jerky with the apple's core, and just as I finished, the girl next to me stopped shaking, and her apple dropped to her feet.

I put my finger under her nose, but I couldn't tell if she was breathing. Her head lolled when I shook her. I lowered my ear to her mouth, and when I couldn't hear anything, panic flooded me. I shook her again and whispered for her to wake, but she didn't respond. I shifted to my knees and tried to lay her down, but before I could, a fist gripped my shirt and pulled me toward the bars.

"Quiet yourself!" Variegate spoke through gritted teeth. When he released me, I fell onto the girl. "Move."

I backed up as far as I could.

He removed a glove from his right hand and placed two fingers against her neck. "She's dead."

I looked at the girl to Variegate, who had already retreated to his rock.

I grabbed the bars and jammed my face between them until my cheekbones hurt. "Wait!"

Variegate turned so fast water sprayed from his cloak as it whipped through the air. "There's nothing I can do. Make sure you clean up that food or she won't be the only body in that cart."

I traded spots with the girl, resting her against the corner. Once settled, Alden bit into the spare apple and handed it off, along with her jerky, passing them around until they vanished.

As the rain slowed, I finally fell asleep.

Variegate woke us by banging on the bars. A moment later, the Howlers emerged from a trail, arguing.

Laufia pointed his long, dirty finger at Variegate. "You take the food?"

Variegate met Laufia half way. "You leave me here all night in a rainstorm to keep watch on these mongrels and then accuse me of taking food?"

They bickered back and forth until Laufia had enough. When Variegate told him to open the cart so they could remove the body, Laufia shook his head and crossed his arms. "The body stays. It will help keep them quiet the rest of the trip."

When we entered Mezzoah, a crossroads town before Warshire, the shop owners had locked their doors and shaded their windows. On the message board, three signs with large letters read: 'NO HOWLERS.'

Laufia stopped in front of a tavern called Grog. He dismounted and cupped his hands around his mouth. "I don't want any trouble!"

No one responded.

He glanced between the other Howlers. "I said I don't want any trouble!"

A faint voice came from inside Grog. "Then you should have thought about that before you shot up Mezzoah, sold our men to slavers, and killed innocent people."

Laufia laughed and shook his head, kicking at the dirt. "I was on the king's business!"

"Your business was with other people. *You* made us your business. We're done with you Howlers."

"Who's the Magistrate? Who's in charge here?"

"You can call me Reeve." The voice formed into a man, tall and strong. A white beard hid his mouth. He walked through the swinging door of the tavern and stood with a blade gripped in his fist.

"Well, Reeve, we're here to have ale while we wait to meet our slaver. I don't want any trouble. I just want to buy supplies." Laufia stepped toward the tavern as he spoke, his gun strap slowly sliding down his arm. "Maybe have a drink, and we'll be on our way. How's that sound?" He pointed his gun at Reeve.

"Sounds like you'll have a hard time getting those items here. There's an abbey up the way. They may have brew and supplies to sell or trade for work. Maybe you can restrain yourself enough to not enslave the men of the cloth."

"You're going to stop all of us with that sticker?"

"I wouldn't think you to fight fair, and I don't believe in guns. A scout alerted me of your arrival, so I had time to prepare." The man threw the sword to his other hand. "Ready yourselves!"

At Reeve's call, doors slammed open and the street flooded with men and women. Men wielded everything from pitchforks to staves, and women gripped brooms and knives in their fists. Above, children lined the rooftops with stones poised to attack. Even an old man who could barely walk joined the stand.

By the look on Reeve's face, it appeared as though he relied on the sheer number of the townspeople to scare off the Howlers. My father had once told me, "If a bear tries to attack you, yell and throw rocks at it and it will back down." This reminded me of that.

Laufia spun in a slow circle, taking in the townspeople. "This is your last warning!"

Reeve took a confident step toward Laufia. "We're willing to die for our freedom, Howler. You won't be able to take us all down."

"You'd better hope you're right, Reeve, because if we can, your women and children come with us, and the men that survive will be sent to Corvee. Then I'll burn this place to the ground myself."

Reeve charged Laufia, but a loud bang sent him to the ground, mid-sprint. As he collapsed, silence stole the air, and then an arrow landed at Laufia's feet. When the arrow struck the ground, everything came undone.

"Get down!" Variegate yelled at us as he charged into the fray.

I tucked my head into the lap of the dead girl, placing my hands over my head as chaos erupted around us. The clash of weapons filled the air, and when I looked up, the Howlers fought two or three townsfolk each. An arrow pinged off the bars and skittered across the ground, followed by a handful of gunshots.

Moments later, a loud horn replaced the din of battle, and the clopping of horse hooves replaced the cries of the wounded.

Thirty or so men charged into Mezzoah. The leading soldiers wore the king's colors with the king's manacles clasped around their necks, securing their cloaks. Behind them, slavers rode in with a handful of guards. The horn faded and the leader demanded silence.

After hearing the story from both Laufia, and then one of the townsmen, a younger man with blood running down his forearm, the guard declared the town to be in the wrong. "These men are contracted by King Sclavus, and you don't have the right to deny them service. Your town will be fined, and I'll have those signs down from the message board."

The damage was tremendous. Two of the Howlers had been killed, Variegate had vanished from the scene, and numerous townsfolk lay dead in the road. The battle did not discriminate. It took women, children, and men. It took people from both sides, but the worst part of it all was the stray arrow that killed Alden.

Chapter 8 – The Trial

Healer Haylan entered the room, placed a flagon of water on the table next to Barloc, and sat by his bed. "I am sorry I did not return yesterday, child. New slaves arrived, two injured, plus another hurt in the battle square. How did the other Healer do?"

Barloc thought about how nervous the young woman had been, though she'd worked fast and efficiently—a girl about his age with pale skin, green eyes, and a narrow jaw. When he had tried to speak to her, she'd ignored him. She'd simply administered the liquid, checked his sutures, and left with the journal. "She was very helpful."

"I am impressed by the amount you wrote. I wonder how much you would have written had I given you more time." She withdrew her journal from inside her robes and placed it on her lap. He could tell by the worn cover that it wasn't the same one he'd written in.

Guilt crawled across his skin at the sight of the journal. "You read it all?"

"I did."

He suppressed the questions that flooded his mind. The dull throbbing in his right hand proved further that he didn't have to be at the mines to feel like a slave.

"They are expecting you out there, but you are not going anywhere until I talk to you about what you wrote."

Barloc looked away from her and scolded himself for placing so much detail on the pages. Since the first word he'd scratched, he suspected he may have been writing his eulogy—each letter posing as a nail in his coffin.

"Firstly, I want to tell you that I am sorry for your friend and your father. It was an awful story to read."

Barloc focused back on the white spot, feeling comfort in the off-colored smudge. As he scanned the ridges, he realized why he liked it so much. The shape resembled, even if just a little, the flower his mother pinned to her blouse. Again, his finger twitched wanting to go for it. He nodded, not looking up yet.

"I have lost people, too, child. I have learned that one never truly heals from such a thing.

Again, Barloc nodded, remembering Alden before fishing was a matter of him eating and more for fun.

"But I also want to make it clear that even though it all feels unique to you, it is not. It *is* tragic, yes, but every slave in the kingdom has lost someone."

Barloc shook his head slowly."Then why did I write all that down? This is all part of Sapper's plan, isn't it?"

Haylan frowned. "I do not follow?"

"Sapper. He promised he would break me. Isn't that what this is? Are you giving him information to use against me?" Red-hot anger pushed up his chest and into his cheeks as Haylan laughed. His fists clenched underneath the blanket.

"I assure you, Sapper has more important tasks to tend to than you. No matter, because you will soon be forgotten. Do not think that you are special. He does this to someone from every purchase."

Relief came with her words, but deep in his gut, he didn't believe her. *Why would he have had Archer attack me? What was the point of all the threats if they were only empty words?*

"I hear stories from slaves, from slavers, and small anecdotes from travelers. Once in a while, a scout or a merchant will come by, and if we are lucky, a Warshire herald will accompany one of the slavers. We do not get a lot of attention because we are so far east. Most of the stories are one sided, so the only way for me to understand what is going on across the kingdom is to inquire in this manner. Now I have a stronger insight on these subjects. For example, I would have never known about Chambers.

"I tend to think that history is like art. The information I gather helps me reveal the canvas. History has already been painted... I am simply trying to see the picture."

"Why not have every slave recount his or her life?"

"Multiple reasons. Hardly every slave is honest and, believe it or not, they tend to not want to help. You are much more reasonable than most. Also, we do not have the resources to recount the small lives of every slave that comes through the gates of Drudgeburg.

We do not have the scribes for that matter. Like I said, it is difficult to get people interested to come this far east. There is not a great deal of opportunity here for travelers.

"But enough about that. I have questions for you." Haylan flipped the journal open and dipped the quill in ink. "What happened to you when you were handed off in Mezzoah?"

"I was tossed in a prison cart twice the size of Laufia's—thrown in with Eleanor and Leon, another boy from Chambers. Though, they divided us after Warshire."

"They took you to Warshire?"

Barloc nodded as he slipped into his memory. Warshire perched high on a mountain. The size of the castle and the city below made Drudgeburg appear miniscule, insignificant. The keep's towers cut into the sky. Long walls, thicker than anything he'd ever seen, stretched down the mountainside, creating a barrier around the lower city. "The castle stood so high and strong that it looked like a fantasy. From the distance, the gleam of rubies and other gems explained why they called Warshire the Sleeping Sun."

Haylan tilted her head, a look of confusion on her face. "You made it *into* the castle?"

Barloc shook his head. "No, I barely made it into the lower city. The gates opened, and I exchanged hands faster than a coin to pickpocket. They divided us, and before I knew it, I was being driven west to the ownership of Rhotec Helory."

"You stayed his slave for over five years?"

Barloc nodded.

"Why is that? It is rare to see someone stay under one ownership for that long."

The cadence of her voice relaxed him. He unclenched his fists and placed them atop the blanket, and he found himself making more eye contact instead of searching for the comfort of the white mark. "I don't know. I did what I was told. I learned fast. I always tried to do more than was asked but not too much."

"Was he an evil man, Lord Helory?"

Barloc wanted to comment that the man was a slave owner but squelched the thought. "He hurt a lot of people."

"Did he hurt you?"

"Of course. He hurt everyone."

She scribbled again. "Were there others that remained as long as you?"

"Yes, but many more who didn't. I'm sure it's the same stories you hear from every place. Men were beaten, tortured, sold, bought, forgotten."

"All right. Now, about this Variegate, did you ever see him after the battle? You noted that he had vanished. Was he killed?"

Barloc closed his eyes and pictured all the people in the town after the battle. "I don't think so. I feel like he would've stood out, though, everything happened so fast."

"Can you remember anything specific about him? Maybe a scar or even the color of his eyes?"

Barloc imagined him sitting on the log, whittling a small piece of wood, but his features came with a fog. "It's interesting that I can tell you everything that was said, but I can't seem to think of anything that stands out other than the fact that he had long hair and was young. Still the youngest Howler I've seen to this day."

Haylan opened her mouth and closed it a few times until she found the words. "It is important. You may not understand now, but you will soon. Please think. Anything will help."

Barloc remembered when Variegate grabbed him and pulled his face into the bars of the prisoner cart, right after the girl had died. "His teeth!" Barloc jolted forward. "His front two teeth overlapped!"

Haylan opened the journal. "What about his hair, how long was his hair? Describe his appearance."

"His hair hung to his shoulders, and his beard was kept short but thick. Dark... maybe black. His eyes were dark, too. I was honestly scared to look at any of them directly. I really don't know past that."

Haylan finished writing and closed the book. "That is fine. Perfectly fine." She nodded. "I believe you may have helped after all."

"May I ask why the interest in this man?"

"Youth and kindness are rare qualities among the Howlers."

Barloc rested against the feather pillow. "Am I being sent back to the first day?"

Haylan didn't answer. She tucked the journal back into her robes.

The anticipation worked Barloc's nerves, but he didn't dare repeat the question.

Finally, she uncrossed her legs and sat forward. "Those things are not up to me. I am just a Healer, though I will see what I can do. No matter the case, we need to leave. I wish I had more time to interview you."

"Healer Haylan," Barloc asked as she stood. "Do you know what happened to MJ-1 and MJ-8?"

Haylan's expression fell. She took a breath and let it out slowly. "MJ-1 was murdered at the mines by the hands of MJ-8."

"That's impossible!"

"It is a lot of things but impossible surely is not one. Lord Harbor is to decide the fate of MJ-8 when we arrive."

Haylan helped keep Barloc steady and guided him toward the door. Before she reached for the handle, she said something so low, Barloc almost missed it. "You do not owe those slaves anything. Worry about *your* thirty days and then maybe one day, you can focus on making a difference for others."

Light flooded the small room when the door opened, much like the day of Atticus's funeral. He shielded his eyes and followed Haylan toward the center of the courtyard, and with only a few steps, Barloc's legs stopped shaking enough to walk on his own.

Lord Harbor, Vicar Farlen, Sir Vigor, Madam Constance, and a handful of Green Cloaks gathered before a much smaller wooden structure supporting MJ-1's body. A row of Healers stood beside them, and behind the platform burned Atticus's memorial as bright as the day it first caught fire.

Lord Harbor nodded at Haylan and began speaking to the audience. "Two deaths at Drudgeburg in only a few days! Death isn't uncommon. Life expectancy is short, especially in this kingdom.

"This convocation is being held for two reasons today. First, when a crime is committed, there must be a trial. The second is the funeral for the man who was murdered. MJ-8, step forward."

MJ-8 moved forward immediately.

"You struck a slave with a stone, causing irreversible damage. The Healers worked tirelessly to revive him until he passed away this morning. Had he survived, it would have merely been the matter of sending you back to day one with no food and a couple of lashes, but he perished, so the repercussions need to be clear."

Barloc thought about how long Haylan had remained with him that day, questioning him about his past life. *Had she not been in that room, could she have helped save MJ-1?*

"How do you plead?" Lord Harbor asked.

MJ-8 spoke directly to Lord Harbor. He lifted his head high and puffed his chest out in confidence. "All of those actions took place, but don't you care to know why?"

Lord Harbor considered this. He paced around the Green Cloaks until he stopped before MJ-8. "I set very clear expectations. If I let you get away with this, then how can I enforce my rules to the many that come through Drudgeburg?"

MJ-8 went to speak, but Lord Harbor cut him off. "What I have here is bigger than you. I'm risking a great deal every day I breathe. Whatever the reason you struck that man, it wasn't your place. You were given clear instructions and now we have one dead slave."

Barloc's mouth opened, and it took everything in him to not interject, but he knew his place and held his tongue.

Lord Harbor stood straight and pushed his chest out in the same confident way. "I will recycle you back into the world as a slave. May you remember your actions and where they led you. Tomorrow morning, you will be sold to the Howlers. If our paths should cross again, remember my kindness."

Lord Harbor walked past MJ-8 to Vicar Farlen. He now addressed everyone. "To show you how fair I can be, I will allow another to step in his place. I will allow MJ-8 to start at day one, and I will send whoever steps forward with the Howlers."

An awkward silence shrouded the sea of slaves. Every set of eyes seemed to drop to the ground. The only people still looking up were the leaders. Barloc discovered Master Sapper standing behind Sir Vigor, staring directly at him.

Lord Harbor somehow managed to speak even louder, his voice crashing against the walls like thunder. "I'm offering the opportunity for someone to stand up and be a hero. You will change this man's life."

Barloc argued with himself. MJ-8 potentially saved his life, but if he stepped forward, he would have to face the world again, face the Howlers. If he stepped forward, he'd be powerless against them. He'd never have a chance to retaliate for all they'd done. His dream before entering Drudgeburg was to get as far away from Kuldair as possible, certain he would never return to the kingdom again, but with the notion of freedom, he found himself stricken with the desire to fight back.

These thoughts barraged his mind as Lord Harbor approached MJ-8. Barloc couldn't take it anymore and stepped forward. A few heads turned, and Haylan's words repeated through his mind: *You do not owe those slaves anything.*

MJ-8 turned his head, confused, as if he didn't understand why anyone would step forward to take his place. When he discovered that it was Barloc, he stared for a moment, shook his head softly, and returned his gaze back to Lord Harbor.

Barloc quickly retracted his step, his shoulders sagging with the weight of his decision.

MJ-8's wide eyes told the truth his puffed-out chest attempted to hide. Fear etched deeper into his face with each passing moment of silence.

Barloc scanned the Green Cloaks to see if anyone else had seen him step forward, stopping on Master Sapper.

Sapper smiled, nodded slowly, and winked at him.

Rage swelled through Barloc's body as he stared at Sapper, unblinking, and it wasn't until Lord Harbor finally spoke that he realized what was happening.

"No one. Very well, then. It's done. Take him away." At those words, he faced the platform supporting MJ-1's still body.

MJ-8 walked past, escorted by a Green Cloak. Tears streamed down his cheeks, and when he met Barloc's eyes, a mixture of feelings collided inside of him. Barloc felt anger toward MJ-8 for following him on day one, furious for falling that day at the mines and allowing that bond to be built between them.

Finally, sadness gripped his heart as he watched what would likely be his final friend sentenced to what would surely be his death. Barloc vowed right then and there that he would keep MJ-8's name readily on his lips for when he cut down his first Howler, if he ever got the chance.

The funeral ceremony began, but Barloc tuned it out. Instead, he reflected on his nightmares, and he thought about the slaves that fell to his blade. He decided that MJ-8 was the first of many he would sacrifice to rise to the top.

Lord Harbor's voice cut into his thoughts. "Even though his life appeared insignificant, you can't have a foundation without every stone, and today we bury one of our stones."

Bury one of our stones? The words pulled Barloc from his thoughts, back to the ceremony. *Our? What a strange way to say that. Why are they treating a slave's life like that of the Green Cloak that died?*

Two guards equipped Lord Harbor and Vicar Farlen with burning torches, which they held at the bottom of the platform. In seconds, the unit collapsed under the flames. Vicar Farlen turned back and announced that MJ-1's fire would burn for three days and then be scattered at the mines, not as a sign of disrespect, but a sign of the hard labor he put in there.

Chapter 9 – King of East Reach

"Hold it!" Master Fletcher yelled and swung his ax for a final blow. Slowly, the tree spun, fighting gravity. The heartwood broke with a series of loud pops. "Pull!"

Barloc and three other slaves gripped the ropes wrapped around the thick trunk and ran toward the castle wall. With a final pop, the tree spun on its point before smashing to the ground. Dust, dirt, and leaves exploded into the air. Once the debris cleared, another group of slaves stripped off the branches and piled them off to the side.

He preferred lumbering over mining. Mining required constant slouching while moving stones, causing his back to always hurt. The lack of sunlight, combined with Master Sapper barking out orders, made for a horrible time. While lumbering, he remained under the canopy of trees and received twice the food.

Also, Master Fletcher helped with the work—the first time Barloc had seen this behavior at Drudgeburg.

Fletcher didn't lead with fear like Sapper. He cared about his slaves and the task at hand, which he made clear earlier that morning when introducing himself. "My name is Master Fletcher. I requested additional hands from Lord Harbor, and he supplied. Yesterday we cleared ten trees. I expect no less than twelve today. I know we can do it. You're all strong men."

Fletcher scraped the sky when compared to Sapper, easily twice his height, though thin and gangly. He kept his graying hair slicked back, his eyebrows clung to his face like two bushy caterpillars, and his eyes sunk into his head. His teeth, though intact, held a glossy yellow color, and when he spoke, his voice often squeaked. He liked to talk with his hands and he pivoted slightly with each word.

Fletcher pointed at the castle and brushed a strand of hair from his face. "Lord Harbor needs this lumber as soon as possible. With that said, if you work hard for me, I'll work hard for you. I'll make sure you get that extra meal!"

Fletcher had separated the slaves into three groups. The first cut down the trees; the second removed the branches; the third manned the lumber cart. All the slaves helped lift the tree onto the cart, which they then hauled to the front of the castle.

"On my mark," Fletcher yelled as the cart backed up to the stripped oak.

Barloc slipped his fingers underneath the tree, and when Fletcher reached three, the men lifted and walked it onto the cart.

The process repeated until the sun began to fall. Barloc listened for the slave horn, ready for the day to end, when the soft echo of a trumpet barely met his ears.

Fletcher stopped cutting, straightened up, and wiped sweat from his forehead. "What was that?" The trumpet sounded again, this time much clearer. Fletcher twirled his finger. "Gather the tools and line up."

Barloc grabbed his ax and joined the formation. The guards ran down the line, retrieving the tools and placing them in a haversack, much like the one Sir Vigor used to carry the training weapons on day one. Together, they marched toward the entrance at a pace so fast the slaves had to jog to keep up.

The trumpet sounded once more but much louder this time, and as they rounded the corner of the castle wall, they came upon a group of men in plate armor, wearing King Sclavus's red cloaks.

Fletcher held up his fist, bringing the line of slaves to a halt.

Above the gate, along the battlement, stood Lord Harbor.

The leader of the soldiers broke away from the group and moved toward the entrance on horseback. His mount differed from the rest. He rode on a white horse that stood a foot taller than the others, its mane silvery and long. His cloak was more vibrant than those of the other men, blazing in the setting sun. "I'm here under the order of King Sclavus to investigate one Lord Harbor of Drudgeburg."

Lord Harbor's voice crashed down on the men. "I am he, but who, may I ask, are you?"

His accent changed again, Barloc thought as he stepped slightly out of line to get a better view.

The knight shook his head and scoffed. "Isn't it clear? I'm wearing the king's sigil, surrounded by fourteen men wearing the king's colors. Isn't it obvious who I am?"

Lord Harbor shrugged and placed his hands on the battlement. "Do you not have a name?"

The leader removed his helmet and set it on his lap. His olive-colored skin reminded him of Slaver Martin, though everything else about the man stood for quite the opposite. Long, black hair cascaded over his shoulders. His high cheekbones forced his eyes into a squint, and his jawline squared sharply around his mouth. Though covered in the silver and red armor, his muscles were evident, even at the distance. "My name is Lord Esmund Aziar. I am the head of the King's Guard. These are my men. Now, are we done with this foolishness? I've traveled long and far, and I'm on the king's business."

Lord Harbor nodded as if he finally understood a problem he'd been working out for some time. "So, you would like to parley?"

The king's men moved their hands to the hilts of their blades. The soldiers in the back of the vanguard gripped bows, already strung with arrows.

Lord Aziar laughed deep in his throat and glanced back at the soldiers. He rested his hand atop his helmet and silently stared up at Lord Harbor.

Across the hill, Sapper and his slaves appeared. At the sight of the new arrivals, Sapper broke into a gallop, stopping an equal distance as Fletcher.

Lord Aziar glanced from Sapper to Fletcher and back up to Lord Harbor. "Did you just threaten me?"

"Heavens, no, Esmund Aziar. I was simply asking if you would like to partake in a parley."

Esmund scoffed. "A parley would suggest that you and I are not in accord. It is a term an enemy will use to allow a reprieve from battle to discuss conditions of surrender or other terms."

Lord Harbor lifted his hands again. "Well, since you seem to understand, let's begin. What is it that I can do for you?"

"You can raise your gate and let us in. The day is nearly at an end, and we will need to take advantage of the king's rights. We will need fifteen beds and food. Our men have gone a little longer than they would prefer without a hot meal.... This bloody castle is practically on the edge of the kingdom."

Lord Harbor climbed onto the wall and sat with his feet dangling over the side. He stared off in the distance, as if pondering what to say. "What is this investigation in regard to?"

"We can discuss that privately."

Lord Harbor smiled down at Lord Aziar. "Well, then let's discuss the things we can openly. First, I'm not letting you into my castle, and you don't control the gate, so your choices in that matter are limited. I would prefer you earned your way into my castle by respecting me and my land.

"Second, since we have commenced our parley—"

Lord Aziar slammed his fist against his helmet, scaring his steed. "It's not a bloody parley."

"Second, I am a man of equal respect. You get back what you give, and since we have commenced our parley, your men haven't removed their hands from their weapons." Lord Harbor whistled through his fingers and immediately five men on either side of him stood, wielding bows already nocked with arrows, all pointed down at the king's men. He withdrew an apple from inside his cloak and lobbed it into the air.

All at once, the archers released their arrows, exploding the fruit, raining small chunks over the king's men. The archers had replaced their arrows before the apple debris landed.

Lord Aziar reared his horse. "How dare you!"

"I am only showing you that my men can shoot. I don't want you to get too comfortable with your armed archers. Now, on with our parley. What investigation?"

Lord Aziar ground his teeth, the muscles in his jaw clenching and releasing. "We have received word that you are freeing slaves, which conflicts with the king's decree. Only the king can free a slave, and you don't have that privilege."

"And whose word was it that you received?"

"That's not your business. You should be much more concerned with what you're concealing in that castle of yours. King Sclavus sent us to investigate. For every freed slave linked back to you, you'll be fined one hundred coin. Now, open the gate!"

"I've clearly got slaves, Esmund." He lifted his arms and pointed to both Fletcher and Sapper. "I've worked entirely too hard to allow someone like yourself to enter my grounds and pick apart my land."

Lord Aziar faced his vanguard. "Do you hear this, men? He believes he has a choice in the matter." He did a small gait and rotated back to Lord Harbor. "I'm not questioning the slaves you have, Harbor. I'm questioning the slaves you *no longer* have. This is my last warning. Open the gate or—"

"Or what? Your men are going to cut me down? Siege my castle? Exactly what happens if I don't lift my gate?"

Lord Aziar straightened up and spoke very matter-of-factly. "Then I will return to the king, declaring you a traitor. King Sclavus will then send a small army to lay waste to this," he panned his hand across the span of the castle, "pile of rubble. The king doesn't take treason lightly, nor should he. Now, stop wasting my time."

"Esmund, how long did it take you to travel this way?"

"What does that matter, for I am here?"

"I'm curious about how weary you and your men are that you approach me in such a forceful and rude manner."

"This is over. Open your castle or I will be forced to take action."

Lord Harbor continued to talk as if Lord Aziar never spoke. "Is this how you conduct yourself to your king?"

"*My* king?"

"Esmund, I'll have it be known today that I reject King Sclavus as my king. He stole the throne through lies and treachery. I cannot support a man who uses outlaws to do his bidding." Lord Harbor's chest rose and fell with a sigh, and then he spoke louder than before. "From this day forward, I declare myself a new king. You may address me as King Harbor, King of Drudgeburg, King of East Reach. King of whatever you please. Leave me to my people at the edge of the world, and we can all live in peace."

Tension crowded the area until Lord Aziar exploded into laughter. It took a moment for him to calm down, and when he stopped, he said, "End this farce."

"You'll return to Warshire with a message. What built King Sclavus up will be what breaks him down. I declare our parley over."

Lord Aziar's mouth dropped open, but nothing came out.

"If you make one wrong move, my men will open fire. Leave now."

Lord Aziar replaced his helmet atop his head. "I should've killed you the moment I saw you."

"And one day you'll truly regret not doing so."

Lord Aziar reared his horse once more and rode away hard from Drudgeburg.

Sapper approached the castle and smirked back at the king's men. "King Harbor, is it now? More like a king of fools."

"Well, this certainly changes things." Lord Harbor disappeared, and moments later, the gate ascended.

With one final glance, Barloc watched King Sclavus's men ride over the horizon into the setting sun.

Chapter 10 – Preperations for War

"These two slaves made it through their thirty days!" Lord Harbor yelled from the sorting table. Barloc couldn't help but notice that his accent had once again returned to its familiar drawl. "Now they have to make a choice. They can leave, or they can stay." He turned to the two slaves in large brown cloaks, their features hidden within the hoods. "If you leave, you lose my protection. If you stay, I offer safety, as well as a place in my castle."

Barloc pushed past another slave obstructing his view, desperate to watch. This was the first real sign of freedom since he'd been sold to Drudgeburg, the first real proof, and he didn't want to miss a word.

"The choice is yours. If you choose to go, you keep the clothes on your back, a weapon of your choice, three gold coins, and two days' worth of food."

Lord Harbor paced back and forth in front of the table, speaking more to the crowd than to the two slaves.

"But if you choose to stay, Madam Constance will escort you inside, where you will swear fealty to Drudgeburg, to me. There is no turning back from either direction, and you must choose now. I'll allow you to speak freely if you have any questions to help complete your decision."

Neither of the slaves spoke, so Lord Harbor continued, "SD-3, do you have a decision?"

From the taller slave, a strong, deep voice boomed: "Yes, my lord. I choose to leave. I want to be free and attempt to find my family."

"Very well." Lord Harbor turned to the other slave. "A-4, what is your decision?"

"My lord?" a much softer voice asked.

"Yes?"

"I've never seen any of the slaves return from inside. What happens to them? Where do they go?"

Lord Harbor smiled. "Fair question. That is all part of the risk, A-4. You're choosing your new path. You can leave like SD-3 and risk a run in with the king's men or Howlers, or you can remain here. If you believe that I've been fair, then I welcome you to enter my castle. As I said, there is no turning back."

"I will remain."

Chatter broke around the crowd but died down just as quickly, as if the men remembered they were slaves a moment too late.

"Very well, it's decided. Sir Vigor, ride hard. Three hours should do it. Take SD-3 past the mire and let him off at the abandoned stables. Madam Constance, tend to the other." Both Sir Vigor and Madam Constance led the slaves in opposite directions.

"This group," Lord Harbor pointed toward Barloc and the thirty or so slaves that surrounded him, "will be dealing with lumber. The other three will head to the mines. A lot of work needs to be done, and fast. If you work hard, I'll allow for an additional meal before lockdown."

Lord Harbor left for the inner bailey while the remaining Green Cloaks directed the mass of slaves out of the castle.

Barloc kept so busy, he lost track of time, and before he knew it, the guards fed the slaves lunch. By midday, the groups had processed more than forty trees. The slaves switched duties, and Barloc helped transport the felled trees to the front of the castle. When he cleared the corner, the sight took him by surprise.

Guards and slaves scattered the field before Drudgeburg. Barloc noted more black outfits than brown, maybe twenty people total, while two Green Cloaks monitored the scene. More slaves pulled carts of stone up the hill toward the crest, and the guards wove wooden pikes together, creating spiked bulwarks.

At the drop point, slaves cut the trees into six-foot pointed poles, which they piled onto another cart to be taken up the field for the bulwarks. Another Green Cloak managed the slaves sitting at a wooden table against the castle wall, fletching arrows from branches. The entire castle had transformed overnight.

The sounds of labor faded and he closed his eyes, processing what it all meant. He opened them back up and spun around in a circle, taking in his surroundings.

For ten days, he'd questioned if freedom was real, and not a few hours ago, he'd seen proof, but now he stared at what was surely the making of a battlefield. *How many of the other slaves realize that he's preparing for war?*

He wondered about the Green Cloaks and Lord Harbor more than ever. *Just what is going on behind those walls?*

As Barloc waited for the slaves to get into position to remove the tree from the cart, the bigger picture began to form. They were only clearing the trees that grew close to the castle. As a kid, he'd learned that anything close to a castle's walls could be used against it in a battle. *Did Lord Harbor really believe he could take on a kingdom? Was he mad?*

He followed the line of slaves back around the castle, lost in his thoughts. *What would happen when the king's men opened siege on Drudgeburg? Would the king care to save the slaves, or would they simply destroy the castle and everything in it?*

Chapter 11 – A New Beginning

The sky stretched white and gray with clouds. It had rained through the night, leaving the ground saturated with mud, and a soft drizzle still fell on the slaves as they waited for Madam Constance to speak. Once again, things changed for Barloc when she announced three names, including his. The three slaves stepped from the crowd to stand before Sir Vigor, Madam Constance, Sapper, Fletcher, and one other Green Cloak.

Madam Constance spoke loudly, addressing the sea of slaves that filled the bailey. "We will repeat the tasks from yesterday—this side to the forest, this side to the mines. It will be slippery, so everyone must move with caution. We had multiple injuries yesterday, and our Healers simply cannot keep up." She took a breath. "If you hurt yourself, it is likely that you will be working alongside your injuries."

Sir Vigor moved with the other Green Cloaks, who led the slaves out of the castle grounds.

Madam Constance ordered that Barloc and the other two slaves follow her.

As they walked across the muddy yard, he worried that he had done something wrong again. Never since becoming a slave had he been targeted so much, but all his worries left at the sight of the pavilions.

"Congratulations on arriving at your tenth day. It's always a surprise to see how few make it. MJ-7 step forward."

Their eyes met, and for a flicker of a moment, in the timespan of a blink, he thought he saw her lips curl into a smile, but when he wiped the rain from his eyes, she only stared at him. He quickly stepped to the guard waiting underneath the tent.

The guard worked at removing his wrist manacles, and while he did, Barloc watched the final bit of slaves funnel out of Drudgeburg. Rain ran off the edges of the tent, cutting a line into the muddy ground below.

Once the guard finished, Barloc stood and extended his arms, moving them in all directions. He remembered his first day and how nice it felt to receive lighter fetters with longer links. A part of him wanted to view the situation through a narrower scope and focus on the fact that he still had shackles on his ankles, that he remained enslaved. Instead, he focused on how much closer he was to freedom.

Once the final slave's manacles hit the table, Madam Constance stepped into the rain. "Follow me."

Small roofs had been erected over each of the funeral pyres, tall enough to keep from catching fire and wide enough to divert the rainfall. Each time he stepped, the muddy ground kissed at his cloth boots, and by the time they arrived at the inner gate, his clothes hung heavy with rain. Steadily, nature attempted to dampen his mood, but the excitement of advancing kept his concerns at bay.

Madam Constance approached the inner portcullis and raised a fist. A moment later, it ascended. The framework resembled the main entrance though a much smaller version. As they passed through, Barloc observed the layers of thick, black grime along the edges of the above murder hole and the scorch marks on the ground below, unable to stop himself from wondering what had happened.

They arrived at a slightly smaller yard than the outer bailey. A crudely crafted wall, made from different types of stone and wooden planks, spanned the left side. Everything about it appeared random except the placement. It clearly segregated the main keep from the slaves.

Smaller versions of the long, thatched bunkhouses stretched along the same makeshift wall. Slaves, guards, and a couple of Green Cloaks filled the yard, keeping busy. Madam Constance worked her way toward a familiar looking man Barloc remembered seeing on the day Atticus had died.

"What do we have here? Fresh meat, aye?" The man crossed his arms and flashed every tooth in a smile. He stood Barloc's height and only slightly thicker. His white and brown hair was cropped short like his beard, and he wore the same green cloak, black boots, and leather gloves as every other master in Drudgeburg.

Madam Constance introduced the man as Master Tarak. "From this day forward, Master Tarak will be your overseer. It's not like it was out there. Things run differently in here. He'll explain everything." Madam Constance bowed her head to Tarak and faced the three slaves. For a moment, it was as if she wanted to say something, but instead, she nodded and disappeared through the gate.

Tarak beckoned them closer. "Come on. I'll get you set up." He waited until all three slaves were within arm's length before walking alongside them. "Contrary to what Madam Constance said, the same rules apply here. You don't speak unless you're spoken to, and you do as you're told." As they walked, Barloc noted that the rain had tapered to a soft mist. "What you will be doing *is* different, but if you do what you're supposed to, you won't have any problems. It's as simple as that."

Different booths lined every inch of the walls, all the way to the bunkhouses, barring a wash station tucked away in a corner. A path cut through the courtyard like a mineral vein, and battle squares occupied any open land. At the very end of the bailey stood a large wooden arena.

Guards and slaves sparred in nearly every battle square. Tarak walked past each until they arrived before a callboard where a series of ladders stretched upward, each rung supporting a different name. Barloc took in the different letters and numbers making the list of slaves. The sight weighed heavily on his mind. He'd gone from being a mule for Lord Harbor, hauling stone and lumber, to a common animal, being used to fight for entertainment.

"The way this works is simple enough. You fight!" Tarak laughed with such animation, he doubled over.

When he finally calmed down, he stood and wiped sweat from his forehead. "If you participate, you have to challenge one person a day, as long as they are placed equal or above you. If you win, you swap spots on the ladder. When you get to the top rung, you battle me. If you do well, then you lose your fetters and move on. In a way, you fight for your freedom.

"As you can see, there are two ladders connecting to one, so there are roughly ten contestants at any time fighting for the top spots."

Tarak laughed again. "Don't worry, though. This is for people who want to expedite their freedom, beat on guards, and for our entertainment. The most important part is the constant training for our guards. If you don't want to be part of the tournament, you will be used as practice dummies and perform other tasks around the yard, like cleaning out everybody's chamber pots. If you choose not to fight, your remaining twenty days will be spent with me.

"If you mess up or fail, you start back at the beginning. If you really screw up, you go out to the slop yard.

"Now, we will go from station to station and test your proficiency with each weapon. By the end, I'll assign you a Focus. Each Focus will be what you use in practice and the arena."

Tarak led them to the first booth, and on the way, Barloc took the chance to inspect the arena more closely. The walls stood slightly taller and more solid than those of the battle squares, and the surface, even wet, appeared hard, unlike the soft mud that covered the rest of Drudgeburg. Two long benches lined one side in stadium fashion. He pictured Lord Harbor and the other Green Cloaks sitting around, watching the slaves get beat down, betting on who would survive and who would fail.

A small line of slaves and guards shot arrows down the long range and into hay targets at the end. "Let us through!" Tarak shoved a gap open between them. "This is the only warm up guaranteed to happen each day. Every man will stretch by using a bow. You will do no good sparring with the guards if you're stiff. Ten shots per person, per day. You, boy, step forward." He pointed at Barloc.

Tarak handed him a bow. Only once in his life had he touched one, and he hadn't been strong enough to pull back the string. He lifted it up, tightened his left hand around the grip, and placed an arrow on the rest. He pulled back, almost forgetting to nock the arrow. After he corrected it, he pulled back once more.

Barloc's cheeks warmed when Tarak laughed. He took a deep breath, and once he felt confident, he let the arrow fly. It ricocheted off the booth's support beam, almost striking one of the guards.

"That was some of the worst shooting I've seen!" Tarak rolled with laughter and slapped his knees. The constant laughing annoyed Barloc. "Go ahead and take your other shots."

Barloc attempted to steady his aim, and by the fifth shot, he managed to land one in the hay.

Tarak stopped laughing, leaned into his ear, and lowered his voice to a whisper. "You need to lock your elbow. Lower your grip so your thumb isn't obstructing your sight. I favor reaction shots, myself. You'll need more strength if you plan to hold it up so long." He stepped back. "Now, keep your target in your sights, pull back only when ready, and for the love of all women, stop closing your eyes when you release. You're going to kill someone."

Barloc followed his instructions and focused on the target. When ready, he drew back and released. The arrow grazed the target and landed in the hay wall behind it. By the tenth shot, his arms thrummed, and when he stretched, he wondered why the slaves would be forced to do such a straining task every day. It was as if Tarak wanted them tired for combat, not stretched.

Tarak made them watch a spar while he explained the rules. Each match had a goal. Either the slave had to hit the guard in the chest with the practice weapon, or he had to prevent the guard from doing so to him, all before the sandglass ran dry. He told them that the only differences between a spar and a challenge were the audience, the arena master could augment the match however he saw fit, and losing had more of an impact than a practice spar. Losing three challenges disqualifies the slave completely, returning him back to the beginning of the remaining twenty days.

Even though the information was overwhelming, the concepts seemed basic enough: follow the rules closely and don't lose.

After practicing with each weapon, Barloc was assigned the sword as his Focus, and he was forced to participate in a spar by tapping a guard's chest before the time ended. He almost did it, too, but between the archery and practice, he fought fatigue as much as he did the guard. Each time he swung, his chest hurt from where his ribs were damaged, and each time he lunged, pain assaulted his foot from where his toes were broken.

Once the horn sounded, and the day came to a close, Tarak directed the slaves to the arena where they sat across the front row. The elevated row behind them filled with the guards. Barloc had been wrong. Where he'd pictured Lord Harbor and the other Green Cloaks sat slaves and guards. Before them, Tarak stood in the center of the arena, facing the audience.

"Each morning, your name is scratched next to the slave you are to challenge," Tarak spoke to Barloc and the other two new recruits. "I'll only explain this once, so pay attention. You climb the ladder until you get to the top. If you do it properly, the process takes ten days. You have the choice of challenging someone ahead, though if you lose, that's a strike against you. After three strikes, you're removed from the tournament and brought back to the beginning of my section.

"There's one exception to this rule. You can bypass all the slaves and challenge me directly. Now, when you choose this path and lose, you automatically gain three strikes, you're pulled from the tournament, and thrown back at the beginning."

On both ends of the stands, two Green Cloaks distributed bread. On one side of the arena, a slave waited, and on the other, the sandglass sat fixed to a tall pole. Another Green Cloak stood by, ready to start the time.

"Today, we have a slave challenging me directly." Tarak burst into laughter and backed to the side. "Send him in!"

A Green Cloak pushed the slave into the arena, who tripped over the wall and fell hard on his shoulder. Once he stood, he focused on Tarak.

"Unfortunately for you, I find it arrogant to skip rungs. I don't like it, but you obviously think you have a chance." Two wooden swords flew into the arena, landing at their feet.

Barloc watched with both excitement and fear for the slave.

"The rule is simple. If you can tap my chest with your sword, you win, but I'm not merely defending." Tarak twirled the sword in his hand and sidestepped.

The slave mirrored him, though the chains around his ankles reduced his movements. He lunged forward, driving straight for Tarak's chest.

Tarak laughed, and in one fluid motion, dropped down and tripped the slave.

The slave fell forward, losing his sword, squirming to retrieve it, but everything ended before he could find his feet.

Tarak stepped over to him and slammed his wooden sword into the back of his head.

Barloc shifted his eyes between the still slave and the sandglass, the bottom barely covered.

Tarak wiped his hand across his forehead and threw his practice sword down. "Strange how that goes, isn't it? You saw the sandglass and the training weapon and expected a long, drawn-out duel. You wanted to see the slave make a heroic move, land a blow on my chest, and succeed, but here's proof that this is not how it works. In a real fight or battle, there are no turns, you don't get the luxury of training weapons, and you absolutely don't get to make numerous attempts."

Tarak rolled the slave onto his back with his foot, the man's chest rising and falling in a soft, easy motion. "And not everyone gets to keep breathing at the end of it." Tarak stepped over him and exited the arena.

Chapter 12 – The Battle Square

The slave horn vibrated the bunkhouse, waking Barloc with a start. He expected the door to burst open and guards to guide him out to the sorting table, but they never came. When he lifted his hands to rub his eyes, the missing weight of the chains almost scared him. He turned his wrists back and forth, certain it was all a dream, but when he glanced around the bunkhouse, the dream quickly became a reality. He lay on the lower bunk of a much smaller building, and no one had secured his ankle fetters to the bedpost.

Barloc joined the other slaves as they rose from their beds and lined up at the door. Even though guards weren't present, they moved as though they were—silent and in single file.

Master Tarak stood outside with two Green Cloaks and a handful of guards. "Head to the callboard to select your challenger, then line up at the archery booth.

Once done there, move to your Focus." He crossed his arms tightly and nodded at the slaves as they passed by.

Barloc's name had been chalked against the wood on the lowest rung, next to the name 'OD-7.' He followed the other slaves as they walked past the board and stood in line at the archery booth, and as he waited, he realized that Tarak hadn't accompanied them. Only a single guard stood watch, silently against the wall.

Barloc landed three out of the ten arrows into the target, but even with repeating Tarak's instructions, he couldn't shoot the arrows straight.

No one escorted Barloc from the archery booth, either. He simply moved toward his Focus: Sword and Shield Combat. On his walk, he counted the people, including slaves, guards, and Green Cloaks, ending at thirty-two. The guards and Green Cloaks scattered the yard, either sparring or surveying, while Tarak escorted a new slave to the arena ladder.

This scene seemed much more chaotic when compared to the outer bailey, likely because of the constant movement and the lack of open ground. Slaves shot at the archery booth, stood at their Focus, or sparred. A few weaved in and out of the buildings carrying buckets.

When he arrived at his Focus, Barloc stepped behind the one slave standing in line. In the battle square behind him, another slave attempted to tap a guard's chest. He moved deftly but carelessly, waiting like a cat for the right time to pounce, only to miss.

The guard didn't fight to disable, rather worked the slave down by deflecting his sporadic onslaught. He kept his form tight, and after each attack, corrected his stance and waited for the next.

A loud crash rang in Barloc's ear, and when he turned, the metal sign above the booth rocked back and forth from where the guard below smashed it with a training sword.

The guard passed the wooden sword to the next slave in line, who then entered the battle square, where another guard twirled a long staff, either attempting to intimidate or to prove his skill.

A Green Cloak stepped to their square, announced that the slave had to tap the guard's chest, and flipped the sandglass. This slave appeared more cautious than the previous, but it didn't matter. Barloc didn't see the fairness in dueling a guard with a long staff when the slave only held a short wooden sword.

Regardless of the disadvantage, the slave attempted his best. The guard did all he could to swipe the slave's feet from under him with each attack, and this repeated until the slave threw his weapon down and dropped to his knees, giving up.

Again, the crash rang in Barloc's ear. A guard forced a wooden sword into his hand and pointed at the square. Barloc gripped the weapon, then tossed it fist to fist. Chips and dents lined the off-balanced piece of wood. He stepped into the square, where a guard waited for him. The man in front of him gripped a sword much like Barloc's own.

The Green Cloak pointed at Barloc and turned the sandglass. "You'll defend yourself. Keep him from hitting your chest."

Barloc stood momentarily confused. The Green Cloak left abruptly, and the guard advanced, crouching low to the ground with both arms out to his sides and his sword at the ready.

Barloc backed away, keeping close to the edge of the arena. His confidence picked up as his mind played out different moves he could make, but nothing worked.

The guard teased him by lunging forward and retracting at the last moment. Three, four, five times he did this, working Barloc's guard down without even touching him.

Barloc circled the arena, growing dizzy, until he saw his opening.

The guard swiped Barloc's feet out from underneath him, pinned his arms down, and pointed the sword at his chest without touching him. Their eyes met and the guard winked and stepped back. He moved to the opposite side of the arena and waited for Barloc to stand.

By the end of the match, Barloc's body thrummed with pain. He didn't understand why the guard teased him. Four times he pinned Barloc down, but Barloc refused to give up, and each time he became a little better. In the end, though, it didn't matter. Barloc lost and stepped to the sideline.

He watched the many spars around him but focused on the guards, attempting to pick out any patterns. None of them seemed to fight the same way. Some moved more aggressively, while others kept their defense. Out of the eight duels he only saw one slave succeed.

On his next turn, he dueled against the guard with the staff. Fortunately, he'd seen him fight three times and learned that he relied on keeping the attacker on the ground as much as possible, using the staff to swipe the slave's feet out from under him.

Barloc copied the form of the sword guard, and though his confidence scraped the ground, he truly believed he stood a chance when the guard failed to bring him down. He skirted the border and focused on the guard's shoulders, noting that the staff took more effort, hoping to predict his next move. Repeatedly, Barloc lunged at him and fell back. As the sandglass emptied, Barloc felt he'd mastered the guard's moves.

He ran forward, taking long strides left, then right, then left. The staff moved faster than he expected and slammed into his ribs. Pain burst across his chest, and before he could adjust, the guard jabbed him in the stomach, sending him to the ground.

Finally, the guard sent the staff into Barloc's side.

When Barloc finally caught his breath, he looked up just in time to see the sandglass's last grains fall. He limped to the sideline.

Barloc searched his arms and legs for cuts, and his head throbbed. Not long after the beating, the guards fed the slaves and gave each a huge tumbler of water.

After a few more duels, Tarak called for everyone's attention. All the slaves, guards, and Green Cloaks moved in a circle around him. "F-4 and OD-13, step into the square."

The arena ladder flashed through Barloc's mind, where he saw the slave names atop each rung. He'd completely forgotten that he would have to fight a challenger. *OD-7.* The thought that the last two fights were only practice depressed him. He shifted to see the battle square more clearly.

"Defend yourself, OD-13. Begin!" This battle went about as well as Barloc would've guessed. Both slaves ran at each other swinging mad. OD-13 held wooden daggers, while F-4 wielded a chipped-up wooden mace. OD-13 attempted to roll under the swing of the mace only to have it strike him in his back, and before he knew it, F-4 smashed the blunt side of the mace against OD-13's cheek. Blood sprayed in a cloud, and F-4 jumped back, not hitting the slave's chest.

Tarak circled them. "Finish it already!"

OD-13 lost both of his daggers and covered his mouth. F-4 lifted the mace high above his head and sent it onto OD-13's chest. The slave screamed on contact.

Tarak stepped into the arena. "You're a fool." He grabbed the mace from the slave's hand. "Why would you do that?"

The slave responded with a smirk.

Tarak's jaw worked in his closed mouth. "I asked you a question, F-4. Why would you maim him when he was clearly done?"

F-4 straightened up and said, "Is an enemy ever really done, Master Tarak?"

Tarak exited the arena. Two guards stepped in with a Green Cloak and removed OD-13. "F-4 wins and moves on."

The next fighters moved more defensively. It took a little bit for one of them to attack. Both men fought with swords, and the fight took nearly the entire time. Even then not much happened.

Next Tarak called Barloc into the battle square. "MJ-7 and OD-7, enter." He pointed at Barloc. "You will tap his chest. Begin!"

Barloc's heart raced and his adrenaline began to flow, but even through that, exhaustion attempted to creep in. His opponent wasted no time. Barloc saw hunger behind the attacker's eyes, so he kept his distance, attempting to learn the slave's moves.

The slave fought with a longsword, which worked similarly to the staff. Barloc doubted his ability to win with each step he took. He moved slower this his opponent, and when he applied any pressure to his foot, pains pulsed through his broken toes. The chains around his ankles held a weight that he hadn't felt since marching across the kingdom.

OD-7 attacked. Barloc watched the slave's shoulders lift, and just in time, he sidestepped the arcing longsword.

OD-7 jabbed Barloc in the side and sent the sword into his already hurt ribs.

Barloc screamed in pain and lost his stomach. For a moment, he wanted to stop moving and lie there. Maybe he would be able to see Haylan again if he got beaten badly enough, but instincts forced him to move, and he retreated to the edge of the arena.

When Barloc turned, the butt of the longsword smashed into his nose. He fought to keep his balance, to keep from falling out of the ring. Blood washed down his chin and soaked into his tunic. He grabbed the slave's wrists and shoved him toward the center, stealing the opportunity to move from the square's edge.

With a burst of energy, he charged OD-7 with his sword out.

The slave made to move but slipped on Barloc's vomit, adding more force to his attack. The sword smashed into Barloc's chest, forcing him into the air, flailing his arms. Barloc's sword left his hand and the back of his head smashed hard against the ground.

Barloc lost. The slave was supposed to defend himself, not destroy his opponent. He closed his eyes, furious with himself. *Strike one on my first day.*

At that moment, between all the pains and the loss, he wished he'd chosen to clean chamber pots.

"Get him up!" Tarak yelled. Hands grabbed Barloc's arms and lifted him to his feet. The other slave's longsword lay on the ground next to his. Tarak stepped in between them, waving everyone away. "Clear out, already!"

Barloc limped toward the edge of the battle square.

"MJ-7 wins and moves on!"

Barloc stopped and turned back to Tarak, confused. *How could I possibly be the winner?*

Tarak crossed his thick arms. "Is there a problem, MJ-7?"

Barloc shook his head. "I just don't... I don't understand how I won."

"Well, by all rights, I suppose you should've lost, but a rule is a rule. When he slipped on your puke, he lunged forward knocking your sword from your hand. Your sword landed right on his chest. It was as if the fool was giving you the match. Had he just defended himself, he would've won. Now, leave the square!"

Barloc transitioned from feeling defeated to elated and one day closer to freedom. He watched the rest of the duels, studying the slaves. He realized that it wasn't the guards he needed to understand. Had he watched the slaves all day, he may have done better, but now he knew, and now he wouldn't take his eyes off them. It was the fights against the slaves that mattered, and now more than ever, he would have to cut down one slave at a time as he fought his way to freedom.

Chapter 13 – A Theif in the Night

Barloc searched the darkness certain he'd heard something, but after a moment of silence, he attempted to drift back to sleep. He replayed his last fight from the battle square, noting what he could have done differently. Images flashed through his mind in a strange limbo between sleep and consciousness when he heard it again: the sounds of someone whispering, the unmistakable thud of boots stepping across the wooden floor, and the soft rattle of chains.

As the figure approached his bed, Barloc squeezed his eyes shut, wondering who it could be. In his grogginess, he thought maybe Sapper or MJ-1, but they were gone. MJ-1 had died and Sapper was busy harassing someone else. Surely his tired mind only played tricks on him. He took a slow, even breath and opened his eyes.

A man clamped a hand tightly over Barloc's mouth and lifted a finger to his lips, signaling silence.

Barloc attempted to identify him but couldn't make out any features through the dark clothes and masked face.

The man removed his hand from Barloc's mouth. "Are you with me or against me?" His whisper sounded like gravel under feet.

Barloc glared into his eyes, unblinking. "I don't even know who you are."

"Your freedom. I've come to rescue you, but you must do everything I say. If you make a sound, I'll kill you where you stand. We have to move fast. We don't have long." He straightened up and scurried to the exit.

Barloc sat off the side of the bed, but before standing, he listened for any commotion from outside and heard nothing.

The man pulled the door open and vanished with the other slaves at his tail.

Barloc took a step but stopped. The thought of freedom made his legs want to twitch forward, but the idea of a masked man behind its claim rooted him down. *If I don't go, he may kill me.* He glanced around the empty bunkhouse before allowing the twitch to guide him forward.

Barloc quickened his pace, and once at the door, he peeked outside, spotting the hue from torches scattered across the battlements and the glow from Atticus's funeral pyre in the outer bailey. He stepped from the building and ran to where the last slave disappeared behind a bunkhouse.

When Barloc arrived, he glanced from slave to slave, each appearing to be equally confused. The silence grew heavy, and Barloc's concern shifted to paranoia.

The masked man crouched low, glancing around the side of the bunkhouse. "Let's go! We don't have much time." He crept along the shadows until he ambled across the yard and disappeared behind a training booth.

The slaves followed but less gracefully, their chains banging the ground as they ran.

While the man checked to see if they were clear, Barloc considered the idea of freedom. He realized he didn't even know what it meant anymore, so he weighed the risk against the payoff. *I would just be forced back into hiding from King Sclavus, the Howlers, and all of Drudgeburg.* His home town had been burned to the ground and his father murdered, so he had nowhere to go, and he had no idea what this man had planned for him. If he were caught, he'd be sent back to the beginning, sold to the Howlers, or worse, sent to Corvee. This thought made him wonder about MJ-8 and where he ended up.

When the man waved them onward, Barloc reached out and grabbed the slave in front of him. "We need to go back."

"Why would I do that?"

Barloc shook his head. "Something's not right. We don't even know who he is."

"He's my freedom, that's who he is." The slave walked away.

Barloc cursed under his breath and followed them to the archery booth.

When he arrived, the man nodded. "Good. We're all here. Now, we need to climb." He pointed to where two ropes hung down from the battlements. "Once up top, wait for me."

The first slave didn't hesitate. He grabbed the rope, twisted it around his wrist, and pulled himself off the ground, his chains banging against the wall.

"Wait," Barloc whispered. The group faced him. "Why are you breaking us free?"

The man scoffed. "Why does it matter? I'm saving you."

Barloc pointed up. "So, we climb this wall? To what? To where? What's next once our feet hit the other side?"

Another slave stepped past the masked man and grabbed the free rope. He twisted it around his arm and looked back. "I'm gettin' out of here. You can sit here and talk till the sun comes up for all I care."

"Going where?" Barloc asked, but the slave ignored him.

The man balled his fists and stepped toward Barloc."Shut your mouth, slave!" His voice rose to a quiet yell. "I told you not to *speak*."

Slave? The way the man said the word took Barloc by surprise. He shook his head and crossed his arms. "Why won't you answer my question—"

He lunged at Barloc with his hands outstretched, reaching for his throat. Barloc barely sidestepped him, but the man still managed to grab his shoulder.

Barloc dropped to the ground, slipped from his grip, jumped up, and ran for the yard. From behind him, the clear swipe of a blade whispered as it left its sheath, which made him run faster. His chains rattled and clanked, and it took all his concentration to not fall. Pain pricked at his chest and foot with each hard step.

Barloc gunned for the closest booth and grabbed one of the training staves.

The man stopped before him and shook his head. "Why would you do this? I've risked everything to get you out and you're ruinin' it for everyone."

The yard remained empty, but he knew people had to be around. "I can't see why you'd risk anything for slaves—"

The man lifted his blade and flashed it in the dim light. "I guess that doesn't matter for you because you're not going anywhere!" He lunged forward and jabbed the weapon at Barloc.

Barloc swung the staff, clipping the man's arm. He searched for anything that could help, spotting the metal Focus sign above his head—a red painted steel shield with the image of a long staff scratched into it. Before the man could attack again, Barloc swung up as hard as he could. The crash echoed long after the hit, and when he lowered his weapon, the man had already backed away, his attention flicking between the sign and Barloc.

As the crash faded, voices echoed from across the yard. The man turned and ran back to the ropes, where two slaves helped pull a third onto the top.

Barloc dropped the training weapon and ran into the center of the yard, falling to his knees, and placing his hands above his head. The slave he had attempted to stop emerged from behind the booth and kneeled beside him.

Green Cloaks appeared from the door cut into the makeshift wall, Tarak in the lead. "What in blazing bulls is going on here?" His chest heaved as he worked to catch his breath.

Barloc pointed toward the ropes. "Some man tried to set us free."

"What?" Tarak glanced in the direction Barloc pointed.

"A masked man. There are ropes hanging from the battlements. Slaves followed him." Barloc nodded toward the slave beside him. "We tried to stop them, but he attacked us."

The other slave nodded, not saying a word. Before Barloc finished his explanation, the Green Cloaks charged the wall, but the man had already disappeared, leaving the three slaves behind.

The Green Cloaks rounded up the slaves and brought them before Tarak, whose voice rumbled low and quiet, to the point everyone had to lean in to listen. "You want to escape, huh?" He paced much like Lord Harbor, and even in the dark, his muscles clearly worked through his neck and jaw. "Some phantom shows up in the middle of the night, and you three think it's wise to leave with him?"

Tarak pointed at one of the slaves. "You, explain yourself."

The man swallowed hard. "I—I—I—" His nervousness wouldn't allow him to speak until he took a deep breath. "I don't know, Master Tarak. I—I just followed him. I was sleeping and—"

"Enough!" Tarak swiped his hand through the air. "Enough." He passed his attention between the Green Cloaks to Barloc and the other slave. "Why didn't you go? What stopped you?"

Barloc looked to the other slave, who shifted his attention down, reminding him of MJ-8. "Several reasons, but mainly that it didn't make sense. I've worked entirely too hard to risk my freedom."

Tarak nodded and addressed the other slaves. "You three obviously thought it worth the risk." He spoke to one of the Green Cloaks. "Get Madam Constance, and tell her we have three slaves set to head back to the slop yard."

The Green Cloak nodded.

"Hold them until she arrives," Tarak told the other two Green Cloaks, who quickly hauled the slaves away. "As for you two. You're out of your bunks, and you made it all the way across the yard. You've broken the rules, too. No, you didn't attempt to escape, but you still broke the rules."

Barloc held his head high and didn't break eye contact.

"You're both on slave wash and chamber pots the moment the sun rises. If you manage to mess that up, you'll start back at the beginning and you won't be eligible for the tournament. You two aren't bad slaves, not from what I can tell, and you both put decent effort into today's challenges. Go now, sleep off what you can."

Barloc bowed and nodded. "Thank you, Master Tarak."

"If you find yourself out of your bunk again without my permission, you'll find your wrists a bit heavier, if you get my meaning."

When they returned to the bunkhouse, the slave whispered, "Thank you."

Barloc looked down at the floor. "I tried to save them."

The slave's hand rested on Barloc's shoulder. "You can't save everyone."

Barloc nodded, attempting to push past the effect the words had on him, thinking of his father, Alden, and MJ-8. "Why did you come back?"

"You seemed intelligent, not scared. Had you been scared, I would've gone with them, but it was like you *knew* something."

"I assure you I didn't."

"Thank you anyway."

Barloc lay down on his cot and closed his eyes. He wasn't sure he'd fall back asleep, especially knowing how empty his bunkhouse had just become, but either way, he realized that his punishment was a day of rest, a day to not get beat on, and that made it all worth it.

Chapter 14 – A Howler in Drudgeburg

While cleaning chamber pots, Barloc had the opportunity to watch the slaves spar. The quality of fighters proved to be just as random as the guards. Only a couple seemed to have experience with combat.

The entire day, Barloc moved around the yard, listening for slave names and matching faces with weapons and styles. He learned that everyone's technique, up until Master Tarak, could be studied. He'd managed to view ten different spars, and by the end of the night, another challenge against Tarak, who fought cleaner, allowing the slave to succeed with his advances but parrying at the last moment. He also let the sandglass run down, and even when the slave gained ground, Barloc had believed it to be part of a show. Up until then, he'd thought it all a farce, but by the end, Tarak announced the fight satisfactory and allowed the slave to advance.

Through the night, Barloc attempted to place himself in the guards' shoes, wondering what he would've done against each attacking slave. His mind traveled to the challenge with Tarak, and he felt confident in making it to him. At one point, the thought occurred to fight more than one challenger a day. No rules were against that, and the only action that seemed to alter Tarak's mood was when a slave felt he could skip all the challenges.

When Barloc stepped from the bunkhouse that morning, he knew it would be fight after fight that he had to win.

Before the archery booth, a Green Cloak assigned each slave their challenge, who would then move on to shoot. "If you desire to challenge anyone above you, step forward when I call your name and point to the desired rung with the stick." The Green Cloak fell into the pattern of announcing the challenge and sending the slave to the archery booth, until Barloc stepped up and pointed to the slave above him and then the one above that.

The Green Cloak glanced up at the board and back down to the parchment. "Which one?"

"Both."

The Green Cloak faced Master Tarak, who stood on the adjacent side of them. Tarak passed his attention between the ladder, to the Green Cloak, to MJ-7. "You want to engage in two challenges?"

Barloc nodded. "Yes. I'm not trying to skip anyone, simply fight them faster."

Tarak pursed his lips. "You're that confident you can win?"

"I believe so. I can only try."

Tarak stepped from his post and stopped in front of the board, arms crossed. "What happens if you fail the first match?"

Barloc didn't respond.

"If you lose and can't perform the following challenge, then you will be disqualified from the tournament and returned to the beginning."

Barloc nodded. "I'm not trying to be cocky. I'm not a great fighter, and I just want this over with."

Tarak uncrossed his arms and belted out a raucous laugh. "It's your fate you're sealing, not mine. You did a mighty fine job on those chamber pots, so you won't hurt my feelings!"

While Barloc waited for his turn at archery, he inspected the wall where the ropes had hung down, where the slaves were caught attempting to escape. Had he remained silent, they may have. Deep rivets from the metal claw of a grappling hooks cut into the edges of the battlement, and he wondered why Lord Harbor didn't have additional security if it were a reoccurring problem, but before he could think any more on it, the bow fell into his hand. Archery went about the same as it had the previous days—half landed in the target, half in the hay wall behind.

Barloc expended less effort while fighting the guards. He didn't want to waste energy, and losing against the guards didn't have any bearing on his outcome, though winning might. He didn't want to risk gaining more enemies, so even while he sparred the guards, his hungry eyes ate up the slaves he was scheduled to fight.

By the time Barloc's first challenge arrived, his confidence soared, but Tarak's announcement applied a great deal of pressure.

"Today, MJ-7 has requested to take on two challenges. Pull your reigns, though, boys. If he loses either of these, it disqualifies him from participating in the tournament completely and sends him back to the beginning where he will do an additional twenty days! That's forty days with ol' Tarak here." Tarak's laughing engulfed Barloc, whose face flushed, and as if Tarak read his mind, he spoke directly to him. "Surely you knew there would be something else, MJ-7. If not, everyone would try to fight more than one each day."

The first fight ended fast. The slave relied on sleight-of-hand, by using his left hand to initiate the maneuver, while the real attack came from his right. Barloc had seen him do it three different times throughout the day.

Tarak laughed, anticipation thick in his voice as he ushered the beaten slave from the battle square. "You will defend yourself, MJ-7. Now, fight!" He flipped the sandglass and backed out of the square.

The slave attacked as if his life depended on it. Barloc panicked because he'd seen the slave fight multiple times, and not once had he moved so fast. *Maybe he caught me watching him? Does he know of my plan?* Barloc backed around the square, faster and faster, keeping his eyes on the slave. It was arrogant of him to think that he was the only one smart enough to watch the others fight.

The slave charged him nonstop, swinging hard with every other step. Barloc retreated as fast as he could, but the slave had gained too much momentum, making it almost impossible to properly block his assault. The force of each blow threatened to knock him off balance, but as they continued in this manner, the slave's swings slowed.

Barloc circled the battle square, blocking anything that made it near him, working to tire his opponent, and not until he was forced to his knees did he understand that he had to disable the slave—stop him from overpowering the fight. The rules became a little clearer in that moment. Yes, the slave had to touch Barloc's chest; yes, Barloc had to defend himself, but for Barloc to win, he had to disable this man from being able to hit his chest.

The slave bore down on Barloc, drawing his sword back. As a last-ditch effort, Barloc swung his weapon across the slave's knees. The force turned one inward, dropping him to the ground. Barloc jumped to his feet and kicked the slave's weapon away.

The slave rocked back and forth, clutching his leg. Barloc stepped to him and kneeled. In his softest voice, he said, "I'm sorry." It wasn't until a Green Cloak guided Barloc from the square that he heard Tarak announce him as the winner, followed by his obnoxious laughter.

Barloc sat off to the side and watched the rest of the challenges. He remained focused on the fighting styles while he rubbed his arms and legs, and it wasn't until the shimmer of a white robe and two familiar faces that he pulled his eyes from the fighting.

Healer Haylan, Sir Vigor, and Madam Constance crossed the yard and approached Master Tarak. After a moment of talking, Tarak waved MJ-7 over. "Walk with them back to the slop yard."

Barloc's stomach tightened. *I did everything I was supposed to!*

Tarak must have seen the fear and confusion on Barloc's face, because he burst into laughter and slapped his back. "No, you're not going back out there for residence. They simply need a word with you."

Madam Constance's crisp, green eyes lingered on him. After a moment, she smiled and turned toward the outer bailey. "Follow me."

He walked in the familiar march behind Madam Constance, his chain scraping along the ground, sounding so solitary and alone. Haylan walked beside him, and Sir Vigor remained behind. Confusion weighed almost as much as fear when he rounded the gate to see seven Green Cloaks in the center of the yard standing before Atticus's funeral pyre.

MJ-1's funeral pyre had been dismantled, a blackened circle the only sign that it ever stood there. He wondered if the slave's ashes were really scattered at the mines.

Madam Constance cut straight across the yard to the group of Green Cloaks, which opened like a mouth, waiting to swallow the newcomers.

Barloc scanned everyone's faces, only recognizing a couple for certain: a man from the day of the bells, Master Fletcher, and Lord Harbor. Haylan took a spot by a man chewing on a stem of grass.

Lord Harbor glanced back at the inner bailey. "When Vigor and Tarak arrive, we'll finish this. Hold the slave horn until we're done. I don't need everyone in the place watching." As he finished saying this, they emerged from the inner bailey.

"Finally," Lord Harbor said at their approach. "The reason I've called you here is because of an ongoing investigation. It has been clear for some time that we've had a rat, an informant, selling our information, and today we rectify it once and for all."

Barloc glanced around confused. *What does this have to do with me? Why am I the only slave here?*

"Why is it you believe King Sclavus is sending scouts?" Lord Harbor asked to no one specifically. Everyone remained silent. "Well?"

"Because he would only have a reason to scout if he *knew* he had a reason," Madam Constance said with venom in her voice.

"Well said, Constance." Lord Harbor spun and spoke to everyone. "Let's skip the pageantry, ladies and gentlemen. I know who you are. I know what you've done, and I'm asking you to step forward before I call upon you."

The Green Cloaks glanced between one another, each waiting for someone to move. Their jaws clenched, they fiddled with their clothes, and sweat beaded across every forehead.

"Last chance," Lord Harbor said. "Step now or kneel later."

Still, no one moved. The silence screamed like an argument in Barloc's head. Every movement could have been a step, until a boot finally moved forward. The man's face sat etched with worry lines, sweat dripping down his nose. He stepped clear into the center of the circle.

The bald man spat out the grass that rested between his lips. "It is I you're looking for."

Lord Harbor crossed his arms. "Why?"

The man kept his eyes on Lord Harbor, fidgeting with his hands. "I only wanted to stay alive. I had no idea where you were going, and I had to cover myself, but I stopped once I realized your words were true. You can understand that, I hope?"

Lord Harbor reached out and grabbed the bald man's cloak. He pulled him to only an inch from his nose. "You could've ruined everything!" He let the man go and stepped back. "You still may have."

The bald man straightened his cloak and bobbed his head slowly. "How did you find out?"

"As the stars would have it, and a long shot it was to hit a target so small, Haylan has been speaking to a slave who happened to describe you as a Howler without knowing what he was doing." Lord Harbor rounded on Barloc. "This is him, correct?"

The abruptness took Barloc by surprise. He glanced between them, confused.

Lord Harbor grabbed Barloc and pushed him before of the bald man. "The Howler! This is the man who took you from your home town, this is Variegate?"

When Barloc locked eyes with the bald man, everything crashed down on him. The man replaced a stem of grass from his pocket, and when he opened his mouth, Barloc saw the overlapping teeth. He resembled nothing of the Howler that had kept them alive, but the grass... and the teeth. There was no denying it. Barloc nodded.

Variegate lingered on Barloc for a moment and turned his attention back to Lord Harbor. "I want to make it right. I believe in you, and I'll fight by your side until my last breath." Variegate's voice came out strong, and he didn't break eye contact with Lord Harbor. "I only gave information early on, but it's also how you've grown so well informed. I traded small things in return for small things." He removed the grass.

Madam Constance scoffed. "This doesn't excuse your behavior. How could we possibly trust you again, Vern, or Variegate, or whatever your name is?"

"Allow me to earn your trust. I promise that I stopped long ago. That's why you haven't seen me ranging, that's why I've had no new information, but how was I to tell you of my actions? You would've killed me."

Lord Harbor shook his head. "Atticus is dead because of scouts, scouts that were only there because of information you sold!" Lord Harbor looked away. "How could I possibly trust a sword that has cut me? Why temper an old blade when I can forge a new one?"

"Please, my lord...."

"Tarak, Vigor, take him to a cell. In two weeks, bring him to the slop yard. If he can survive thirty days there, then *maybe* I'll let him back out into the world."

"Plea—"

Lord Harbor finally looked at him. "I'm letting you live! One complaint and my offer disappears. If you mean the words you speak, perform your penance in silence, or I will introduce you to the gibbets. Understood?"

Variegate's mouth pumped opened and closed, silent words attempting to form, until Vigor and Tarak grabbed either arm. Tarak stripped him of all his weapons and bound his wrists.

"One last thing, Variegate. Atticus was a friend to those who wear the green. Think about all you've done as you become a slave for me, because you will be working for them as you fight for your freedom."

Vigor and Tarak pulled him away.

Variegate shrugged off their hold and turned to Lord Harbor. "My lord!"

Lord Harbor kept his back to him.

When Variegate realized that he wouldn't turn around, he said, "He was my friend, as well."

After a long moment of silence, the group dissipated, the slave horn sounded, and Barloc returned to finish out his day.

Chapter 15 – The Final Challenge

As Barloc exited the bunkhouse, he knew how it felt to be sentenced to the gallows, thinking each step was one closer to his end. Of course, it wasn't that dramatic, but his mind reeled with the possibilities of the day ahead. He planned on challenging everyone that remained. Not only did he desire to get it over with, he understood the risk that his opponents would soon learn his weaknesses.

The slaves stared at him a little differently that morning. Barloc figured it was because he'd won two challenges the previous day, or maybe that he had been pulled from the yard, yet returned, unlike so many others.

When Barloc arrived at the ladder, he tapped the stick on each rung above him, and with each tap, the slave's face and fighting style briefly passed through his mind. He knew them all.

Tarak grabbed the parchment from the Green Cloak. "*Seven*? You barely stood against two, and now you think you can take on seven?"

"I've got no choice. I have to do it now... before it's too late."

"You *do* have a choice. You can slow down and take it one day at a time."

Barloc shook his head. "I'm no fighter, Master Tarak. I risk too much having the slaves ahead of me learn that."

Tarak nodded vigorously and laughed. "Well, I can't pretend I'm not interested. I'll let it go on, but if you fail, add fifty days to your stay here at Drudgeburg."

He had expected some sort of added repercussion, but Barloc truly believed it was his only chance. He nodded and bowed slightly. "I understand."

"You know... you could've just done your normal days and cleaned chamber pots without fighting at all, right?"

Barloc thought about it and glanced over the names, but before he could agree, retract his request to fight so many, Tarak spoke through a toothy smile.

"Well, you *could* have, but now you *will* fight. Take this day as a lesson to think before doing." He smiled. "To the archery, then!" Tarak slammed his hand on Barloc's back, pushing him forward.

He forced his way as fast as possible through archery, managing to land six of the arrows, and as he walked toward his Focus, he felt he finally understood what Tarak had meant by trigger shot.

By the time his turn in the battle square arrived, he noticed that guards and slaves alike kept their eyes on him. Tarak paced in the center of the yard, watching the various fights, but even he gravitated toward Barloc.

When Barloc stepped into the square, he immediately kneeled and laid his weapon at his feet. The guard appeared confused. Barloc exited the arena. In both directions, slaves, one-by-one, laid their weapons down, following suit, and before long, the sounds of fighting dissipated, until no one fought at all.

Tarak paced back and forth with his arms crossed, eyeing up all the slaves. After a moment, laughter erupted. "Never in my day!" He doubled over and slapped his knee. "Let's get on with it, then. To the arena!"

Tarak called MJ-7 and the first slave to enter. "I'll keep this one basic. You," he pointed to Barloc, "tap his chest." Tarak spun the sandglass and stepped outside of the arena.

Barloc recalled the slave's moves: *F-5. Fights with a long staff and relies on keeping people at a maximum range.*

The man swirled the staff, tucking it under his arm while sidestepping. Barloc advanced but backed away just as quickly. The slave noticed Barloc analyzing him and charged, swinging wildly. Barloc continued to retreat, but an idea dawned on him. He flipped his sword around and gripped it like a spear. The man didn't seem to notice or care; he continued to swing and rotate the staff, screaming while he pursued.

Barloc launched the sword at the slave, which barely missed the spinning staff and bounced off his chest, falling to the ground.

F-5 stopped spinning his weapon and looked down at the sword, his face bunched up in confusion.

The crowd remained silent alongside Barloc.

Tarak's laughter announced the end of the challenge. "F-5, step from the square. DM-17, enter."

DM-17's fighting style flashed through his mind as he tightened his hold on his sword.

Tarak gripped the sandglass and teetered it back and forth.

Barloc focused on DM-17, waiting for the fight to begin, and it wasn't until Tarak cleared his throat that he broke his concentration.

Tarak smiled at them both. "Drop your weapons. You will perform hand-to-hand combat. If you tap the ground, you're out. If you fall limp, you're out."

A Green Cloak stepped into the ring and took away both their weapons.

"Fight!"

Barloc stared at Tarak, confused, but the moment the sand hit the bottom of the sandglass, DM-17 approached him. Barloc knew how the slave used a sword, not bare hands. He attempted to loosen up and follow DM-17's movements, but hand-to-hand was an entirely different style, hard to predict.

As each of them landed blows against the other, Barloc's chest and foot hurt more than any time since injured, and it didn't take long for him to mess up. Blood filled his mouth and his vision spun from a strike to his head, but Barloc ended it with a kick to DM-17's stomach and a headlock that cut off his air supply until he feebly tapped his hand.

For the next fight, two Green Cloaks brought in a pedestal twice their height, placing it in the center. Another set a block atop and Tarak flipped the sandglass. "Bring me that block."

Barloc raced to the thick pedestal, pulled the slave down, who had already began climbing, and instead of going up, he managed a similar headlock until the slave fell limp. While he climbed the pole, blood leaked from the claw marks etched deep into his forearms. After retrieving the block, he slid back down and threw it at Tarak's feet.

The next slave had to tap Barloc's chest, which Barloc defended cleanly, though he moved slower from fatigue. Halfway through the fight, Tarak sent another slave in, forcing Barloc to fight both at once.

Fueled by adrenaline, Barloc charged forward, swinging mad. He aimed to maim, to disable. The only chance he had to win was to land clean, hard hits on his attackers. In his fury, his wooden sword smashed one man's nose, spraying blood across the arena floor. The other slave struck Barloc's leg, damaging his right knee, but by the end, Barloc managed to take them down. He bled from various cuts, his right leg pulsed with pain, and his right eye barely opened. He had to lean on his sword while Tarak laughed on the next challenge.

Two Green Cloaks moved hay targets to one end of the arena. Tarak directed Barloc and the new challenger to the opposing side. "You get one shot. Closest to the center wins."

Barloc's chest raced more from this challenge than any prior. He was horrible at archery, but every morning, the challenger proved to be one of the best, landing nine or ten into the center rings.

Barloc stood next to the slave, nocked his arrow and lifted the bow level with his opponent's. His heart pounded in his ears, and sweat ran down his face. His damaged eye made it almost impossible to see.

The challenger pulled his arm back, ready to fire.

Barloc took a chance and threw his weight into the slave's side. The arrow popped from the bow and shot into the air. The slave tumbled over the small arena border.

Barloc quickly threw up his bow, forced his eye open, and let his arrow fly. The arrow landed in the very edge of the target, so close it poked out the side.

The challenger regained his feet and tackled Barloc, swinging his fists viciously. Barloc took three hard hits before the Green Cloaks removed the furious slave.

The laughing stopped, fingers prodded him, and his consciousness waivered in and out. The nightmare from so many nights ago returned, and he fell down the pile of slaves toward the open mouth of Sapper. Sapper. The origin, the problem, the reason Archer was dead and MJ-8 exiled. MJ-8, his silent friend. The man who risked everything to save him, and Barloc had returned the favor by casting him out. *MJ-8. MJ-8.* The name repeated itself in his mind and finally he forced his eyes open. It took all he had to stand.

Tarak called the last slave into the arena.

Barloc fell and tried to stand once more.

The challenger entered, gripping a longsword, swinging it in a similar fashion as the first slave with the staff, and when Barloc lifted his sword, the weight forced him to stumble.

Somewhere in the distance, Tarak announced that the slave had to tap Barloc's chest.

MJ-8.... I didn't even know his real name. A sudden sorrow overtook him.

He opened his eyes and tried to lift the sword once more but fell to his knees instead. The slave approached, cautiously, and pointed his weapon inches from Barloc's chest.

Barloc blinked up at him through his one good eye and watched the slave throw his weapon aside and lower down in genuflection.

Tarak entered the arena. "You're willing to lose for him? You're one day away from your final challenge, and you're throwing your sword down to this slave you don't even know?"

Barloc blinked hard, hissing from the pain in his right eye.

The slave nodded and stepped from the arena.

Tarak pursued. "I'm not done talking to you!"

The slave stopped and rotated back.

"Why? I demand to know."

The slave cleared his throat and pointed at Barloc. "This is no challenge. He can barely hold up his head." He took a seat on the lower bench.

Tarak picked up the longsword and threw it from the arena. "All right, then," he said, pacing back and forth. After nodding to one of the Green Cloaks, he kneeled in front of Barloc.

The Green Cloak made his way across the yard, away from the arena.

Tarak grabbed Barloc's shoulder, steadying him. "For your final challenge, MJ-7, you expect to defeat me, yes?"

Barloc remained silent. The spinning in his head slowed, but the throbbing across his body increased as his adrenaline abated.

"I've seen you walking around watching, studying. The other slaves seem to cheer for the guards to get beat, or for them to overthrow me, but not once did I see that in you. You don't stand a chance against me."

Tarak lifted Barloc to his feet, who swayed like tall grass in a windy field.

"I could take you down blindfolded. I've spent way too much time fighting to lose to someone like you.... No, today you'll have a challenge like never seen before, and it's all your own fault. You could've done it one day at a time, but you wanted it all now. You chose this path, now you can walk it." No laughter followed, the air now taught and palpable.

The door in the crude wall slammed open, and the Green Cloak returned, forcing a fat man with a sack over his head toward the arena. The man staggered toward them blindly.

Tarak returned to his spot by the sandglass. "Bring in the weapons!"

A guard walked two steel swords into the arena. Two swords with long, sharp blades. Their appearance cut through his fatigue. His heartbeat quickened, and he turned to Tarak, but the guard and fat man arrived. The Green Cloak pushed the brown mass, tripping him on the edge of the arena. He fell onto the hard-packed ground with a grunt.

"Please," a sobbing, pitiful voice pleaded from underneath the hood. The guard removed the cloth, and Barloc recognized him immediately: Slaver Martin.

Tarak tapped the sandglass. "You each get a sword, and you'll fight to the death. If the fat man wins, he'll be one day closer to his freedom, and if you win, MJ-7, you'll move on. Now, fight!"

Tarak rotated the sandglass.

Martin scrambled for the sword, sending up dust as he crawled.

Barloc scooped up his own blade and backed away.

The slaver stood, wiping sweat from his eyes. "What kind of farce is this? You'll all die for what you're doing here."

How did this man end up here? I watched him leave a fortnight ago. As Slaver Martin backed away, pointing the sword in Barloc's direction, all the fury from pulling him on that palanquin across the kingdom forced Barloc to grip his sword tighter.

Slaver Martin turned to Tarak. "You dare throw me down here with this filth, as if we're equals?" He spat.

Tarak's laughter returned. "Today, you are."

Barloc lunged forward, driven by blind fury. His memories piled up: the lashes across his back, the starvation, and the night of holding a tarp over the slaver and his guards, while he froze in the cold rain.

Slaver Martin forced a fake laugh. "Killing him is nothing. He's a slave. I've killed hundreds, but I assure you, the day King Sclavus comes to free me, I will enjoy running *you* through, personally, *Master Tarak*. I will enjoy killing every one of your lot!"

Barloc shortened the distance by half.

Martin retreated. "You get away from me, you spume! Bow down!" He tripped but returned to his feet. He gripped his sword with both hands, a man of inexperience, and swung hard at Barloc, who sidestepped and waited for Martin to collect himself.

Martin let out a war cry and charged. Barloc barely parried the attack. He slapped the flat side of the blade against the slaver's back as he maneuvered around him. Martin whimpered, turned, and prepared to attack again.

"You beat us!" Barloc swung the sword toward Martin. "You humiliated us!" He swung even harder.

"You killed slaves for no reason!" He swung again, their swords connecting in a fury of high pangs.

He lunged forward, forcing Martin on his back. It was no challenge. The weapon fell from Martin's hand, and Barloc pointed his sword at the slaver's throat.

Barloc fought every desire to push the blade into Slaver Martin. He screamed as loud as he could.

The slaver cried, begging for Barloc to stop, to spare him, to let him live another day.

Barloc caught his breath and threw the sword away. With one final glance at Master Tarak, he walked to the other side of the arena and stepped out.

"Where are you going, MJ-7?"

"I'm done. You can have me for fifty days, for a hundred. I'm not killing him for sport." Barloc looked directly into Tarak's eyes but yelled for everyone to hear, "You people have it all wrong. This isn't right!" He pointed to the slaver. "I refuse to stoop to your level. I will not kill him; I will not kill anyone for something menial as a *tournament*." Barloc turned away.

Tarak's voice boomed through the air, all humor vacant. "Stop! You two return the slaver to his cell." His footfalls neared Barloc, who kept his back to him. "Face me."

Barloc remained still.

Tarak stepped around him and lifted his chin. "You defied a direct order, MJ-7. You were to fight to the death." Tarak leaned closer and forced eye contact. "But you chose honor."

Tarak put an arm around him. "MJ-7, you're more a man than I ever thought. Faced with someone I was certain you would retaliate against, you rose above your hatred for what was right. You move on, MJ-7."

He waved a guard over. "Take him to Haylan." Tarak gripped Barloc's shoulder and shook him slightly. "You did well."

A Green Cloak and a guard guided Barloc toward the Healer's hut. Barloc stopped halfway and looked back to see Tarak lecturing the benches, and he couldn't help but smile.

Chapter 16 – The Whisperer

Healer Haylan held a small spade over a candle flame, her features dancing in the flickering light and the fog from being forced awake. "What have you gone and done to yourself, child?"

Barloc blinked hard, allowed his eyes to focus. The hartshorn worked its way through his senses, and when his vision finally cleared, he realized that he lay in the same bed and room as before, crimson rags littering the blanket and table around the candle.

"I did not believe you could outdo yourself, MJ-7, but you did not disappoint." She smiled and pulled the metal away from the flame. The tool pulsed a soft red. She gripped it using a bloody cloth. "I cleaned your wounds. You are bruised badly. I wanted you in my care for two days, but the Whisperer wants you by nightfall. He believes these to be scratches." Her voice rose and fell as she traveled through her sentences, and she spoke heavily with her hands, more than he could ever remember. "He says there is not enough time for you to be wounded. Now, this will hurt. You have a gash behind your ear that needs cauterizing. Roll on your side." She pulled him toward her.

"Who is the Whisperer?"

She smiled. "You will find out soon enough."

As he rolled, pains exploded across his body. Her weight pressed on him, and without warning, the hot metal seared his skin. He screamed and bit down on the thick piece of leather she'd slipped between his teeth. The smell of burnt hair flooded his senses, and when her weight lifted, he rolled onto his back.

"You are fortunate it is behind your ear, out of sight, child. It could have been on your face, and you would forever have to shave in fancy designs like Sir Vigor." She smiled, set down the tool, and wiped her hands.

"I don't remember coming here."

"No, I suppose you would not. You did not even make it all the way across the yard. They had to carry you, and then you slept through the night. Now, I have to know what kind of fool would take on an entire army of slaves all at once."

Images from the fights passed through his mind. They already felt like a dream. "I had no choice."

"Master Tarak was quite impressed with you, though he said you fought like a fish out of water." She laughed. "He said you flopped around like a fish out of water, just slippery enough to keep popping out of everyone's hands. You could have died, you know?"

Barloc closed his eyes and pictured the final challenge against Slaver Martin and how very random it had seemed. He knew the slaver had left through the gates, yet there he sat in one of Drudgeburg's cells. "Can I ask you a question?"

Haylan nodded.

"Why did you bring me in front of Variegate and tell him I was the reason he got caught? Won't he try to kill me now?"

Haylan sat back, pensive. After a moment, she shrugged and said, "I am not sure, child. I hope not, of course. But Lord Harbor needed to make sure it was him. I would have never thought one of our own to turn on us like that. Not after what we have been through together."

"So, you don't believe him. You don't believe that he's changed?"

Haylan shook her head. "He is too old. Changing minds is a young man's errand. No, it takes a special person to stoop so low to become a Howler."

"He's not that old." Her response reinforced disappointment in him. He wanted Variegate to change. The man had saved his life once before. His emotions rose to the surface, so he shifted the subject. "What do you make of dreams?"

"What are you going on about, child?"

Barloc pictured the pile of slaves, the faceless figure, and the way he was thrown down to Sapper. "Do you believe dreams can be real?"

She blew out the candle. Darkness enveloped the room. "Are you asking me if I believe dreams to be a prediction of things to come?"

Barloc nodded, excited she understood.

She shook her head again. "No, I do not. Being a Healer, this is a question that presents itself quite often." She peered at the wall above Barloc as if traveling into a memory. "No, I believe in direct results, child. The shamans and some islanders feel that dreams are a divine connection to faith and are the deity's gift to allow a glimpse into the future, but I suspect, at best, that a dream can reflect your subconscious fears. Why do you ask?"

Barloc explained the details of his nightmare and how it had returned for multiple nights, justifying different events against the dream: the faceless figure against the masked man who tried to set them free, and how if he were caught, he would have been thrown back to Sapper; he explained how he felt responsible for MJ-8's exile, MJ-1's murder, and then all of those slaves he'd literally cut down to advance. By the end of connecting everything he could, Haylan nodded. As she stared at him, his ears warmed, and he shifted uncomfortably on the bed.

"Do you not see? All coincidences. I assure you that you will have plenty of faceless figures attempting to hold you back, and I hate to say it, but your freedom depends on the people you cut down."

The answer added weight to Barloc's worry.

"You have so much more to focus on than childish fears." Haylan stood and crossed her arms. "Rest. You are going to have some interesting days ahead of you."

Barloc didn't see Haylan again that evening. Instead, one of the younger Healers escorted him, another he'd not yet met. The sun had long since left the sky, leaving the outer bailey dark and empty. Small effulgent glows scattered the battlements, and the slaves were already in their bunkhouses.

Barloc lingered on the blackened circles where the funeral pyres had been. He thought about MJ-8, and his stomached tightened. Even that felt like a lifetime ago.

The young Healer placed her hand on his arm and nodded toward the inner bailey. "Let's go," she said, her voice hardly audible.

Barloc followed her through the inner portcullis and stopped as soon as soon as they entered. "Wait here," she said and disappeared through the gate. The same torchlight lined the inside battlements like on the night of the masked man, except now guards accompanied them.

"Nice of you join me," a man's soft voice said from behind him.

Barloc jolted forward, and when he turned, he encountered the silhouette of a tall, hooded man, dressed in long, black cloak covering every portion of him. A dark mesh mask shielded his features.

The man stood motionless, appearing like an apparition of death. The figure's voice hissed from behind the hood. "I am the Whisperer. You don't know me, but I know you, oh, yes, I know you *very* well."

Goosebumps scaled up his arms and back, but he didn't break from staring at the mask. He didn't want to show fear even though he felt it. There was something about the mask; he couldn't help but think of his nightmare.

"Come with me." The Whisperer glided toward the door in the makeshift wall, the door where Slaver Martin had come and gone. His black cloak barely whipped behind him, giving him the appearance of floating. Once they arrived, a guard's head popped over the wall, then disappeared. A moment later, the door opened and they entered.

Barloc struggled to keep up, his chains scraping against the ground as he jogged along the Whisperer's long stride. They passed by another stretch of bunkhouses, stopping at a tent in the far corner, where a guard stood, waiting with huge pliers gripped in his fist. Two fires burned in sconces on either side of him, just enough light for Barloc to see. A small barrel sat in the center, and behind the guard leaned a tall mirror as large as Sir Vigor, and then to the sides of that hung a stash of the guard's black armor.

The Whisperer held his hand out, indicating the barrel. "Sit."

The guard immediately knelt and removed Barloc's ankle fetters.

"Listen carefully. I am the most valuable person in Drudgeburg. You will never see my face, though, you know me. I am a man of many trades. One day I may be disguised as a slave, the next a guard. I have even been one of the many masters you see scattered around the castle. I am a man of several faces.

"I saw you arrive on your first day. I worked alongside you. I have watched you sleep. I have watched all the slaves sleep."

Barloc tried his best to keep up, to understand, but the man's quiet voice distracted him equally to the fact he hid behind a mask.

"My job is to listen, to find people who are against our Lord Harbor. I discover the unworthy of freedom, and I reveal them."

Barloc's memory instantly reviewed every face he'd come across since he arrived at Drudgeburg. He had no way of knowing who this man could be.

"You're moving onto a different task. You'll now don the black of the guards."

The guard hung the pliers on the rack with the armor and moved to the Whisperer's side.

Barloc glanced behind him at the hanging armor and back to the Whisperer. *Don the black?*

"You're assigned to bunk nine," the Whisperer continued. "You *must* follow instructions. You sleep, you wake, and you receive your quest. It's simple enough.

"You're only allowed to do what I just said. Everything else is against the rules. You're not to hurt a slave under any circumstance. If one is acting out of line, you'll detain him and nothing more. The masters will deal with the punishment." The hood bobbed slightly as he spoke. "That's it. You're a guard. Turn, disrobe, and don your new armor."

With his back turned, the Whisperer's voice moved around him like mist. "If you value freedom, you'll remain silent at all costs. You'll do your task and only that. If you take one step out of line, you'll return to the beginning."

I'm a guard? Barloc faced the mirror, taking in his appearance. This was the first time, for a long time, that he'd seen himself outside of his reflection in a puddle, and he hardly recognized the man staring back. The fickle light of the fire made his features even more defined. His clothes hung off him in tatters, each article dirty with bloodstains. He lifted his arms to see that his muscles were more defined than he could ever remember. He'd forgotten how much longer his hair had been before Drudgeburg, thinking on his first day when they shaved his head. Cuts littered his entire body, and the sun had worked his skin like a piece of leather. His blackened eye looked much worse than it felt, but even through all this, he could see a resemblance to his father. He rotated around and looked up at the mask. "What do you mean I'm a guard?"

"It's something Lord Harbor never says early on, because he doesn't want to ruin the surprise. It's all part of the plan."

It wasn't a direct answer to his question, but he understood. *All the guards are slaves.*

The Whisperer withdrew a curved blade and pointed it at Barloc's mouth. "Guard your words like you'll guard these slaves, or you'll be short a tongue. If a guard makes a mistake, he's sent back to the beginning, unable to whisper."

Barloc stared at the blade and turned back to the mirror. He stripped his clothes off and replaced them with pieces of black leather armor. The gear was oddly light, not much more restricting than the loose slave clothes. By the time he finished, the Whisperer left and the guard waited in silence to show Barloc to bunk nine.

Chapter 17 – A Different View

Barloc spent most the night contemplating how far he'd come in such a short period. He lifted his legs every so often, trying to remember the last time he felt the freedom of no chains, thinking of his father's death and the Howlers' slave cart.

He ran his fingers down his shin and along the deep indent where the manacles had clamped around his ankles. All his hair had been rubbed off, and the skin was smooth like polished armor.

Sleep came in fits, and each time the nightmare returned.

The door opened with a creak, and a torch entered the bunk followed by a man's head that poked in and left without a word. The two other guards sharing bunkhouse nine stood, stretched, and ambled after the torchlight. Barloc followed.

Outside, a Green Cloak rummaged through a

purse hanging across his chest. He removed a parchment and brought it dangerously close to the flame. After squinting at it, he softly announced the guard's names and gave them their quests. "MJ-7, you will join the slaves at the mines. Wait for your escort here."

The mines? Barloc's eyes widened and he stopped breathing. Images of Sapper and MJ-8 assaulted his mind. *How would he treat me as a guard?*

He remained still, panicking, until the soft voice of the Whisperer cut through his fears.

"No, I'll take him today. Special request."

Barloc searched for the voice, but the glow from the Green Cloak's torch made it hard to see him standing in the shadows.

The Green Cloak tucked the parchment into his bag. "Very well." He retrieved a small burlap sack from a pile beside him and passed it to Barloc. With a nod, he grabbed the remaining sacks and walked to the next bunkhouse.

The bag held a half loaf of bread, a ball of grain, and an apple. He stared for a moment before closing it back shut, his mouth salivating.

The Whisperer glided forward. "Normally we give you a task away from the inner bailey so the slaves you recently battled don't recognize you. It messes with the system, though it happens. Nothing they can do about it, really, but it's best we keep words worthy of a whisper to a minimum.

"I want to show you something." He lifted his arm and guided Barloc toward bunks four and five. "If you don't eat and walk, you won't eat at all."

Barloc immediately opened the sack and grabbed the bread, gnawing out a huge chunk. He followed the Whisperer, focusing very little on his surroundings. He wanted to eat before that privilege was revoked, and it wasn't until his first bite that he realized how hungry he'd been.

They slipped behind the fourth bunkhouse to an extremely narrow path directly into the castle wall. The Whisperer stopped at the entrance and turned around, crossing his hands over his stomach. "Finish your food quickly and drop the sack there." He indicated the ground by the door.

Barloc nodded and finished the bread in a few bites. The grain took a little longer to chew, and he wished he had water almost as much as he wished the Whisperer wasn't watching him eat, but after an awkward few minutes, he dropped the apple core into the sack and threw it on the ground.

The Whisperer nodded and disappeared into the castle wall.

Two steps in and everything fell into complete darkness.

"Drudgeburg is a very strange castle," the Whisperer said, and after what sounded like two rocks beating together, a spark turned into a flame, and a torch appeared in the Whisperer's fist. Even with the flickering light, Barloc could barely see the man holding it. It didn't help that he wore a long black cloak and a mesh face mask, blending him further with the darkness. "Much more to the eye than one would expect." The flame rotated and began moving down the narrow passageway.

The dampness and musty scent overwhelmed him in the small confines, but before long, the path opened wide enough for them to walk side-by-side. Occasionally, light filtered in from a crack, but almost the entire trip, the torch led the way. The hallway finally lit up when they arrived at a small and uneven staircase, barely etched into the wall, leading up to the battlements.

He now understood how the guards and Green Cloaks traveled around so easily. Too many times it felt like they appeared out of nowhere, and he'd always wondered how they climbed atop the battlements. He had never seen ladders or similar structures, yet guards walked the castle walls day and night.

The Whisperer indicated the hall they'd just walked from with his free hand. "When we found these tunnels, it shaped the way we run things here... helped me a great deal, anyway."

When we found these tunnels? The words replayed in Barloc's head, but he moved past them, nodding as if he understood.

"The tunnels course through the curtain wall, though there are even more inside the keep." He nodded toward the stairs. "Let's go up top."

When they emerged atop, Barloc was taken by surprise once more. The battlement came up to Barloc's stomach at its lowest point, leaving plenty of room to maneuver around without being seen.

The Whisperer stepped to the wall and peered over. "This is one of my favorite places. I can see across the field that way," he pointed to his right, "and I can watch the entire yard from here. Better yet, you see how the walls curve there." The Whisperer pointed again. "Any voice nearby will echo off this wall, and even if I can't make out what they're saying, I can at least know that someone's speaking. That's when I slip back down for a closer inspection." The mask rotated to Barloc for a moment, and he suspected that the face behind it smiled.

The slave horn sounded from its mount high on the wall above the inner bailey. A Green Cloak stood with the end of the horn at his lips, and a moment later, the vibrations traveled through the castle walls.

The Whisperer moved toward the inner bailey. "I want you to see this."

Below, the guards spread out in what seemed like a random pattern across the yard, though he now understood how the system worked. The Green Cloaks assigned the guards tasks, just like they did Barloc before the Whisperer had stolen him away, and they spread out to their assigned post. Barloc admired it.

The slaves dumped out of the long bunkhouses like ants from a hill.

The Whisperer pointed at them. "See how they scurry about?"

Once the slaves arrived at their spots, Madam Constance stood from her seat at the sorting table and announced that all but the last bunkhouse would be going out. She sent one group to the field, one to the mines, and one to the forest, and before long, the slaves filtered through the front gate, led by some very familiar faces: Sapper, Fletcher, Vigor, and another Green Cloak he'd seen around the yard.

Madam Constance didn't speak until the march of what sounded like an army left the echoing confines of the outer bailey, and only then did she read from the parchment in her hands.

The remaining slaves wore various pieces of gear, and at a quick glance, Barloc knew roughly how far they'd come. When Madam Constance spoke, he fully understood what the Whisperer meant by being able to hear nearly everything.

Madam Constance's voice, though soft in its own way, arrived at his ears as if she were standing beside him. She announced the slaves' names and gave them their tasks, spreading them across the yard from the livery, to the crops, to repairs and chamber pots.

The Whisperer stepped back and crossed to the other side. Barloc joined him at the battlement. He believed he could even make out the entrance of the mine from his position. Walking with carts filled with stone made it seem like forever away, but from his new perspective, it wasn't far at all. Sapper led his crew of slaves and guards there, already cresting the first small hill. Thoughts of being stuck with Sapper made him wonder if Haylan had been right, and if she were, Sapper would've already found a new slave to pick on, but if she were wrong, Sapper would've had him working alongside the slaves dressed in guards' armor. In that moment, Barloc was thankful for the Whisperer's company, no matter how creepy he appeared.

Barloc scanned the field in front of the entrance, discovering that it had transformed into a battlefield of sorts. The workers spread out to their different spots, and across the hill, almost as far as he could see, stood a long line of bulwarks with huge spikes sticking out in all directions. The tall grass waved across the field, but from that angle, it looked like a meat tenderizer had been smashed across the surface. Small paths cut through, and every few feet, holes dotted the entire field.

They returned to the stairs, lowered themselves back into the castle wall, and traveled until they emerged into the outer bailey. Once outside, Barloc realized he stood behind one of the long bunkhouses he was just looking down on.

"Madam Constance is expecting you."

Barloc nodded and checked for the best way to exit from behind the bunkhouse. When he turned back to say his thanks, the Whisperer had already left. Barloc moved around the bunkhouse and walked the stretch of the yard to meet Madam Constance.

When he first stepped into the open, he remembered his first day. He felt like he was doing something wrong walking out like that, no chains linking his limbs together, but now he wore the black of the guards. This thought changed the way he walked, and when he approached the sorting table, Madam Constance smiled.

Behind her stood five more guards, Master Tarak, and another Green Cloak he'd seen at one of the arena matches—Master Dharah.

Madam Constance continued to smile. "Good to see you, MJ-7. You look like hell."

He smiled and tried to push open his swollen eye. When his cheeks lifted, they burned from the cuts, scrapes, and other damages from battle. He thought about the man in the mirror and silently agreed with her. He did, indeed, look like hell.

Barloc bowed. "Thank you, Madam Constance." For the first time since becoming a slave at Drudgeburg, he didn't feel that he had to look away. He absorbed her beautiful smile and was happy to return one, no matter how ugly it may have been.

And in the blink of an eye, her smile faded and she guided him to the other guards. "Stand with them."

Two carts arrived shortly after Barloc, each pulled by horses. Four additional steeds approached, guided by the guards from the stables, and then Lord Harbor emerged from the inner portcullis with another Green Cloak Barloc hadn't seen before.

I wonder if that's the Whisperer. Barloc watched the man walk, trying to see if he could spot a similarity, but nothing stood out.

Lord Harbor stopped by Madam Constance. "We're all set?"

She nodded. "Yes, five guards, three Green Cloaks, and yourself. Two carts. Gear for everyone."

Lord Harbor mounted his steed and rotated back to the group. "Why aren't they equipped?"

Madam Constance nodded once. "I was leaving that to you, my lord."

"Very well. You," He pointed to the guard at the end. "Dispense those weapons. You get the horses ready. The guards will ride on the carts. Everyone else mount up." He faced Madam Constance. "I entrust the castle with you."

She smiled and nodded once more. "Of course, and it's in good hands. You be careful and swift." She bowed.

"Sir Vigor will oversee the slaves. You make sure this place doesn't fall to pieces. The ride takes two days. One to, one fro. I may need time convincing the people, but I don't think that'll be too much of a problem."

Lord Harbor's gaze lingered on Madam Constance. Barloc thought he saw his lips move, a whisper, something only for her.

Barloc's stomach tightened, an instant pang of jealousy, and his face flushed at the realization. He'd never felt jealousy like that before, and he tried to shake it away, watching Lord Harbor spur his horse and ride to the guards and masters. "Let's go."

The guards mounted their steeds less smoothly than Lord Harbor, Tarak, Dharah, and the unnamed, and together they rode, the carts trotting behind. The gate lifted, the drawbridge lowered, and before they crossed, Barloc turned to see Madam Constance stepping from the table to see them off.

Chapter 18 – Dreston

Barloc sat at the table alongside the other guards, Green Cloaks, and Lord Harbor. He took in the interior of Dreston's inn, realizing that he'd never been in one before. He sat quiet, drinking his first ale in a long time, since being a boy with his friend Alden, and though he'd been presented with all the comforts of an inn, he'd never felt more out of place.

Lord Harbor finished his beer, slammed the empty mug on the table, and wiped away the foam caught in his beard. "Your ale tastes like piss, Rosa."

She grabbed the empty mug, pulled it away, and straightened back up. She wore her auburn hair in a ponytail and kept her bangs long and tucked behind her right ear. Small pockmarks sprinkled her right cheek, but her lips were full and her eye lashes waved through the air when she blinked. A tattoo of small vines and flowers wrapped around her arm and wrist, and her clothes, though filthy and worn, curved with her body. "No one asked you to drink it."

Lord Harbor smiled, but it vanished just as fast. He shifted on the stool, placing his elbows on the table, and lowered his voice to a whisper. "We leave by morning light, and your lot needs to come with us."

Rosa pushed back from the table and stared around the inn. After a moment, she shook her head and glanced between Lord Harbor, Tarak, and Dharah, and then at all the guards. They circled the table, leaving Harbor and Rosa in the center of either side.

"You want me to abandon my bar, my town, and my people, to hide away in your castle at the end of the world?" She ran her finger around the brim of Lord Harbor's mug. "I know what's coming your way, Harbor. I'm no fool."

Harbor pursed his lips and nodded, but spoke as if she'd just agreed to join him. "I'm willing to take on all that will come, but the men must fight and work. The women will have jobs, too. Even the children."

Rosa smiled, still running her finger around the mug. "Why are you so convinced that anyone would follow you to certain death?"

Lord Harbor spread his hands and leaned back from the table. "Certain death is staying here, and you know it. That's why you're entertaining this. The moment Esmund Aziar finds out that you've been supplying us, *helping* his enemy, he'll enslave everyone at Dreston. Then the Howlers will burn it to the ground and piss on the ashes."

Rosa stood now and placed her hands on the table, leaning in to Lord Harbor. "If we go with you, Lord Aziar and his men will still do the same. They'll just do it at your castle instead of my town."

Lord Harbor rose and matched her stance. "Rosa, you've been a friend to me. You've helped my cause and kept my people healthy. One day I hope to repay you, but I won't be able to do that if you're dead. I knew if I only sent my men to get you, there would've been no chance, so I came myself." Lord Harbor looked around at his men and nodded.

Barloc stood with everyone else.

Lord Harbor straightened up. "I'll need an answer by morning." He walked past Rosa and ascended the stairs. Master Dharah faced Tarak, Barloc, and the other guards. "Head to your rooms. I'll be on watch for the first half, then Master Tarak."

***

"Ready your swords!" Master Tarak yelled from somewhere in the hallway.

Barloc jumped from his bed and exited the room, nearly running into the back of another guard.

Tarak's voice boomed again, "Check all the rooms! Bring anyone you find out to the hall!"

Doors slammed all around, followed by furniture and chairs scraping across the floor.

After a moment, Barloc remembered he was part of the search party; he *was* a guard. He ran into the room across from his and scanned every corner, flipped over the mattress and pulled back the curtain. He didn't know what—or who—to look for but searched for anything out of the ordinary.

"Clear!" a voice called out, followed by another, then two more.

Barloc exited the room and announced his clear.

"Grab your gear and follow me!" Tarak's voice faded fast as he barreled down the stairs.

In the bar area, the tables had been scattered around, some knocked on their sides, and a man sat tied to a chair in the center of the room. The guards and Green Cloaks circled him, Lord Harbor sat directly in front of him, and Rosa stood behind her bar.

Master Tarak approached them. "The building's clear."

Lord Harbor spoke to Tarak without looking at him. "This was a set up. I'm not sure how involved we are. Tarak, take a guard and scout outside."

Tarak stepped forward. "But, sir, I don't know that we should separate. If there's one Howler, there's sure to be more."

Lord Harbor glanced up at him. "I didn't ask you what you thought. I gave an order."

Tarak's face tightened, and for a moment, Barloc was sure he would lash out, but instead he nodded and pointed at the guard nearest him. "Come with me."

Lord Harbor glanced around, scanning each of the guards until he rotated back to his captive. "Remove his gag."

Master Dharah stepped forward and untied the dirty linen from around his head.

"How many more Howlers?" Lord Harbor asked, but the man swore he worked alone.

From behind them, Rosa slammed her fist on the bar. "He's lying!"

The man threw his head side to side. "You're the most wanted person in the kingdom. I can't possibly be the first to try and bag you."

Lord Harbor drummed his fingers across the back of his chair. "How did you know what room I was in?"

The man paled and shot a glance toward Rosa. Just as he opened his mouth, a blade landed in his throat with a wet *thwack* and his body fell forward. Everyone in the room turned with their weapons ready. Rosa stood behind her bar straightening her skirt. "More are coming. That one's a Howler for sure. I remember his face. We need to leave. Now."

Lord Harbor jumped from his chair and flung it aside. "Why would you kill him?"

Rosa untied her apron and ducked down behind the bar, pulling out various items and scattering them across the floor. "We'll have to kill a lot more if we don't go now. Remove your cloak, Harbor. They'll be looking for your Green Cloak!" She set an old, wooden box onto the bar, opening it with in a frantic rush. From inside she pulled a long necklace with a locket dangling from it and tucked it into her blouse. She looked up to see everyone staring at her. "Go, now!"

Lord Harbor nodded and removed his cloak.

Barloc realized that this was the first time he'd seen a Green Cloak without his cloak on, and the thought that they all wore the same black leather as the guards gave him pause.

Tarak entered with the guard. "I didn't see anyone, but something's not right. We should move." He stepped into the room and looked down at the corpse. "What the hell happened to him?"

Lord Harbor locked eyes with him and then glanced back to Rosa. "We'll discuss that later."

Barloc followed his gaze and saw the burning glare they gave each other, much different than the one at the table the night before.

Tarak nodded. "We need to guard up and move out. Check the windows. Ready your weapons."

Barloc removed the small sword hanging on his hip. This was the first time he'd been equipped with a real weapon outside of the arena when Tarak wanted him to kill Slaver Martin. He held it in his fist and glanced around to the other guards who did the same.

Rosa disappeared into the kitchen and returned with a pot and large metal spoon. "I'll alert the town and get all I can." She ran out of her bar and into the streets, banging the spoon against the pot, screaming out after every few hits, "Gather all you can carry and come to the bar!"

"Keep an eye on her," Lord Harbor said to Master Dharah.

Dharah crossed the room and glanced out the window. "Somethin' flighty going on, boss."

Rosa continued to repeat her phrase and bang the pot. Slowly the murmur of a crowd gathered before her.

Lord Harbor neared the door. The guards followed with Tarak and Dharah in the rear. "I'll stay with the people. Dharah and Tarak, wear your hoods so no one can tell who's who."

Barloc followed the group into the street and was surprised to see so many had already gathered. He scanned the crowd for Lord Harbor, unable to pick him out.

Rosa stood on the porch to the inn and announced that they were leaving for Drudgeburg, and everyone would have to follow new rules if they decided to join. "If you stay in Dreston, you will likely die or fall to slavery. I don't have time to explain, but I've never led you wrong, and I don't intend to now."

Her words were met with small pockets of chatter, a few questions that received no answers, and a handful of people who broke away from the group, claiming things like they would rather take their chances living with hungry wolves.

Rosa commanded a group of people to fill the two carts with supplies from the stores, and when the group finally began marching, Barloc scanned the crowd once more. Their numbers were about forty strong, including the guards and Green Cloaks, and for a moment, he wondered which bobbing head belonged to Lord Harbor.

The old, feeble, and children either rode pillion with riders or were thrown onto the carts. They moved snail-slow, and when they crested the hill out of Dreston, Rosa stopped and pointed over the crowd.

Small flickers of flame exited the forest surrounding the town. The flickers grew and danced around the buildings, and shortly after their appearance, gunshots echoed from the distance, trailed by screams. All around Barloc, people sucked breaths in, sighed, or let out a sob as the flickers grew into flashes that transformed into rolling flames. In seconds, Dreston burned as bright as a star. A few people tried to break away from the crowd only to be pulled back.

Barloc's stomach twisted at the sight of the flames because no matter how hard he tried to fight past them, images of Chambers, his home town, burned in his mind. The screams from Elly, the girl from the cart from so long ago, echoed in the flames.

"Let's go," Rosa yelled. "We need to move fast! They can see us for certain."

Slowly at first, people began to run away from Dreston, and like a dam breaking, they pushed one another, shoving each other to the ground in their desire to get away. Those who tripped in the darkness were quickly trampled. The sudden movements scared the horses, some rearing up, knocking the riders loose.

Small torchlights broke away from the town and floated in their direction, and after a moment, Barloc charged to the front of the line. "They're coming!"

Master Tarak's deep booming voice rose over the mob. "Group up! Guards, get everyone together!"

Again, it took Barloc a moment to realize he was included in the command. He immediately corralled the people together.

Tarak circled around the group. "Calm down and walk or we'll all die!"

Slowly the group reformed and fell in tighter.

Tarak got behind them and pointed toward Drudgeburg. "The sun will be up soon. Keep moving as a group! If someone falls, pick them up, but no matter what happens, we need to keep moving. If they attack, throw rocks, sticks, blades, hell, the shoes on your feet. Anything you have to dismount them."

The group had moved halfway down the hill by the time the riders appeared. Small flames spread out on either side of them. Barloc's heart raced like the horses' hooves.

An arrow flew from the group and hit a rider with a wet thump. The Howler flew back off his horse and collapsed on the ground, the torch flying from his hand, catching the tall grass on fire. Another rider charged from the other side, and a second arrow buzzed over Barloc's head, but it missed the rider and disappeared into the darkness. Rocks flew from the group at the Howlers, but to no effect. The rider neared them and swung his sword down, cutting across a man's chest. He screamed, but before the rider could do more damage, an arrow landed in his shoulder. The horse reared and retreated away from the group.

Three more Howlers approached on horseback. A gunshot blasted from a Howler standing off on the hill. It struck a woman directly behind Barloc. Four more charged at them on foot. The clashing of swords sounded all around, and as a man approached, Barloc gripped his weapon, ready. Another gunshot filled the air.

A rider seemed to materialize from the darkness, nearly knocking into him.

Barloc reeled back and threw his blade forward, embedding it deep in the horse's leg. The horse screamed a near-human scream and fell with a crunch, sending the rider into the mob. Instantly, the flame extinguished, and the man's screams muffled until they stopped.

The remaining Howlers retreated, diving into the tall grass, and even though more flames appeared at the hill's crest, they didn't pursue, and after a moment, a soft cheering mixed in with the harrowing cries of those around him.

Tarak spoke over the din. "Place all the injured on the carts. We need to ride hard to the castle. Swap the horses for rested ones as soon as you get there and return with empty carts. Go, now!"

Everyone moved fast, lifting the hurt and dead onto the carts. Barloc watched this but continued to glance at the burning grass, sure they would be ambushed once more, but nothing happened.

When the sun finally rose, the light revealed how bad their situation truly was. Blood splattered across the group, on the young and the old, but worse was the wear on their faces.

He continued to walk, watching those around him. *They lost their home, their friends and family, and now they were under the care of the most wanted man in the kingdom.*

Chapter 19 – Emancipation

Barloc stood alongside other guards and Green Cloaks at the entrance of Drudgeburg. Together they circled the crowd from Dreston, blocking their way into the castle. He scanned the people's faces, searching for a sign that a Howler hid among them.

At the head of the crowd, Lord Harbor and Rosa stood atop a cart that was pulled in front of the entrance. Madam Constance and Sir Vigor flanked either side, both watching intently.

Lord Harbor waved his hands in wide arches. "Listen up, everyone!" He waited until the murmuring died down. "I know you're all very tired, but we need to do this properly. If Rosa can't vouch for you, you'll be taken to a cell where you'll stay until further notice. Not as punishment, mind you, but for *our* safety."

The crowd broke into concerned whispers, everyone turning to their neighbor, their faces distorted with confusion.

Barloc watched them closely, his hand on the hilt of his blade. *Not even a day has passed. Now they're being threatened with a prison cell at a known place that deals in slaves.*

Rosa flapped her arms to quell the crowd. "If I don't know you, and you don't wish to stay in a cell, then there's no room for you at Drudgeburg. Lord Harbor has agreed to offer you a weapon, a sack of food, and a few gold coins to help you out."

The crowd grew louder with complaints, but Rosa continued to speak over them. "One last thing. There's a strong chance this castle will be sieged by King Sclavus's men very soon, and when that happens, we will need to defend it. In fact, we'll be required to. Lord Harbor has made it clear that anyone who remains and doesn't participate will be considered an enemy."

Small conversations broke out amongst the people, and Barloc overheard a handful of voices claiming they had nowhere else to go or that they trusted Rosa, but more than anything, he saw tired people with their heads hung low.

"Those who choose to leave, please step up here," she held her hand out to her right, pointing at Sir Vigor, "and collect your items. May your fire burn bright." She jumped down from the cart and took a spot next to Madam Constance.

Barloc found her long, red dress a strange contrast against Sir Vigor and Madam Constance's green cloaks. It popped like a rose among bushes, though dirty and bloodstained.

A handful of people broke away from the group and lined up before Sir Vigor. First two, then another, and then a family of four.

Rosa spoke to the mother, but Barloc couldn't hear what was said. It didn't matter, though, because all of them left.

This time, Madam Constance stepped forward and spoke over the crowd, her voice much more commanding than Rosa's. "Once inside, you'll wait in the outer bailey for instructions. Lord Harbor will be out once everyone is fed. He'll make an announcement, and then you'll be shown to your quarters."

After Rosa verified each person, Sir Vigor and Madam Constance stripped them of anything that could be considered a weapon.

Barloc's eyelids drooped from the weight of the past few days. His knee throbbed, his foot hurt, and his ribs stung when he breathed in too deeply, but now that he'd finally stopped moving, he couldn't tell which was worse. He never really had the chance to recover after the challenges, except for the brief time with Healer Haylan.

Only one more person stepped from the line, deciding not to enter the castle, claiming that he couldn't trust a man who would disarm him and then promise safety. This man received his sack, kept his own sword, and marched away from Drudgeburg.

When the last woman walked through the gate, the guards, Rosa, and the Green Cloaks followed. Inside, meals were already being distributed. The Healers weaved between the people, patching up their wounds. Even Vicar Farlen joined the crowd, helping with prayers.

A bell rang across the yard, and as a group, everyone stared up at the tall tower. Slowly, slaves flowed in from all around, and eventually, the outer bailey swelled like the days of the funerals.

Sir Vigor stood at the entrance, Madam Constance and the other Green Cloaks gathered by him. "Everyone, face this way!" His voice, once again, carried across the yard like the slave horn.

Lord Harbor swiftly walked across the curtain wall above them, stopping at the gate, wearing his green cloak once more. He stared down at the crowd until the bell stopped ringing. "Look around, all of you." He spread his hands apart. "Do it, look at those next to you and consider what you see."

Nearly everyone surrounding Barloc continued to stare at Lord Harbor, confused, and as if a spell broke, they inspected those around them. There was no longer a divide of guards circling those from Dreston, but a mixture of everyone. Even the Green Cloaks and Healers peppered the crowd in no distinct order.

"What do you see? Slaves? Free men and women? Guards? Masters?" Lord Harbor paced, his hands hidden in his cloak, occasionally casting his attention down at the people. "It's strange that we all start and end at the same place, yet we walk such different paths. It's stranger yet that we stand so close we can smell each other's breath, but we are divided by titles... imaginary lines drawn to claim that one person is better than the next." Harbor climbed onto the wall and kicked his legs over, sitting on the edge.

"I have some things to confess. I've tried to master a plan around it, but I think the best course of action is honesty. It's time to come clean. A war is on the horizon, and by the end of my speech, I will offer you a choice. But for now, you will listen to what I have to say.

"This kingdom is divided by the very lines I was just speaking of, but it wasn't always this way. Some of us old enough to remember King Ulrich are brought back to a time when Howlers were called criminals, slavery was illegal, and the common folk were respected as the backbone of the kingdom."

A few voices murmured but quickly fell silent.

"Now we have some sort of reversed ascendance, making the criminals the leaders and the common folk the criminals. Small resistances around the kingdom pop up now and again but are quickly squelched, leaving fear to rule us all. When people stop fighting for what's right, they are accepting what's wrong.

"Sclavus has a very common saying associated with him: 'If you're not with me, you're against me.' It's simple yet powerful.

"This kingdom needs a leader that the people vote into the position or a family with a noble name, like King Ulrich. Without votes, you risk a dictatorship or something of the like, and a dictatorship *is* tyranny.

"As many of you have heard, or even seen, I've taken charge and begun freeing slaves. Word, as it inevitably does, has reached the king, who has grown comfortable in his throne. He sent a handful of men to clean up the issue, though I rebutted them. I claimed myself as a king of East Reach, a king of the end of the world."

More conversation spurned from the group, but Lord Harbor lifted a hand to indicate silence and closed his eyes. Everyone fell quiet. After a moment, he opened them again.

"I'm no king and I never want to be." Lord Harbor stood and walked along the wall's edge. "I'm simply a man who's fighting for what I believe to be right."

He teetered dangerously close to the edge, took another deep breath, and let it out in a long sigh. "My name is not *Lord Harbor*; my name is Martell Eldridge. I was the son of a blacksmith from a poor town called Trappe. When Sclavus came into power, I was among the first to fall to the Howlers, and being among the first, it was one of the worst. The Howlers attacked my town with a type of bloodlust. They killed our fathers and mothers and shipped the children and young adults off with the slavers. They raided our homes, taking all our belongings for their own. I became a slave."

He untied his green cloak and let it fall, revealing black leather armor from head to toe. "I was tossed between owners and camps until I was sold to Lord Edgar Harbor, the lord of this very castle. I was one of ten. My blood, sweat, and tears have soaked into the very dirt you stand on."

He unstrapped his left bracer and let it fall atop his cloak.

"Edgar was out of his mind. One moment he was kind, but the next... not so much."

He dropped the other bracer.

"What drew the vow to my lips was when he strangled a slave to death simply to watch him die, and we could do nothing about it. The slave was one of my only friends, a man named Darim."

He worked at the sides of his tunic, unstrapping them from base up.

"I spoke to each slave that night while the hatred was fresh on my heart and devised a plan to overthrow our master. After seeing what had happened to Darim, they eagerly agreed. I told them my vision of staying in Drudgeburg, and that I wanted to fight against King Sclavus so this could happen no more!"

He removed the tunic, revealing bare flesh. Defined muscles cut across his chest and stomach. Dark, curly hair covered his torso, and thick, bumpy scars painted his flesh. Slowly, he rotated, revealing his back to show scars resembling crags in a mountain. Long, deep, red and purple gashes cut up his spine.

"I killed him myself. He came out one morning, drunk before the sun came up, and started shoving a slave around the yard.

"After I killed him, we fell into a state of panic. We lost two of the nine remaining slaves, but the rest of us stayed. The following day, a slaver came to the gates demanding to see Lord Harbor. He was delivering three slave men and two women. That was when the idea hit us. I donned Lord Harbor's clothes and purchased the slaves. The slaver left, happy and well paid."

Barloc couldn't help but stare at Sir Vigor and Madam Constance. *They were slaves the whole time?*

"Almost one year ago, I sat with my newly appointed council and we devised a system that would help us build an army to fight King Sclavus and the Howlers. The system relied on the slaves working their way up a chain by doing a quest a day. They mined resources to keep up on maintenance to the castle, fight in the battle squares to help train everyone in battle, then become the very guards that kept the slaves in line.

"If they spoke, they'd be returned to day one. As the slaves progressed, they saw more and learned more, but it wasn't worth it to risk of being sent back to the beginning."

Barloc's mind reeled with the past few weeks.

"It's worked so well up until now, but while we were marching back from Dreston, I realized that I would be no better than Sclavus if I held you here to die and you not even know what you're dying for. We have a chance to fight against slavery, against Sclavus. We have a chance to make this right once more. Raise the gate!"

He stretched his arm out and indicated outside the castle. "I open the gates to you. If you choose to leave, enter the world and find your place, then go. I can't hold you against your will... not to fight for me, for my cause. Not anymore. All of you are free to go."

Lord Harbor stepped down to where only his top half could be seen.

Barloc closed his eyes, remembering his life since the day the Howlers had burned his home and his journey through slavery. *MJ-1 and MJ-8. Master Tarak and Slaver Martin.* Anger met sadness and confusion.

A man's voice called out from the center of the crowd. "Lord Harbor, or Eldridge, or whoever you are, do you think you can beat them?"

Lord Harbor stopped collecting his armor and faced the crowd below. He stared for a moment, blinking hard. "Might as well call me Lord Harbor. My family name died the moment Sclavus entered into power."

The man spoke again, and this time the crowd spread out around him. "Lord Harbor, do you think you can beat them? Sclavus's men?"

"I do. I'm going to try, at least. I refuse to die as a slave when I can die fighting for something I believe in." He turned his back once more and walked away, his cloak and gear under his arm.

The same man stepped forward and yelled out a chant at the top of his lungs, flapping his arms to try and get those around him to join. "Har-bor, Har-bor, Har-bor!"

The energy floating around Barloc forced a smile on his face. All this time, he'd wondered if Lord Harbor had been genuine, all this time he'd questioned so much, thinking it all a game, but now he saw that it was true and authentic. *I'm... free.* The thought stuck hard to his mind, and as the chant grew louder, so did the name. *How could I possibly walk away now?*

Slowly, other voices joined in, and Barloc found his lips and voice working on their own, singing the name. Men who had moved for the exit turned back, and by the time Lord Harbor made it halfway across the curtain wall, every single person on the ground clapped in unison and chanted his name.

Chapter 20 – The Calm before the Storm

By nightfall, a transformation happened unlike anything Barloc had ever seen. Only a handful of people had left after Lord Harbor revealed his true identity and behind them the gate was sealed shut. The slaves' fetters were removed and thrown into a pile, and they were given free reign of the outer and inner bailey, as well as the stock of clothing, armor, and weapons. Even the handful of men and women Rosa couldn't identify when arriving at Drudgeburg were pardoned from their prison cells, though there was no sign of Slaver Martin or Variegate.

Those who were slaves, lords, and common folk on that prior morning now sat around a huge bonfire, drinking and eating. The invisible social lines that Lord Harbor had spoken of vanished while they sat under the shade of the same idea: freedom.

Barloc took a swig of ale and surveyed the outer bailey from his seat at the sorting table. Everyone danced and drank and laughed as if they found all the happiness they'd lost over the years.

The Green Cloaks remained to help keep order, but it didn't stop them from enjoying the festivities, though Barloc noticed a few of them missing. He couldn't find Sapper, Tarak, or Sir Vigor anywhere in the yard and assumed they'd retreated to inside the castle.

"It's quite the sight, isn't it?" Madam Constance sat next to him at the sorting table.

Barloc almost dropped his drink, pulling away from his thoughts. He cleared his throat, but when he went to speak, he stopped and stared into her eyes, the firelight flickering in the reflection. She wore her hair pulled back into a ponytail, reinventing her entire appearance.

She tilted her head and stared at him, confused. "Is something wrong?"

Barloc looked away, shook his head, and finished his beer. "Feels like a trap, doesn't it? Seeing all these people relaxing when we know what's coming."

Madam Constance glanced around the yard. "You're a very smart man, Barloc Maghild. And you're not wrong for being concerned. I've seen it go two ways. Some leaders allow their soldiers to bathe in merriment prior to a battle. At the very least, they're required a night of peace and solace to clear their minds."

Barloc nodded. "Makes enough sense."

"But in our case, I would say that happiness is more important to the rest." She rotated in her seat, offering him her full attention. "It's not a secret that we aren't a castle full of trained soldiers. The king's men will be on horses and covered in the finest armor.

We have limited resources and hardly any mounts. Our people are mostly farmers or tradesmen and have learned how to fight using wooden weapons in makeshift battle squares, but do you know what we *do* have that the soldiers don't?"

Barloc scanned the yard, his eyes passing over a fat drunk man, a woman hanging from his neck, barely wearing any clothes, and a gangly young boy dressed in the black leather of the guards. Another man covered in muscles but passed out drunk, drooling on the ground. More of the same met his eyes until he returned his attention to Madam Constance. "Diversity?"

She laughed, her smile spreading wide across her face. It'd been the first time he'd seen her truly smile, and it could have been a sunrise of its own kind. The anxiety associated with his concerns slipped away at the sight of her shining countenance.

She nodded. "You're not wrong there, but what I mean is that we have people driven by passion and hunger. We have men and women who've been beaten and tortured and raped. People who've had every freedom stripped away, and now they have a fighting chance." She nodded as if agreeing with herself. "There's nothing scarier than a pack of starving dogs, and not to suggest that we're all hungry dogs, we *are* starving for life, for freedom."

Barloc fought the urge to ask what she knew about being a hungry dog, but he thought of Lord Harbor standing above the gate, admitting that they'd all been slaves. He nodded.

"You still seem angry."

He continued nodding.

"The deception? The freedom? Are you so upset that you're not in fetters?"

Barloc didn't respond, though his cheeks grew warm.

"Or is it me that you're angry with? Do you wish me to leave?"

Barloc shook his head and locked eyes with her. "No."

She smiled again. "Let's talk then."

"What about?"

She shrugged and shifted a little in her seat. "Whatever you want. Ask me anything and if I'm able, I'll tell you. I want you to know that you can trust me."

Trust? "What does my trust matter?"

Madam Constance nodded and stood. "It would appear I've misjudged you."

Barloc stood with her. "No, you didn't. It's just... you must understand. I was your slave not even a day ago, and everything up to this point has been that of a game. I'd like to talk." He sat back down and added, "Very much."

She glanced over her shoulder toward the fire and then at the closed gate of the castle. She sat down. "Well, go on and ask me anything."

Barloc nodded. "The man who snuck in the other night to try and break us out. Was that a set up?"

Madam Constance started nodding halfway through his sentence. "Yes. It's one of the many tests we do to help gauge the slaves. It's how we decide on who will be a guard in what area."

Barloc closed his eyes and pictured the deep grooves cut into the castle wall where it was clear that a grappling had been used numerous times before. *That would explain why the yard was so empty, and why Master Tarak had been fully geared and ready in the middle of the night.*

"Okay." Barloc took a breath. "The Howler, Katiph. What's his deal? Why are we selling slaves to him if the Howlers are one of the forces we're fighting against?"

"Another great question." For a second she smiled, but her cheeks fell back down just as quickly. "That's one of Lord Harbor's plans. It's a hard plan, and I wish I could fight against it, but it really is a great idea."

Barloc sat forward, his curiosity baited. "What do you mean?"

"We enlist certain slaves that make it through the thirty days. We take them into the keep, and we fill them in on the plans once we know they can be trusted. Then we offer them the option to go back into slavery." Her head sagged with her shoulders, her eyes shining with tears. "I've lost some friends back into the very system we're fighting against."

Barloc shook his head. "Wait, what? Are you telling me that those two old men were slaves that made it all the way through the thirty days just to go back into slavery?"

Madam Constance's eyes opened wide at his rising voice. "Be quiet! You can't just yell out all our information. I'm telling *you* this. These things I'm revealing can't be spread. It risks too much." She glanced around to make sure no one listened in. "They weren't sent there as much as they chose to go—"

"But who would *choose* to go back into slavery?"

Her lips tightened into a thin line. "If you'd let me finish, then you would've known by now."

Barloc nodded, glancing down at his empty mug sitting on the sorting table. "My apologies."

Madam Constance watched him for a moment as if deciding whether she should continue or not.

"They make it through their time and learn about our cause. Not all of it, of course. Not any one of us knows everything. Not even Lord Harbor. He issues out specific tasks and jobs to each Green Cloak to limit the information from being spread. He doesn't want any one person to know everything just in case they're captured and tortured." She held up her hand when Barloc went to speak. "These slaves that make it through are given the option to participate around the castle or they can help the future cause of our freedom by being sold back into slavery with a specific mission, ultimately with the top down goal of King Sclavus's murder. There are enough members of that hierarchy spread out across the kingdom that all who are eliminated are one less obstacle for our cause."

Barloc processed her words while watching the fire. "But... how do you communicate with them to know they're doing the right thing? How do you know that they aren't captured and turned?"

"Well, I think that this is how the information floated back to the king, actually. It's a gamble for us, but it's one we must take. We now have numerous men and women all over the kingdom. Some lie in wait, searching for the perfect moment to strike, some die on their journey by overzealous slavers. It's a gamble, but if we can infect the system, we win by having people willing to die for our cause, for freedom."

Barloc shook his head. "That was more than I was expecting."

"This goes much deeper than you or I will ever know."

"I can't help but wonder why you're telling me this."

She put her fingers on his chin and turned his head to her. "We're running low on good people, and you fit the mold. Everything you've done up to this point is defining of what we're looking for in leadership. Lord Harbor is still unsure of you, but I see something that I rarely see in anyone."

Tingles climbed across Barloc's body, and he fought the urge to shiver. "So, the kingdom is being loaded full of slaves that are willing to die in order to kill a handful of villains?"

"I wouldn't say *full,* but I would say even if we all die in battle at Drudgeburg, we have enough gears turning to hopefully keep this machine of an idea going at least for a while."

Barloc smiled. "This is quite the system. Take slaves and use them to build an army. Train them and slowly shape them into soldiers who will inevitably fight for you to the death. I must admit that I'm impressed."

She smiled. "Please don't repeat any of this. I'm still trying to sell you to Lord Harbor... oh... maybe that's the wrong choice of words."

Barloc laughed and so did Madam Constance.

"What else would you like to know?"

"What's your name?"

"Mad—er. Asha."

"Asha Constance?"

She nodded. "Asha Constance Locke."

"What were you before all this?" Barloc indicated the crowd around the outer bailey.

"I was the daughter of a farmer. My mother was teaching me to be a seamstress, but my father was determined to educate me on how to farm."

Barloc nodded. "Your turn. What do you want to know about me?"

"I read the journal entries, so I know a great deal about you already."

Barloc flushed with embarrassment and anger. Something about her peering into his life without his knowledge made him uneasy. "Why all this banter? What is the purpose if you already know so much about me?"

She smiled. "I want *you* to know about *me*, Barloc. I see the way you look at me. I would've thought it impossible for us to act on anything due to the circumstances, but... here we are."

Barloc's stomach twisted. *Am I that transparent?* The awkward tension forced him to act, though he had to remind himself that he did so as a free man. He took her hand into his. "Then tell me what I should know." His heart raced and his cheeks warmed with a different type of heat.

She gripped his hand in both of hers. "Very well. I thought that my life was over until I met Lord Harbor. He helped us break free, and here we are on one of the last nights we may ever see again. I find your courage and honor extremely attractive, and I can't help but want to know more about you. I'm not much older than you, and I'm experienced enough now to express myself when the time is right. I don't know that I would call it love, but I would absolutely declare my interest in having future conversations with you."

Barloc's mouth watered alongside his eyes. In all his life, he had never heard a woman outside of his mother spoken to him with such care.

He pulled her closer. Her hand shot up to his cheek, and he stared at her features, wondering if he should kiss her. She licked her lips as if preparing, but he didn't want to overstep. Before he could properly register his actions, he closed his eyes and leaned in for a kiss.

Their lips connected and though he lacked the experience, he followed her lead. She pulled him closer, and he found his hand shifting to her back, holding her tighter than he'd ever held a woman, terrified the moment would end.

"Constance!" A deep voice startled them apart. Lord Harbor stood with his hands behind his back, watching.

Madam Constance straightened her cloak and stepped away from the table. She bowed to him. "My lord."

Lord Harbor passed his attention between the two. "I need you in the castle. There are a few more items we need to review before we close out the night. Dharah is on your watch." He glanced back at Barloc, his jaw working back and forth in his closed mouth. Without another word, he turned on his heels and walked beside Madam Constance toward the keep.

Barloc watched Madam Constance—*Asha Constance Locke*—walk away beside Lord Harbor, and before they cleared the fire, he saw her soft features glance back one more time.

Tired of watching the fire, he walked toward the bunkhouse, and as he went, he glanced up at the stars, remembering the spot the Whisperer had shown him.

He decided to travel up top, searching for the recess in the wall. It took him much longer in the darkness to navigate through the small tunnels, but he eventually found the opening.

Atop the wall, he discovered that a handful of people had also found their way up, all either guards or Green Cloaks, and that was when he found Master Sapper, staring out at the battlefield, away from the festivities.

Barloc quickly thought to turn back, to go down, but instead found himself approaching. "Master Sapper." He placed his arms on the wall and stared across the battlefield.

Sapper grunted and drank from his mug. "Hero," he said curtly.

"Are you all right, Master Sapper?" Barloc wouldn't step any closer. He couldn't help but think back at the nightmares and the mines. A pang of anger flashed through his stomach at the thought of MJ-8.

Sapper pushed air through his nose.

Barloc waited another moment and took a step back but stopped when Sapper spoke.

"Everything we worked for is gone."

"I don't understand."

Sapper lifted his hand and spread it across the land before him. "All of it. Thrown away. I thought we really stood a chance, but we needed more time, and the fool Harbor had to open his mouth. That's what I get for trusting a slave."

He drained the contents of his drink and tossed the mug over the wall, hearing it *ting* as it hit the hard ground below. "We really had a chance to bring down Sclavus... put an arrow in all of his rabid dog Howlers."

"Master S—"

"I could see it, ya know? The way he was falling into his own mind, not sharing his plans with us. He'd tell Vigor one secret and Constance another. Then he'd give me another. Not any one of us are important enough to know it all."

"You don't think we'll win?"

Sapper finally faced Barloc. "I wanted to kill ya."

"I suspected this, yes," Barloc said, inching away.

"I don't know what Constance saw in ya. A skinny little wretch. Who knows the truth? Sure as hell not me." Sapper approached him.

Barloc casually rested his hand on the hilt of his blade. "I don't understand."

Sapper ignored him and reached his hands out. "But ya know what? I see it now. I saw ya... ya cared for the slaves. Hell, they were never slaves to ya. They were men, and ya recognized that. Ya stood up for what was right and ya risked yer own life to save that MJ-8."

Barloc's stomach churned at the mention of his name, especially from the man who essentially condemned him.

Sapper placed his huge hand on Barloc's shoulders and peered into his eyes. "I almost killed ya because of my issues." Sapper leaned in closer, and for a moment, Barloc thought he was going to kiss him. He went to push him away and in that very moment, Sapper lost his gut, sending it to splatter at Barloc's feet.

He wiped his hand across his mouth and leaned against the wall. "I never claimed to be perfect." With his arms out for balance, Sapper moved to the stairs and slowly descended.

Barloc stepped to the wall where Sapper had stood and stared out at the field. In the dim moonlight, the silhouettes of the bulwarks bit up from the field, and the grass swayed peacefully as if waving to the sky above.

I kissed Madam Constance and Master Sapper opened up to me. Maybe I'm already dead.

Chapter 21 – The Sorting

The slave horn vibrated the castle walls, jarring Barloc awake. He jumped to his feet and carefully stepped over the dried remains from Master Sapper's stomach. The previous night replayed in his mind, and he remembered nestling into the Whisperer's corner at the end of the evening, not wanting to travel back into the dark tunnels within the castle's walls.

The horn's echo faded away, and he peered over the edge, into the outer bailey.

Unlike the morning with the Whisperer, everyone emerged from all over the grounds and shuffled around without order. Some returned to their places in front of their bunkhouses— Barloc suspected without even realizing—and many held their hands to their heads in anguish from the night before, but before long, the crew of Green Cloaks arrived from the inner bailey. Fifteen in total, led by Lord Harbor and Rosa, followed by the Healers and Vicar Farlen. His eyes fell upon Madam Constance, who marched behind Sir Vigor, her hair down once more.

Barloc broke away from the wall and ran to the stairs, moments later emerging from behind one of the long bunkhouses.

Lord Harbor stood atop the sorting table, adorned in his green cloak. He spun in a slow circle, scanning the crowd, until he lifted his arms to call for quiet. "I'm glad everyone could enjoy themselves. I want you to think about that enjoyment and ask why you shouldn't have that every day. I want you to believe in our cause. It's not to drown in merriment but to live. As slaves, we were unable to experience laughter and fun. We constantly lived in fear and never experienced love." At this, he reached his hand toward Rosa, who took it with a smile.

Something about the sight sent a quiver through Barloc's stomach. *Then why did he have to interrupt Madam Constance and me?*

"But now we prepare to secure this freedom. Today, my Green Cloaks will take the lead of a Focus. As I announce each Focus, approach the Green Cloak associated with the one you will best benefit in the oncoming war." Lord Harbor glanced around at all the people before continuing.

"Those skilled in battle, meet Master Tarak at the red marker over here." He pointed behind him.

Tarak broke away from the group to stand at the designated spot. Once there, he cupped his hands around his mouth and yelled, "Any weapon, any style. If you have something to offer in combat, come to me. I mean anything. We'll also need those who can cover the murder holes in case we're breeched."

All around, people worked their way across the bailey toward Tarak. Mainly guards approached at first, but a few former slaves and free folk from Dreston trailed.

Barloc decided to wait, wanting to see the whole scene play out before choosing.

As the crowd moving toward Tarak slowed, Lord Harbor continued. "Anyone who is of the cloth, join Vicar Farlen at the white marker."

Only an old man and one little boy with his mother emerged from the remaining people. Vicar Farlen accepted them with a hug.

"Not many. Very well. Next, I need anyone skilled in the arts of healing to meet Healer Haylan at the blue marker. She will gear you in vials and train you fast and hard. This may be one of the most gut wrenching tasks in the war. The Healers risk their lives while tending to the wounded. They must understand the many vials and lug them around the field, while dodging trouble. Those able, please step forward."

The remaining crowd thinned as a surprising amount of people gathered around Haylan.

"Master Fletcher will take those who can help make arrows and keep the archers stocked. This tends to be a great task for children. It keeps them safe, they're quick on their feet, and even quicker to learn. That will do it for today. Those are the Focuses. The remaining men and women can join Madam Constance, where you will be given your tasks."

Barloc slipped past those too young, too old, or too scared and fell into the crowd surrounding Master Tarak.

Once the outer bailey emptied of the spare people, Lord Harbor faced the flags. "Everyone!" He waited for the many faces to turn toward him. "We don't know for certain *when* this war will happen, and we don't know *how* it's going to happen. The only thing we know is that it *will* happen. From this point forward, no one is permitted to leave the castle unless it's under *my* direct orders. We now prepare for battle. The merriment will slow, mainly because our stock of ale is running low." He laughed, which echoed across the crowd. "Be rested, keep your head cleared, and follow the orders given. We don't have long to uncover your skills. Work hard."

Lord Harbor lifted his right fist high into the air. He glanced around at each flag's crowd, and bellowed as loud as he could, "For Freedom!"

The outer bailey blew up in cheers and shouts of "For Freedom!"

Lord Harbor sat down on the table next to Rosa and fell into conversation. The remaining Green Cloaks dispersed around the yard, some moving to the battlements and others joining the various groups.

Master Tarak led the group toward the inner bailey. "Let's go!"

Barloc followed the mass of people, and once there, everyone spread out as best they could, filling the area more than Barloc could've imagined possible.

Tarak and Dharah stood together in the center of the bailey. Tarak cupped his hands around his mouth once more. "I want my guards to line up behind Master Dharah here. You'll help train. Everyone else stand behind me." He pointed at the ground. "Right there."

As he got situated, Barloc thought back to his first day at Drudgeburg and how Lord Harbor stretched them out in a similar fashion, as if they were on display.

"These are the men that made it through my gauntlet once before. I trust their ability to train you." Tarak turned toward the line of guards. "In my bailey, authority is still present. Green Cloaks have the final word, and if you cause a problem, allow me to say that the stockades will be my last choice." He pointed at the Focus booths lining the wall. "Guards, make your way to your Focus."

Barloc walked to the booth with the sword and shield banner where seven other guards stood alongside him.

Tarak addressed the remaining people. "Now, try to follow along. I don't have the patience to repeat myself. Above each booth is the symbol of which Focus the booth is for. Find your home. The more archers we have, the better, but anything will do. There's a place for everyone. Step up to your Focus and wait in line. You'll be matched up with a guard to test your skills. Now, go on and get to your spots."

Some of the people appeared confident and marched right up to where they believed they were best, while others meandered slowly around, seeming lost. Barloc's booth quickly became one of the fullest the fastest. The line stretched down the vein of the bailey.

Additional Green Cloaks joined them, increasing their numbers to five. Dharah, Tarak, Sir Vigor, and two he didn't know.

Barloc discovered a woman standing toward the center of his line. This took him by surprise, but when he searched the rest of the bailey, he found women mixed throughout. There weren't many but still more than he would've ever imagined.

Tarak called all the Green Cloaks to the center and huddled with them. After a moment, he addressed the entire bailey in the loudest voice he could. "I'll not have any joking around. If I catch you causing trouble, starting fights, or going too far in any manner, you'll deal with me directly. This isn't a game. Our lives depend on how well you do.

"With that said, the Green Cloaks will manage the battles and gauge the fighters. You'll be given the very simple task of tapping the opponent's chest with your practice weapon during the time of the sandglass. First, I want the trainees to tap their guard's chest. *Tap*. They will alternate each fight. If you have questions, ask one of the Green Cloaks. Now, begin!"

A Green Cloak came by Barloc's booth and instructed the trainees to surround the battle square to observe the fights. The first guard collected two practice swords and gave one to the first trainee as he walked by. The guard twirled the wooden sword, testing its balance. Once satisfied, he nodded at the Green Cloak who turned the sandglass.

The trainee fumbled with the piece of wood at first but quickly became comfortable. He advanced on the guard. The man stood with a shaven head and dirty, tattered clothing hanging from his thin frame. He was exceptionally skinny, but his footwork provided proof of his knowledge with a sword. Each attack the guard performed was easily parried, but the same happened when the man assaulted the guard. Neither really advanced in the fight, for they appeared to be equally matched.

Before the sandglass ran out, the Green Cloak called for them to stop. "That'll be enough. You there," he pointed at the trainee. "Go see Master Tarak in the center of the yard." The trainee bowed slightly at the guard, thanked the Green Cloak, and stepped from the battle square.

Many of the spars that followed didn't go as well as the first, though a few were beyond exceptional. On Barloc's turn, he grabbed the sword from the previous guard and stepped into the ring where he faced the woman that had been standing in their line.

Her long, dirty-blonde hair had been pulled back into a ponytail, and where her features seemed soft at first glance, her face was covered with small scars. The woman had calloused hands, clearly visible from across the battle square, and she wore a long dress with a tight top.

She smiled and tucked the wooden sword under her arm. "Wait a moment." An accent unlike one Barloc had ever heard drenched her voice. "I gotta gat rady. I wasn't espactin' ta beat on a pup."

The men around the battle square laughed.

Barloc's cheeks warmed.

The woman pulled at the strings around her corset. The sides popped and she lifted it over her head, leaving a loose, white blouse behind. She took her dress in her hands and pulled it up to her mouth. After biting into the cloth, she tore at it until it became a skirt that hung just above her knees.

A few of the men cheered, some laughed, but all watched. When she finished, she grasped the sword in her right fist and nodded.

The Green Cloak stood at the sandglass and teetered it in his hand. He glanced at Barloc and then back at the woman, lifting his eyebrows. "You're sure you want to do this?"

She laughed. "I got no problem swattin' him down."

The Green Cloak nodded and went to turn the glass but stopped. He faced Barloc. "Are you certain *you* want to do this?" He quickly glanced at her and back. "She's fierce."

The men laughed again, but the Green Cloak rotated the glass without a response.

She advanced on him, swinging her sword hard and fast. The force of the attack took him by surprise even though he had watched her prepare. He made no effort to assault her back, rather focused on deflecting her onslaught. Every move she made grew harder to keep up with. She stood taller than him and fought with a confidence Barloc hadn't seen before, other than maybe in Master Tarak.

She laughed and taunted him. "Come on, pup. I'm jus' a little girl." She advanced.

"I don't," he parried another blow, "want to hurt you, my lady."

The men circling laughed even harder. Their battle had apparently attracted more onlookers from the surrounding booths.

She smiled again while advancing. "I plan ta spank ya with this sword."

Barloc retreated and blocked another attack. His arms grew tired, and as much as he didn't want to disarm the woman, he knew he had no choice. Honor would only go so far in a real battle.

"Come on, little one."

Barloc glanced around, wishing someone would end it. His arms grew heavier with each parry, and his knuckles bled from where one of her strikes slid down the wooden blade and smashed into his hand.

Her confidence flourished, and Barloc knew that he would lose if they continued to dance in this way. He waited for her arms to lift before he dropped to the ground swiping his legs into hers.

She fell with a clatter and a grunt of surprise, and when she landed, her sword dropped from her fist. She scrambled for it, but Barloc managed to grab it first. He pinned her down with his foot and pointed both at her chest. "You're a good fighter," Barloc said. "You're fast."

The woman smiled, wiped her forehead, and stood. The crowd around grew silent as they watched.

She dusted off her clothes. "I don't need ya blessin'."

Tarak's voice shattered the cheering. He stepped into the battle square and crossed his arms, sizing her up. "You obviously know how to use a sword, but you have no sense. I could've taken you down in seconds. You can't rely on speed to win. You need to slow down and use your wits."

She spat on the ground and crossed her own arms, meeting Tarak's eyes. "Ya know how it is, do ya?"

Tarak laughed. "I know that he parried every attack and then disarmed you. Had you been a man, I wonder if you could've lasted that long." He spoke to the entire crowd, slowly rotating in his spot. "In battle, you can't rely on gender to belay your opponent. They aren't here to court you, they're here to murder or enslave you. Whichever comes first."

The woman's face turned red, but she didn't take her eyes off Tarak. Tension filled the air.

Tarak stepped in front of her. "Doesn't change the fact that you can fight. Hell, I would wager you could take on most the yard here and win, and that says something. Good job. I'll have you practice...

slower and more thought out. Grab a weapon and join me in the center."

Barloc stepped from the ring and passed both swords to the next guard.

The rest of the day panned out for the better. Nearly everyone who approached a Focus had some skill with the weapon of choice. Only a few had to be reassigned, and another group was taken back out to the outer bailey where they were given other tasks. Tarak only had to break up one fight that escalated to fists, and by the end, he called for everyone to gather around the center once more.

"I think we got some good practice in. I have an idea for tonight. I'll allow some challengers to go against one another in the arena. It'll be the same type of situation we just went through. The winners will be given as much food and ale their bodies can manage this evening. The losers will clean the chamber pots on the morrow."

That evening everyone from Tarak's group crowded around the arena. Members from the kitchen floated around the crowd and handed out bundles of bread and fruit, while the Green Cloaks stood at each corner, keeping watch. In the arena, people volunteered to fight one another with practice weapons, hoping for a hot meal.

Barloc sat back and watched while chewing his bread. *They can keep their hot meal.* The sun began to fall, darkening the sky, and for the first time since stepping into the battle square that morning, Madam Constance popped into his mind. He wondered how he would go about seeing her. *Where would she even be?*

After a few minutes of thinking on it, he decided to ask Tarak. According to Lord Harbor, they weren't slaves anymore, so he should at least be able to scout out his new friend, assuming he wasn't taking her away from her duties.

When Barloc went to stand, a hand forced him back down. "Sit," a voice spoke in his ear.

He knew the owner instantly, and when he turned to confirm, the Whisperer towered over him, still dressed head to toe with his face hidden behind the mesh mask.

The Whisperer stared for a moment longer before speaking. "I've been watching you today."

"Is that so?" Barloc asked and attempted to stand again but was quickly pushed back down. "I thought we were all free? Why the mask still?"

The Whisperer laughed. "We're far from free, MJ-7. Once the war begins, meet me at the entrance to the keep. I have a special task for you, understand?" His mask pointed toward the arena.

"What do you mean, report to you?"

"Ignore everything else, even orders directly from Lord Harbor, and come straight to me. I'll be waiting for you at the entrance to the keep, where you received your armor." The Whisperer's hand lifted from Barloc's shoulder. The hooded figure bowed and disappeared among the people.

Barloc watched the spar another moment but still decided to approach Tarak.

Tarak smiled. "The great MJ-7. You're not in the mood for some hot food?" He directed his hand to the arena.

Barloc shook his head. "I was... well, I was looking for someone."

Tarak crossed his arms. "Oh? And who is that?"

Barloc stared at him a moment unsure if he should continue. *What's the worst-case scenario? I've been enslaved for my entire adult life.*

Tarak cracked a smile. "Confident in the arena. Useless in a conversation."

Barloc shook his head. "Madam Constance. I'm looking to speak with her."

He nodded and smiled. "Ah, well, you're not in good luck for that meeting. She's preparing for war. We had a scout return earlier claiming the king's army is on the move."

Barloc nodded. "Thank you." He walked away. Knowing the king's army was marching toward them made him increasingly uneasy.

He glanced up to the sky, seeing nothing but bright stars and a near full moon. He decided to return to the Whisperer's corner and spend what would most certainly be one of his last nights in peace alone.

Chapter 22 – First Blood

Barloc woke with a start at the certain call for help. He sat up, listening intently, only hearing the occasional snores from the bunks below. The sudden thundering boom of footfalls rushing upstairs forced him to his feet.

The flicker of flame danced off the stone as Master Sapper emerged from the stairwell, gripping a torch. Sapper barely stopped long enough to acknowledge him before running the length of the wall toward the entrance.

Barloc peered over the edge and across the field. At first he saw nothing, but then flames surfaced along the horizon, much like the night in Dreston when the Howlers appeared at the tree line. The dark silhouette of a rider rushed down the main road, the man atop slumped forward, his arms around the horse's neck.

The flames on the horizon multiplied until there were too many to count. They blended together, creating the illusion that the field was on fire.

Sapper jammed his torch into one of the guard's hands and gripped the wall. "Open the bloody gate, already!" He leaned over the edge at the rider's approach. "What's happened?"

The man pushed up, swaying atop the horse. "They're here."

Sapper jumped back from the wall and ran toward the stairs. Barloc followed. When they arrived below, the rider had just entered the outer bailey, hanging from the horse's neck.

Sapper pulled the Green Cloak down, nearly dropping him to the ground. Various arrows poking out from his back broke off on the horse's flank. Blood covered his front and had begun pooling underneath him. It reminded Barloc of the day Atticus had died not far from where they stood.

The man looked up at Sapper while clutching his stomach. "He sent scouts ahead to search for us. I don't know what happened to Brea or Sticker. They're—" He hissed in a tight breath. "either caught behind the army," he coughed blood into his lap, "or they're dead. I think it's the latter."

Sir Vigor arrived and stared at the wounded man. "I'll get the Healers and Harbor."

Sapper kneeled and leaned in close, gripping one of the man's hands. "What happened?"

"Howlers got me. They knew I was there. Surrounded. I couldn't get out. They—" he coughed again, spraying blood and saliva into the air. "They sent me away to warn you but shot me in the back as I rode away."

Lord Harbor ran across the bailey with Haylan and Madam Constance at his heels.

Barloc finally spoke. "Lord Harbor's coming."

Sapper glanced up at Barloc, seeming to only then realize his presence.

When Lord Harbor arrived, he lowered down beside Sapper. "How many?"

The man stared off just over Lord Harbor's soldier. "My vision." He reached his bloody hands up to his eyes.

Lord Harbor shook him. "How many strong?"

The man blinked rapidly and dropped his hands. His movements slowed a great deal. When he spoke, extra seconds found their way in between the words. "Couple... thousand...."

Lord Harbor nodded and released his grip. "Anything else?"

The man coughed, still not bothering to cover his mouth. He rested his head on the ground, staring up past everyone to the stars. "Yeah...." He closed his eyes and took long shallow breaths. "Run."

Lord Harbor stood and so did Sapper. They looked at one another for a moment, but before either could speak, the wounded man called out Lord Harbor's name.

Lord Harbor kneeled back down. "What is it?"

"Fire a lit arrow at max range." He swallowed hard, unable to keep up with the blood filling his mouth. "Lord Aziar will do... same. Meet... in middle... conditions."

Lord Harbor didn't respond. He stood once more and nodded at Haylan, who stepped in and quickly went to work, first popping a vial free and then dropping gratuitous amounts of liquid into the man's mouth.

She cut the bloody leather, but before she could even remove the tunic, his chest heaved a couple of times, his head rolled to the side, and he died.

Silence stole the yard around them until Lord Harbor finally spoke to Sapper, his attention passing between all who surrounded him, including Barloc. "Establish order. Get people armored. Set them into ranks."

Master Sapper made for the stables. "I'll get our horses."

Lord Harbor threw his arm out and stopped him, shaking his head. "Tend to the people. You know what to do."

"Are ya not going out there?"

Lord Harbor pointed at the dead man at his feet and shook his head. "This is proof," he lifted his hands toward the army behind the castle walls, "that those men have no intention of a parley. This is all planned."

Master Sapper crossed his arms. "Then why don't we take advantage of it and plan the ambush ourselves?"

Lord Harbor shook his head. "This is no coincidence that they showed up in the middle of the night, torches lit. This is no happenstance that they shot a handful of arrows into Piper's back. That is war. There is no parley. If we ride out there, we would be lucky to even see Esmund. Whatever their plan is, whether it's a rain of arrows, soldiers hidden in the grass, or a flat-out charge, there is nothing positive on the other side of that wall. He wants to see how stupid we are."

Master Sapper's face scrunched up in frustration. He uncrossed his arms and nodded. "Aye."

Lord Harbor reached out with both arms, placing them on either of Sapper's shoulders. He leaned down and stared into his eyes. "It's time."

Master Sapper nodded and pulled Lord Harbor into a hug, patting his back in a series of hard thumps.

Lord Harbor stepped back and bowed slightly. "Maybe we'll see each other on the other side, hey old friend?"

Sapper nodded and stuck out his arm. They gripped each other's forearms and shook slowly. "On the other side."

And in that moment, the scene melted away. Their contact broke. Lord Harbor marched toward the sorting table, and as if on cue, the bell filled the air, followed by the deep blast of the slave horn.

People emerged from their bunkhouses and awoke from their various places around the yard, groggy and confused. Green Cloaks appeared from all over, commanding them into groups.

Lord Harbor climbed atop the sorting table and spun in a slow circle, looking over the people. The crowd gathered around him, and like a wildfire, whispers carried across the yard drawing everyone's attention.

Barloc scanned the crowd, spotting Madam Constance standing beside Rosa and Sir Vigor. He wanted to approach her, but Lord Harbor began waving his arms and calling for silence.

"People of Drudgeburg, cast your eyes upon me!"

When the murmuring died down, Lord Harbor clapped his hands together. "We've come a long way to get to the position we're in now." Cheers broke out, but he flapped his arms to indicate silence. "We've come from all reaches of the kingdom. Poor, wealthy, criminals, farmers. You name it, and it's standing in this bailey. Though, none of that matters anymore, because tonight, tomorrow, or at any point in this war, we are brothers and sisters. We are one."

Cheers met this, and Lord Harbor allowed them to ring through the air. "The time has come. King Sclavus has sent his men to eradicate us, to throw us back into chains, or send us to Corvee. We have the chance to break free beyond these walls and live like we once did, live free like our mothers and fathers. If we don't make a stand now, then we may never stand again. The kingdom has fallen to King Sclavus's rule, and he's become more powerful than any of us, so we *must* band together if we're going to secure our freedom once more."

Lord Harbor nodded along with the cheers. "I don't have some great speech that will make you better fighters. You are what you are, and you're all here to fight for freedom. I did my best to strengthen you by hauling stones from the mines, by gathering lumber from the forest. I attempted to fine tune your combat through the battle squares, focusing on your talents, and because of it, nearly everyone here understands the basics. I attempted to feed you all the essentials to bulk you up and make you fiercer.

"The stones you believed were punishment and slave labor are now scattered across the field, hidden in the tall grass. As the king's men charge us, their horses and soldiers will trip and break their legs upon them. The lumber you cut now make up the barriers lining the battlefield. We've placed copious amounts of gunpowder-filled barrels behind each wall, awaiting their charge. Our arrows are plentiful. All this because of you."

Barloc found himself cheering alongside the rest of the bailey, thinking of the stones he'd hauled from the mines and the large piles he'd helped create outside of the castle wall, always wondering what they were for.

"Listen to your commanders, your Green Cloaks. Fight with the passion I know lives inside you all! Fight for freedom!"

The crowd cheered the words back.

Lord Harbor lifted his fist and repeated, "For freedom!"

Their second cheer slowed quickly as the whiz of a fiery arrow arched high above them. It descended upon the crowd and collided with a shirtless man, landing directly in his chest. The crowd backed away from him.

An eerie silence fell over the bailey followed by the whiz of another arrow.

Lord Harbor jumped from the table. "Archers into position! Hold no quarter. Keep no prisoners. If they're here to fight, then they're here to die!"

The arrow landed on the ground a few feet from Barloc, burning bright up the shaft. Above them, three more fiery arrows entered the keep, followed by another wave of five. Barloc ran with the others, attempting to work his way through the crowd.

He searched for Sir Vigor's head, hoping to find Madam Constance beside the giant, but the urge to locate her was quickly replaced with the Whisperer's words: *Once the war begins, meet me at the entrance to the keep.*

Chapter 23 – A Man's Last Whisper

The ground shook as Barloc forced himself through the inner bailey, squeezing between frantic people until he finally emerged into the guards' quarters.

A bearded, skinny man asked for help collecting swords he'd dropped on the ground, but Barloc ran past, only stopping once he came upon a circle of guards with the Whisperer standing in the center.

At Barloc's approach, the Whisperer's hooded and masked head dipped in a nod. He spun in a slow circle, addressing each man. "Looks like we're ready. Follow me." He stepped through the group, walking toward the tent where Barloc had received his guard's gear.

The ground and walls shook again, and the echo of crumbling stone crashed down like a distant avalanche after a boulder struck the curtain wall.

The Whisperer's pace quickened until he stopped at the tent. "We've a special mission, easily one of the most dangerous. We'll be going out there in hiding, waiting for the perfect moment to strike. We have the opportunity to make or break this war, but one wrong move and we'll all die, and this will have been for nothing."

The men glanced between one another and back to the Whisperer.

He lifted one of his arms to indicate the rack behind him covered in black leather armor, then lifted his other arm to a barrel full of swords. "Behind me stands a rack of armor and the best tempered steel we could find. Equip what you need."

Barloc joined the other guards, searching for any gear he could replace, finding only a pair of gauntlets, quickly slipping them over his wrists, receiving help from another guard to tie them on.

While the men rifled through the rack, helping one another equip their armor, the Whisperer spoke to them from the sidelines. "You're welcome to back out of this mission now. If you care to join the fray in another fashion, do so before moving forward with me. There's a good chance that you won't return, so go now if you want to leave. Report to Sir Vigor. He'll find something for you to beat on."

No one responded outside of equipping more gear.

Barloc leaned his old rusty sword against the rack and held his new one out before him, turning it in the light. The steel gleamed clean in the moonlight, a strange comparison to the one he'd held moments ago. It stretched a few inches longer than his previous with near perfect balance.

Once everyone finished, the Whisperer paced before them, his hands behind his back. "Last chance."

No one moved until Barloc stepped forward. "I'm here to fight for our freedom, and if this is the best way for me to be used, then I'm not going anywhere."

Beside him, another guard nodded. "Aye."

All at once, the remaining four men spoke their accent.

The Whisperer nodded. "Very well." He reached up to his neck and unclasped his cloak. It slipped to the ground with a whisper, piling up around him. He stood in the same black leather armor as the rest of the guards, except for the cowl tucked into his tunic, hiding his features.

He lifted his hands and stopped with his fingers at the base of the mask. "I can't fight behind this veil, but I'll warn that you'll all know my face the moment you see it. It's been my cause to find the most trustworthy and skilled men out of all the slaves, which I have, and they're standing before me now." He pulled the fabric loose, dropped it to the ground, and slipped off the mask.

The moment their eyes met, Barloc understood. He nodded as events connected in his mind. The man standing before them had been the same who attempted to free them when he'd arrived at the inner bailey. This man was one of the guards on the day Katiph had purchased the two older slaves from Master Sapper, and he was the Green Cloak that had marched MJ-8 away on the day of his trial. A tangible silence strung between them until a crash from the outer bailey shook the ground again, and in that instant, everything began.

The Whisperer placed his hands on the two daggers strapped to his sides. He straightened up and glanced between the men, nodded, and took off toward the far corner of the guards' quarters.

Barloc fell into the middle as they marched in a line, much like the night the Whisperer had attempted their escape.

The Whisperer crouched low to the ground, continuously looking around the yard, and it wasn't until they slipped behind the last bunkhouse that he stopped and faced them.

The first guard in line spoke. He wore a thick, short beard like so many in Drudgeburg, and his eyebrows were bushy. His voice sounded as though it were being filtered through gravel. "Whisperer, where are we going? The fight is that way." He pointed over his shoulder toward the outer bailey.

The Whisperer placed a finger over his lips, and when he spoke it came out as a true whisper. The men leaned in or turned their heads to hear better. "Don't bother calling me the Whisperer anymore. My name's Ronin. I'm done with the pageantry."

Everyone, including Barloc, nodded.

Ronin leaned in closer. "Once we leave these walls, the game has changed. We need to move fast and silent. I'll lead, but if you see anyone who is not one of us, kill them on sight. We don't have the luxury of taking prisoners or dealing with miscommunication. From this point on, we don't speak unless necessary. Understood?"

The men nodded again, but a new tension filled the space between them. *Not an hour ago, we'd been sleeping and now we speak of murder.*

"You keep watch." Ronin pointed at the man with busy eyebrows and turned away, moving toward the corner.

Barloc watched behind him, listening for any movement, but the only noises that met his ears were that of the oncoming war.

Ronin removed two grappling hooks from beneath a pile of loose stone. He unwound the first and threw it over the wall with ease. Once secure, he tossed the second and faced them. "One at a time. Once over, put your back against the castle wall."

Barloc waited for his turn, hearing the din of an army and feeling the vibrations through the ground and walls, followed by the occasional blast of stone, and the distant echo of other unknown sounds.

Barloc grabbed the rope and attempted to pull himself up like the man before him, but he couldn't find his grip. He tried to snake the rope between his legs but couldn't make it catch, and when he pulled up to about halfway, his hands slipped and he slid back down to the bottom, his palms on fire.

Ronin groaned from atop the wall and dropped to his knees. "Just grab the rope and we'll pull you up."

Barloc wrapped the rope around his arm and held on as tightly as possible. Ronin and another man pulled him up slowly while he used the wall to walk up and keep his balance.

Once up top, Ronin glared at him, red in the face. "Maybe I was wrong about you."

Barloc sat, watching the man behind him climb with ease. He waited to see how they descended, and when it was his turn, he attempted to follow suit, wrapping the rope around his arm and using the wall to scale down, arriving with a much greater ease than climbing.

Before he hit the ground, the six other men already ran along the wall. He held onto the hilt of his blade so it didn't swing back and trip him.

The group stopped at the next corner, but before he could catch his breath, Ronin led them away from the castle and into a small copse of trees, running hard until under cover.

Once there, Ronin stopped and wiped sweat from his face with the back of his hand.

A different guard spoke this time. "Can you at least tell us where we're going? If we're risking our necks, then we should at least know the plan."

The other men nodded, and once more, Barloc found his head bobbing alongside them.

Ronin scanned each of their faces before dropping to his knees. He threw his arms into a thick bush at the base of an oak and removed a haversack, much like the one Sir Vigor had carried the training weapons in. From it, he pulled a torch, a flint, and a striker, then tossed the bag aside.

He handed the torch to the first man in line. "Very well. I'm sure some of you've made the connection, but maybe not. The mines were old and collapsed. That's why we were clearing them and why we broke the groups up so much—so we didn't have people figuring out that the entrance connected to the back side here. Since we cleared that end, we're able to travel through to the edge of the battlefield. That's the whole plan. We go down the tree line here, slip into the mine, make our way through, and assault from the shadows."

The men each reacted differently. Two of them nodded, another shook his head, and another remained silent. The other laughed, and Barloc felt a strange adoration for the plan. He smiled.

Ronin slipped the flint and the striker into his armor and grabbed the torch. "We move through the trees. Make sure you stay under their cover.

Before we go into the mine, however, we should be able to see a portion of the battle. Get a feel for things."

They cut across the field, feeling the vibration of another bolder making contact. Barloc walked slowly, careful not to trip on a root or low-hanging branch and almost bumped into the man in front of him when they stopped in a small clearing.

Ronin stepped toward the tree line and pulled back a branch, revealing a portion of the battle. They hid at the top of a small hill, off to the side of Drudgeburg, just high enough to see past the castle's wall. The fields had been lit on fire and they burned in a long line toward the castle; behind the flames waited the silhouettes of men.

Ronin dropped the branch and pointed over their shoulders with the unlit torch. "We enter there. I'm not lighting this until we're well inside, and once in, we need to move fast. Stay close and keep your weapons ready."

The men had to turn to their sides to squeeze through what resembled more of a crack in the mountain than an entrance. Paired with the sheer darkness, the tight space pressed against Barloc's mind. He inched through, attempting to step over the debris, unable to see the men before him. He gripped his sword to stop it from scraping and catching in the wall. Their breaths echoed in the confines, and just when he wanted to call out, a light exploded in front of him, and the crack opened into a small cave.

Sweat dripped down his face in rivulets, but before anyone could speak, they moved in a single file line, following the effulgent glow of Ronin's torch. Barloc's heart beat against his chest, and he continued to wipe his forehead against his leather gauntlets.

Much faster than he anticipated, Ronin smothered the torch and spoke over his shoulder, "Stay here. I'll go ahead and signal when it's clear."

The rest of the men watched, two of them removing their swords. The light from the moon outside shined into the cave, allowing them to see.

Ronin slowed his pace as he neared the entrance and carefully looked out. After a moment, he turned back, lifted his hand and waved them on. He stepped from the wall and out into the entrance. He kept his voice low but audible. "I was at least expecting a scout, but it looks like Lord Aziar didn't have a—." He stumbled forward, cutting off his own words. He spun on his heels and dropped to his knees, an arrow poking from his back. He crawled toward his men with blood leaking from his mouth, and as if his last words pulled him to his ground, he dropped with a thud: "Kill them all."

Chapter 24 – For MJ-8

Blood snaked away from Ronin and pooled at a dip in the ground. The soft buzz of cicadas filled the lulls between war, and the men's breathing acted as a eulogy to the corpse at their feet. *The Whisperer... Ronin.* Unsure how to feel or what to say, Barloc removed his blade and approached the entrance, crouching low against the wall.

One of the guards, a middle-aged man with a thick beard and wrinkles around his eyes, broke the silence. "What are ya doing?"

Barloc pivoted and spoke over his shoulder while pointing the sword forward. "We kill the scout."

The man shook his head. "And how do ya expect we do that, boy? We just lost our leader, and this *scout* has a bow. We also don't know how many there are. The chances of it being just one is slim."

Barloc lowered his weapon and straightened up.

"We can't hide in this mine while everyone's getting killed!"

Another guard, much younger, stepped from the darkness. "Why not? Haven't we been through enough?"

Barloc pointed his sword down at Ronin's body. "We could've turned around back there and hid in the castle, but we agreed to go with him. If you want to vanish in the night, then go ahead, but I'm moving forward."

The bearded man bucked his chest and stepped directly in front of Barloc, their noses nearly touching. "I never said I was scared." He clenched his teeth, grinding them as he spoke. "Boy." This time the man removed his sword and pointed past Barloc toward the entrance. "I asked how ya expect us to *kill the scout* as ya put it, when we have no cover and he has a bow."

Barloc glanced out across the small field and along the tree line. "He's obviously in those trees, and he's probably waiting for us. There's a chance we all won't make it, but I say we run out at the same time toward the tree line. Different patterns, shift our direction."

The bearded man spun in a circle, speaking to the guards hidden in the darkness. "Ya hear this, men? He wants us to die." Voices mumbled, none clear enough to hear. He turned back to Barloc. "If the archer is good, he'll kill one of us for certain. If he's great, count on two, and being as he's one of the king's army, I'm assuming he's trained, so I could even wager three of us might die before we hit the trees, and that's if there's only one."

Barloc shook his head. "Well, I haven't heard your grand plan. If you want to run, then run. If you want to hide, then hide." He stepped back and spoke to everyone.

"We're in the middle of a war. People are dying. Ronin is dead, and we can't just hide in a mine. On top of it all, they know we're here." He glanced back at the entrance. "I'll go first. We'll need to spread out. Who's with me?"

No one moved until the bearded man stuck out his hand to shake Barloc's. "Yev got balls the size of a bull. Big, *stupid* balls, and I like it. The names Riedell. What ya say, men? Want to go die?"

One at a time, they stepped closer, everyone gripping their swords, except the last.

He stepped forward, his sword still in its sheath, fear etched into his pale face. His head shook back and forth. "I didn't sign up for this. I was okay bein' a slave. I don't want any o' this." He backed away. "I'll take my chances back at the castle." He disappeared into the darkness.

Riedell nodded. "Any other green boys here?"

No one responded.

Barloc led the assault as promised, running as fast as his legs would allow. He pumped them up and down, certain he'd fall. The men behind followed suit, their thunderous footfalls spreading out around him. He zigzagged left and right, attempting to throw off the archer. A whirring passed over him, ending in a thump. He glanced behind him to see one of the five men rolling on the ground, screaming in pain.

He cut left and then right, the tree line nearing. His palms grew sweaty around his sword's hilt. He cut left again. An arrow flew past him so close it grazed his arm, cutting through the leather and his skin. A stream of arrows flew from the trees, and Barloc saw where they came from. *He was right. More than one.* He shifted his target to the right of where the archers hid, driving for the tree line. Fire climbed through his stomach and up his chest.

The archers struck another man, sending him down with a scream.

Finally, he made it, not slowing for the low hanging branches. They whipped his cheeks, cutting him as he entered, and once inside, he pushed his back against the nearest oak. He rested his hand on his knees, focusing on breathing, trying to lose the stitch in his side, and when it began to abate, he searched his surroundings, listening for any movement.

Leaves rustled ahead and off to the side. He held his sword before him and stayed close to the trees. He crouched low, listening. Someone walked around close by, each step an attempt to pad their footfalls, but the dead dry leaves gave them away. Barloc held his breath, trying to stay still, regretting crouching down. His knees burned from holding the position to the point his legs shook.

The footsteps seemed so much closer now, but Barloc refused to move, fighting through the discomfort. His teeth chattered as if from cold, and when the figure moved again, Barloc tightened his grip on the sword, ready to lunge it into the first sign of movement.

Ahead of him, deeper into the forest, the clear pleas of someone being murdered filled the air: "No, no... please sto—" His scream echoed among the trees like the caw of a crow. The person lurking by broke into a run in the opposing direction. Barloc had no choice but to follow. He had to stop the man from returning to camp or hiding and plucking him off later.

He jogged along the trees, careful to jump over fallen logs, until another scream pierced the air. He broke into a run, miraculously slipping through the dense foliage unharmed, until he stepped into a clearing where Riedell stood over a man in king's armor.

Blood ran down the soldier's face. "Please. I... I've got a family. I—"

Riedell kicked his helmet aside and crouched down, sword in hand. "Ya don't think those men you shot down out there had families?"

The soldier backed away, spitting blood off to the side. "They're... slaves. I... had orders and—" But the soldier never finished his plea because Riedell slammed his sword down and into his chest through his neck. The man twitched, pathetically grabbing at this throat, until he fell still.

Riedell leaned down and wiped his blade clean on the soldier's armor. "Two." He smiled.

Barloc stepped toward him, his eyes on the dead man. "He was begging."

Riedell lifted his eyebrows, the moonlight cutting down to illuminate his features in a cynical fashion. He tossed his head from the corpse to Barloc. "Are ya upset that I just killed the man who tried to kill us, who *did* kill our men?" He stepped toward Barloc, slipping his blade into its sheath. "Boy, it's clear yer green in the ways of battle. Ya got the heart, and ya courage, but ya got to have the stomach. Let yer emotions catch up later 'cause everyone on that battlefield wants ya dead and will not care if yer begging or if ya have a family or whatever comes to mind when facing death."

He glanced around. "We still have a man in these woods, but I don't suspect we should hang around." Barloc followed him through the trees, marching at a steady pace toward the battlefield. On their way, they found the corpse of a guard, their last remaining of the seven. An arrow poked out of his shoulder and stab wounds littered his chest.

"Looks like we're it, boy." Riedell stepped over the corpse. "The war's last hope." He laughed quietly and moved on. Each step brought them closer to the battle where they dropped into a position, hiding among the dense foliage.

The battlefield opened before them. On the back lines, soldiers loaded a boulder into the catapult and let it fly. The catapult flung forward and slammed back down, sending the stone onward. It crashed into the castle wall, cutting out a huge chunk on impact. Behind the catapult stood two carts half-loaded with more stones and a small army tending to them. It took almost ten men to move one of the boulders from the cart to the catapult.

The field burned toward the castle, slow and steady. The dewy grass slowed it, but a row of men ran back and forth with torches, keeping it lit. The fire nearly reached the first line of defenses.

Barloc leaned in toward Riedell. "Why aren't we attacking?"

Riedell shook his head. "Don't know. Maybe Lord Harbor is waiting the boulders out as long as he can. Hard to dodge a stone like that on the battlefield." And as if Riedell's words triggered the action, small flames sprouted up from the woods to the right of Drudgeburg, where not long ago Barloc had felled trees, praying he'd never see Master Sapper again. The orbs of flame took flight as if the darkness shot them. They arced through the air toward the slowly creeping line of soldiers, scattering the ground around their defenses.

A pang of frustration rose in Barloc at seeing the poor shots. *We're all going to die if this is what Lord Harbor has in store for us.* "Why would they waste—" His words ended at a series of explosions that went down the line of soldiers, just before the flame, and he answered his own question. He remembered Lord Harbor speaking on the barrels of gun powder. "Smart, but why not let them blow everything up on their own by burning the fields?"

Riedell glanced over at him and back to the battlefield. "I don't know what the Whisperer saw in you. 'Yer just a boy. Ya can't fight, ya charge blindly into battles, and yer extreme on the nerves."

After the last explosion, the small invisible tie still holding the chaos at bay slipped loose. The king's men scattered from the blasts. One of the catapults caught fire like kindling, and another wave of blazing arrows glided through the air, much farther this time, littering the ground. A few landed in the soldiers, dropping them down.

Drudgeburg's drawbridge lowered, and once it hit the ground, people flooded the field. From the distance, what seemed like an endless stream of soldiers entered, but Barloc knew it was only slaves, children, and women.

The opposing end responded, sending in wave after wave of soldiers, mounted fighters in the lead. Barloc sat forward, watching, thinking on what Lord Harbor had said about the stones being scattered across the field. His eyes followed the horses. A handful of them fell, rolled, and writhed on the ground. It wasn't clear if it was the stones hidden in the tall grass or the archers in the trees, but something worked them down. What could have easily been an endless stream of king's soldiers stormed the field, all screaming their own battle cry as they charged.

Barloc watched the remaining fighters exit the castle, and he couldn't help but think of Madam Constance. His stomach soured at the thought, and he missed her, wondering if he'd ever see her again.

Riedell grabbed Barloc's arm and pulled him to his feet. "We need to go. Carry on with our duties. They're distracted, and we need to find their leaders."

Riedell removed his sword and signaled him to do the same. "I believe Ronin would've said the same, but if not, I'll say it now. From this point on, kill anyone but me." He looked at Barloc. "Even if they *plead* for their life. We're at war, and these people want us dead."

Barloc followed him in a half-sprint, half-jog until he stopped suddenly, lifting his fist up for silence. He quickly moved to the side, pulling Barloc with him.

Two men worked their way through the woods toward them, a blonde man in dark clothes leading. The darkness caused his details to blend into the surroundings, but his bright hair and clean-shaven face came through clear enough. He stopped and turned to his partner, his voice high and nasally. "I heard something."

The other man pushed past him. His voice carried a greasy, dirty tone as if he spoke through a cloud of smoke. "Ya been hearing things all night. Just admit yer afraid o' the dark."

"It ain't that. I heard something moving up there." He pointed his gun right at where Barloc and Riedell hid.

Howlers. Barloc wanted to reach out and signal Riedell, but it was clear he knew.

The dark-haired Howler shook his head and turned back to his walk. "Merk. How in all the hells did I get stuck with you?" He slowed again and slapped his partner's chest. They now stood only fifteen feet from where Riedell and Barloc hid. "Though it's an honor for you to ride beside ol' Chip tonight, you could've been back there doing who knows what for Katiph or out there caught in the battle." He lifted his hand and ran a finger down the blonde Howler's cheek, who pulled away. "Don't want to cut up your pretty face." He burst into laughter and continued up the hill.

The two men stepped past their spot, and as they moved, Riedell shifted, rotating around the tree to stay out of sight, but accidentally hit the end of a dead branch and stirred the area.

The Howlers stopped. The blonde one rotated around. "I told ya I heard—"

Riedell pushed Barloc down to the ground in his attempt to get by. He screamed as he ran, his blade in the air, and before either Howler could react, he cut down into the dark-haired man's neck, sending him to his knees.

The Howler dropped his gun and grabbed his throat, attempting to stanch the wound.

A blast exploded between Riedell and the blonde man, Merk. Light flashed from the butt of the gun and darkness fell. Merk threw the gun aside and withdrew the small blade from his hip.

Chip, the dark-haired soldier, grunted and gasped for air through the blood washing down his throat.

Riedell stumbled backwards, holding his stomach, blood leaking between his fingers.

Barloc rose to his feet as Merk lifted the blade, ready to cut into Riedell. He ran at him, sword at the ready. "Howler!"

Merk turned with a dumb look on his face as if he'd forgotten there were two, or maybe he hadn't seen Barloc at all.

Barloc pulled his blade back and jammed it forward like a pike, though he didn't thrust hard enough; the tip of the blade bounced off the Howler's armor.

Merk cut down, slicing Barloc's chest, cutting through to the skin.

Barloc rotated low and swung his blade up, aiming for the gap at the bottom of the armor, embedding it directly into the Howler's stomach.

He backed away, scared the man might fall on him or cut him in a last wind, but instead, Merk dropped to his knees and fell forward with an unsatisfying *thump*.

Barloc wiped sweat and blood from his forehead and took in the scene. Chip lay on his side, eyes open and blank. Merk lay face down, his body propped up in the center from Barloc's sword, and Riedell on his back, breathing in steady, calm breaths.

Barloc crawled over to him and pulled Riedell's hand away from a circle that had been blasted into his armor. Blood leaked out uncontrollably.

Riedell placed his hand back over the wound. "Bastard got me."

Barloc shook his head. "You *did* just charge at two Howlers with a sword. What did you think would happen?"

Riedell closed his eyes. "I... I wanted to scare them. If I had one more second or even told ya the plan...."

Barloc glanced around him. "What do I do now? You can't go on like this."

"Yer right. Hell, maybe I'll die here. I'm tired, anyway."

Barloc sat up on his knees. "I'm sure I can help somehow. We can work back to the mines and get you to the Healers."

Riedell shook his head and opened his eyes. "Ya don't owe me anything, boy. Ya were given the same job as me."

Barloc looked toward the war even though he couldn't quite see through the trees. *Job. People get paid for jobs. What the hell am I going to do now?*

"Boy." His words began to sound forced and labored. "Ya need to find the leader and do what ya can. Go back to that soldier I killed. The one ya loved so much. Take his armor. Put it on, and slip into their ranks. It's the only way I can see it happening, and ya better hurry. These bastards seem to spawn like rabbits, so they're apt to have more lurking around." He laughed, rested his head, and closed his eyes. "Probably smell the blood, dogs that they are."

Barloc glanced from the bodies to Riedell, wishing he'd never been shot, wondering what he would do without the man's instruction. He stood. "What will you do?"

Riedell didn't bother opening his eyes. He waved his hand through the air and let it drop the ground. "Ya know I've been wanting to work on my skills with chainmail. I only ever seem to get to nothing larger than my palm." He smiled. "What do ya think I'm going to do, boy? I'm going to do the same thing *yer* about to do." He paused allowing the words to settle. "I'm going to die. Yer going to die. Hell, most of that outhouse of a castle back there's going to die, but we aren't here for that, right? We're Lord Harbor's play things, but even then... it's not about any of that. It's about the *greater good.* My life tonight is a small payment if this works. Maybe I'll even get a pass on some of the terrible things I've done."

Barloc nodded. He faced Merk's corpse and kicked it. "That's for shooting Riedell." He kicked again. "That's for being a Howler." Again. "That's for my father!" He kicked one final time. "And that's for MJ-8."

Chapter 25 – Into the Fray

Why are there so many damned parts? Barloc rolled the dead soldier over once more. He'd spent entirely too much time unclasping and reattaching different pieces of armor to himself, and as he struggled to secure the pauldrons, he slammed his fists down against the dead man's chest. He set the shoulder pieces aside and removed the cloak and clasp instead, the final item. He threw it over his back and linked the two manacles together, King Sclavus's sigil.

When they snapped closed, a cold chill slipped through his body. *If I die wearing this, people will think I supported him.* He stared blankly at the corpse before removing the cloak and covering the man up to his neck with it, staring into his dead, paling eyes. "I know you're my enemy, but it seems like such a waste of a life." He closed the soldier's eyes, pushing them harder than he needed to. They squished under the pressure.

The new weight of the armor pressed down on him with each step, and he wondered how he'd be able to fight with the barrier of plate. He turned back to the dead soldier whose sword rested on the ground beside his helmet. Barloc realized that he needed to switch weapons just in case someone recognized the false steel.

He returned to the body and kneeled with a clatter, exchanging the sword with his own and scooping up the helmet. He decided he hated the new weight. When he stood, he wondered how many of the soldiers believed in slavery and weren't just saving their own skin by joining the king's forces.

He marched back the way he'd come, hiding in the trees only once while a lone Howler passed by. He wondered what would've happened if he'd just approached him, wearing the king's armor, but it wasn't worth the risk. He stopped at the same spot Riedell had been when they'd seen the gates of war open.

From there, the field sat locked in battle. End to end, the fighting raged on. He knew he could easily step right out of the trees and join the fray, but he also knew it would do no good. If he stepped onto that field this far down, he would only be a soldier, an enemy to his cause.

I need to find their leaders. He traveled back to where the two Howlers lay dead. More blood had leaked from them, but Riedell had backed up against a tree, his head bent forward, and his arms resting limply at his sides.

Barloc shook his head, his eyes stinging with tears. A series of images passed through his mind: Ronin, the scared guard that retreated in the cave, the man who pleaded for his life, and finally Riedell, who'd died with honor while attempting to carry out the Whisperer's plans.

He turned back, glaring down the path he'd come, wondering what had become of Lord Harbor and Madam Constance and all the other lords and masters of Drudgeburg. He scanned the bodies beneath him one last time and stepped over Riedell's legs, toward the battle.

Soldiers streamed into the battlefield, though their ranks began to slow, and it wasn't long before he saw his chance. The soldiers this far back had begun to break their formation, charging ahead with their swords or pikes already drawn. From what he could tell, the army neared its end.

He slipped his helmet over his head, removed his sword, and waited for the right moment. When he ran out, he nearly tripped in the tall grass before joining the group. Together they ran hard, their weapons pointed carelessly outward, and as they crested the hill to look down upon Drudgeburg, Barloc stopped, his sword lowering to his side. A soldier ran by, shouldering him and bumping past. Hundreds of men stood locked in battle, fighting and dying and screaming.

The climate of the situation had changed. There was no more strategy. None of the preparations mattered anymore. The tall grass still burned and the stones across the field did nothing. This was a numbers game and these were trained fighters against slaves. Even the temperature had gone up, trapping his sweat inside the armor.

Barloc searched the battlefield for where to go. It was pointless running in blind. He would be forced to fight his own people. He fought past the urge to remove his helmet and instead scanned the field with a closer eye, but it was near impossible to locate any one person in the middle of so many, until he spotted a ridge to his right where three men stood safely on a hill, launching arrow after arrow into the mass of people.

He ran horizontal to the soldiers still entering the battle. It took a moment to climb the few rocks, but the archers hadn't noticed until he arrived up top. The first man glanced over his shoulder but returned to firing his arrow. The string snapped and the arrow flew into the darkness. Barloc approached him carelessly. The archer nocked another arrow, but Barloc lifted his sword and cut down, slicing the man's arm. The arrow snapped up and off to the side. The man screamed, and before the archer beside him could react, Barloc slipped the tip of his blade into the first soldier's throat. The second soldier grabbed a dagger from his side, but Barloc had lunged forward, sending the already bloody blade into his stomach.

The third archer backed away, fumbling for an arrow. "What the hell are you doing? You're killin' the wrong side!"

Barloc adjusted his grip on the sword.

The man secured his arrow and lifted the bow, but Barloc cut through the wood, knocking the weapon aside. The soldier tripped over one of the rocks and backed away. "Please... I don't understand."

Barloc stepped again, ready to cut him down. "Why do you fight for King Sclavus?"

The soldier backed away, pressing up against a huge boulder. "W-w-what? What do you mean?"

Barloc advanced, changing the way he held the sword, as it were a spear. "Why?"

The man's expression switched from confused to scared. His eyes squinted, and the lines across his forehead became more pronounced. His blonde hair matted to his head with sweat. "I have no choice. You know this. None of us do."

Barloc nodded. He considered the man for a moment. "If I let you let go, what will you do?"

He didn't answer.

Barloc straightened up. "You know... we all have a choice." An explosion blasted from behind him, and it took everything for him not to look away from the archer. "You chose to obey instead of oppose, which is how we're into this mess in the first place. Fear is not an excuse. I'm sorry."

Barloc lifted the blade, wishing the man would stop pleading. Their eyes connected through the helmet, and an instant rush self-awareness, he dropped the sword to his side. *I've killed three people*. He couldn't believe he just now realized that he murdered that Howler. He imagined the warm blood flowing across the back of his hand and stepped away. With a quick glance at the two bodies, he took one more step back and pointed away from the battlefield. "Go. Please, stop fighting and go."

The man blinked a few times, tears pushing out of his eyes. His lips quivered but he jumped to his feet, stumbling as he ran down the hill as fast as he could.

Barloc glanced around, tears stinging his eyes. *He didn't need to die. You did the right thing*. He faced the battle, stepping up to the spot they had been launching their arrows, and observed the field. The pressure from the king's men stood obvious. He remembered the day Lord Aziar had visited, threatening this very battle. The man had been in the same armor as all the soldiers, but his cloak was more vibrant. His horse had been white, while all the others were brown or spotted palominos. He remembered the archers hiding in the back and the way Lord Harbor had met him with so many of his own.

Barloc scanned the field below for the horse, but even then, those that had been mounted, were no more, and just as he was about to climb back down, he saw it. Dead center in the field circled a few men watching a battle. The black, shiny hair of Lord Aziar floated as he parried an attacker's advances, and that's when he discovered the squashed, angry face of Master Sapper, gripping a mace and shield. They danced in a circle while small pockets battled around them.

Barloc descended with a dangerous speed, nearly losing his balance. He charged across the field, slipping between people locked in battle. Faces he knew fought in anguish as they tried to survive against armored men. The clanking of sword, shield, and plate consumed the area. As he ran, he tripped over a dead slave, falling to his knees. MJ-4, one of the slaves that had traveled across the kingdom with Slaver Martin, lay motionless on his back, eyes blank with deep gashes across his cheeks and chest.

Someone shoved Barloc from behind, and when he turned, he was forced to throw his arm up to block the blow of a sword. The blade bounced off his gauntlet with a *pang*.

A man wearing old slave's clothes assaulted him, forcing him back. Barloc deflected the attacks; he knew if he did nothing, he would be killed. He parried again, but this time he swung his sword down, slicing into the man's leg. A piercing scream filled the air, and the slave dropped his sword and grabbed his bleeding shin with both hands. Barloc backed away, nearly tripping over another body, and ran toward Lord Aziar.

When he arrived, Master Sapper and Lord Aziar still exchanged blows, Sapper laughing with each one he tossed aside. "This must be how they train ya in the king's bed?"

"Silence yourself! I'm done. You will die now."

Master Sapper laughed a genuine laugh unlike any Barloc had ever heard, but something changed. Lord Aziar moved faster than Sapper was expecting, and even though Sapper fought to resist, his opponent overpowered him, tossed his sword aside, and pinned him down.

Lord Aziar laughed. "Now, you die!"

Master Sapper's expression shifted from humor to fear as he tried to break free of Lord Aziar's grasp, but even bucking his body did nothing.

Lord Aziar threw his head from side to side. "Someone stab this *slave*, now!"

A soldier nearby buried his blade into the stomach of a Drudgeburg man and turned to Lord Aziar.

Barloc stepped forward, almost forgetting he wore the king's colors, arriving first.

Lord Aziar glanced up, still holding onto Sapper's wrists. "Do it already. Stab him in the face for all I care, but just *kill* him!"

Barloc glanced down at Master Sapper, whose eyes connected with his. He remembered all the times he'd wanted to kill him, and now he had the chance. *What's one more murder in a field of death?*

He shifted his blade so he could drive it downward and hovered over Master Sapper's head.

The other soldier lifted his own blade. "Move aside, little man. You take too long."

Barloc's blade descended at the same time as the other soldier's. It resisted at first, slowed by bones, but once past the spine and ribs, it slipped in and back out with ease.

The battle paused for Barloc as he stared down at his bloody sword. A loud bang filled the air and a pain mixed with pressure exploded across his chest. He dropped his sword and stumbled, straightening once more.

He removed his helmet and dropped it to the ground, gasping for air. The heat inside cooked him, and the fatigue crushed him under the weight of the armor. The breeze chilled the sweat on his face, but the heat emitting from his breastplate reminded him of being fevered.

An arrow poked from his chest, just above his heart. It pierced through the steel and when he looked up, he saw that one of his own men had shot him, only five feet away. *The arrow pierced my plate. I've been carrying this heavy plate around me so I could be shot with an arrow by my own side?*

"What have you done?" The king's soldier that was supposed to have killed Master Sapper sat on his knees with his hands across his stomach.

Tears from pain and confusion slipped down Barloc's cheeks. The world around him spun, and he dropped to his knees. In front of him, the still body of Lord Aziar lay face down. Master Sapper sat up with a gash across his cheek and Barloc's sword in hand. He got to his feet and kicked the soldier over, stabbing him a couple of times until he lay still.

When he turned around, he stared at Barloc for a moment, then shifted his eyes to the body below him.

His voice filled the air. "Their leader is dead! Retreat to the castle. Spread the word!"

Like waves smashing against the shore during a storm, those words slowly washed over the field. Barloc dropped to his hands and then his side. The pain increased with each passing second.

The clinking and clanking of war began to fade. He closed his eyes, knowing he'd done all he could for the cause.

Chapter 26 – The Fallen Leader

The moment of unconsciousness lasted just long enough for Master Sapper to start dragging Barloc's body toward Drudgeburg. The arrow pushing out of his chest broke immediately, sending sharp pains through his body. He coughed up blood and spat it to the side.

"Get up and walk! I can't drag ya the whole way."

Barloc's vision came through blurry, but he fought to stand, only to stumble back down.

Master Sapper pulled him to his feet. "Ya've come this far, Hero. Now ya need to get in and see a Healer."

The slave horn blasted, and though the sounds of battle tapered away, the soldiers still attacked. Master Sapper backed up close to Barloc as they neared the keep. He fought off someone but continued to move. "We've got to go faster."

Two of Drudgeburg's fighters stopped and faced Barloc. Master Sapper screamed. "Leave him alone, he's one of ours! He's disguised!"

Reluctantly, the men nodded and ran into the keep.

The reverberation of the horn faded. Men and women ran past.

Barloc stopped and scanned the battlefield. A divide began to separate them. Small pockets of fighting continued, but the king's soldiers retreated. From above him, arrows arced like blankets, creating a line for the soldiers to stay behind.

Sapper pointed at two men running by. "Make sure everyone gets in!" They nodded and cast confused looks at Barloc.

Sapper scooped him up and charged through the gates of Drudgeburg. The bouncing jarred the stem of arrow in his chest, making it feel as though he'd been shot all over again.

Once inside, Master Sapper dropped him to the ground with a thump.

Sir Vigor approached. "What is this?" When he kneeled, he saw Barloc and nodded.

"He'll die if we don't move fast."

Sir Vigor grabbed him up with ease and walked him to the sorting table. "Haylan," Sir Vigor's deep voice boomed through the air, and a moment later, Healer Haylan stood above him.

"Child, what have you done?" She looked up to Vigor. "Get this armor off him. Be careful about the chest. We can still get that out."

Together they worked the armor away in much less time than it took to arm himself. He lay in only a loincloth, similar to his first day at Drudgeburg.

Haylan popped a bottle from her necklace and leaned down. "This is for the pain." Drops of medicine filled his mouth. She popped another bottle and filled his wound with liquid that numbed him immediately, though only on the surface. The burning felt worse than when the arrow had entered. "You are fortunate."

Barloc didn't say anything, focusing on not breaking his teeth from gritting so hard.

"It is one of our arrows." She looked up to Sir Vigor as if he had the answer.

He nodded. "Dressed like the king's men." He lowered down, sitting on the table. "Why?"

Barloc went to speak but the blood coating his throat caused his words to come out sticky and broken. "Wh-per."

It took a moment, but Sir Vigor understood. He nodded and repeated it out loud. "Whisperer."

Haylan worked while the front gate closed with a clinking sound. Another *whish* filled the air as a wave of arrows flew off in the distance, and the horn faded completely. She removed a pair of metal tongs and pressed them against the shaft of the arrow. "Vigor, please."

Sir Vigor gripped the handles and glanced between them. When she nodded, he pulled away in a hard, strong motion.

A sucking sound filled his head as the arrow left him, the pops of cartilage breaking echoing inside his ears.

Haylan began her work, pressing gauze into the hole and working another vial from her necklace. After a couple minutes, she removed sutures from her robes and worked the stitching into his skin.

Sir Vigor stood. "Harbor's above the gate."

Lord Harbor's voice carried over the silence, across the battlefield, to the king's men. "Your leader's dead. You can still fight, but you'll lose. You can attempt to lay siege, but we'll have counter measures. It's not worth your lives. Collect your men and go."

Haylan helped Barloc sit up. The outline of Lord Harbor stood directly above the gate, next to Rosa.

"We will stay our arrows and allow you to collect your dead. Have honor and retreat. Mark this day as our independence. You don't have to fight for the king. You can make a choice, but not today. Take your men and leave. You have one hour, and if my men see anything outside of this, they will shoot to kill."

Lord Harbor turned his attention to the outer bailey. He stared down, scanning the ground below before disappearing.

Sir Vigor turned back to Haylan and Barloc. "Where's the Whisperer?"

Barloc pictured the way Ronin had fallen with the arrow sticking in his back. He shook his head. It was enough.

Haylan snapped the last vial back to her necklace and straightened up.

Master Sapper returned. "I'll check with Harbor. He'll want to speak with ya. We need to clear up anything we can and prepare. Ya able to walk or ya need the giant to carry ya?" He nodded toward Sir Vigor.

Barloc stood, checking his balance. It felt strange standing in only a loin cloth once more, and as if she read his mind, Haylan spoke to Master Sapper, "Get him some of the slaves' clothes and make him a sling for his arm. He should be fine with that. I gave him enough sedative to hold him over. Be well, child." She bowed and walked away.

Sapper nodded. "Very well, let's go." They crossed the yard, weaving in and out of the many people. So many wounded men and women lay about, leaning on each other. He'd been certain he stepped over two that had already died.

When they arrived at the tent, Sapper had gone ahead, grabbed a few pieces of what remained, and passed them to Barloc. He slipped the tunic over first, wincing hard at the pain in his shoulder.

Sapper grabbed up another piece of cloth and cut it in two with his sword. While he worked the two ends into a knot to fashion the sling, he stared at Barloc. "Ya saved my life back there."

Barloc nodded. "I am *the hero,* after all." He smiled.

When he finished tying up the sling, Sapper stepped closer and helped secure it around Barloc's arm. "Ya've no idea how much I hated ya. Ya seemed so smug and weak at the same time. I was wrong, Hero." Once done with the sling, he stepped back and nodded. "Thanks. I'll hopefully never have to say that to ya again, but thank ya. I was certain ya were going to kill me, even when I realized who was under that helmet." He winked and walked past him.

Barloc followed him through the inner bailey and into the guard's quarters. From there, he approached the keep's entrance where Sapper opened the door and stepped in.

The inside of the keep was nothing like Barloc expected. He had imagined long tapestries hanging down with old house sigils. Suits of armor lining the corridor, and other items rich lords always seemed to have, like huge oak tables etched with a map of the kingdom, but this wasn't the case.

When the doors opened, the ominous glow of dim torches tucked in wall sconces stretched across a huge open room where bunks lined the parameter. It appeared no different than the bunkhouses the slaves stayed in. The smell of an unkempt, musty castle and a room full of sweaty people combined and assaulted his nose.

Barloc followed him past the bunks to another room that opened into a dining hall. The room proved to be just as dark with only two torches on either side and a fireplace keeping the place lit. Huge parchments with maps drawn on them spread across the table. Wooden soldiers scattered their surfaces.

"What's he doing here?" Master Dharah pointed at Barloc. "He shouldn't be seeing this."

Sapper stepped around the table. "Well, things have changed. Where's Harbor?"

Dharah shook his head, his eyes lingering on Barloc. "We normally vote on who sees our plans."

Sapper waved him off. "He saved my life, killed their leader, and knows about Ronin." He sat down in one of the seats down the long side of the table and pointed to the one besides him. "Sit. When Lord Harbor gets here, ya can fill them in and we'll get ya bunked up in here." He locked eyes with Dharah, who now sat, and said, "The least I can do."

They waited for a while in silence until they heard the door open from the hall. A woman's voice called for help.

Sapper jumped up and then Dharah. They ran for the door, but before they could get there, it opened and in stumbled Lord Harbor.

He caught himself on the edge of the table and fell into the chair at the end. He looked up at Dharah. "Go get Haylan and Vigor. I'm not going to make it through the night, if through this conversation, and I need to say some things."

Chapter 27 – Keep the Fire Bright

Barloc stood at the table, torn on what to do. Part of him wanted to rush over and hug Madam Constance, very aware of how happy he was to see her alive and well, but it wasn't clear if she wanted that. Her attention was on Lord Harbor, whose face had paled. Another part of him wanted to run away. He couldn't be more out of place by the council's table, standing over their plans, nothing more than a beaten and bruised slave, but the urge to discover what had happened overpowered his insecurities.

Barloc shifted toward Lord Harbor. "How can I help?"

Lord Harbor shook his head, his eyes lingering on Barloc before meeting those of the Green Cloaks. "Just sit. Everyone. I need... Vigor."

Madam Constance kneeled by Lord Harbor, attempting to inspect the wound, but he swatted her away. "There's nothing you can do. Sit, please."

Madam Constance looked back as if to ask for support, but Barloc remained silent and sat down. She pulled her blood-mottled cloak straight before sitting in the chair besides him.

The door banged open outside and a series of footfalls charged through the outside room until three people entered: Sir Vigor, Master Dharah, and Healer Haylan.

Haylan pushed past Sir Vigor and dropped to her knees by Lord Harbor's side, but he swatted her off just as he had Madam Constance.

He sat forward in his seat, wincing at the pain. "Ale and sit."

Sir Vigor stepped to a table where he poured a tankard of ale and passed it to Lord Harbor. All of them sat.

Sir Vigor leaned forward. "We should have Haylan look at that."

Lord Harbor shook his head and took a deep, long drink. "I've been poisoned and stabbed. I'm—"

Sir Vigor stood, throwing his chair back with the force from standing. "Who did this?"

Lord Harbor lifted his hand for silence. "Dead. I'm dead. Look at me. Rosa. She was working with the Howlers the entire time. Played me like a fool."

Madam Constance twisted her hands together, and Barloc saw blood covering them.

Lord Harbor took another drink. "She'd been planning it, waiting for us to fall, and when we didn't, she panicked. When I stepped into the corridor to return to the keep, she stabbed me. She'd poisoned the blade. And, well...." He nodded at Madam Constance.

Madam Constance wiped a tear from her cheek. "I'd been waiting for him in the outer bailey, but he hadn't come out, so I went and searched for him. I heard a commotion and then Rosa's voice, so I ran in, and when I did, she tried to stab me, but I...." She lifted her hands. "She's dead."

Lord Harbor stared at Haylan. "Give me something for the pain."

Haylan quickly popped off one of the vials without looking and handed it to Dharah, who handed it to Lord Harbor. "Four drops should take care of it. I can numb the wound if you need." She sighed, shaking her head as if she had more to say but knew it was worthless. "The whole bottle should do the trick if the poison takes over. Are you certain it's poison?"

Lord Harbor stood. "Help me with this."

Sir Vigor jumped to his feet alongside Madam Constance, and in only a few seconds, the armor pulled away from his body with a sticky sound. He lifted his shirt to reveal the wound. Dark edges of skin folded over one another like a piece of rotting fruit.

Haylan looked away. "And this *just* happened?"

"Aye," Lord Harbor sat down. "It's poison all right. Like I said, she had this planned."

Sir Vigor lingered but then returned to his seat. "What did she say?"

Lord Harbor laughed through his nose. "That she was sorry, but her alliance with the Howlers was what mattered."

Dharah slammed his fist against the table, knocking over a couple of the wooden figurines.

Lord Harbor nodded. "There appears to be a spy, or there was, anyway. I'm not sure how they were getting out, but information, as it does, seems to float with the clouds. They'd been planning this for months, and someone was informing them." He glanced around. "Where's Ronin?" He passed his attention from Vigor, who looked from Dharah to Sapper to Barloc, the expression on his face suggesting that he just realized who was sitting in front of him.

Barloc glanced around the table, staring into each person's eyes before returning to Lord Harbor.

Lord Harbor lifted his hand for Barloc to continue.

He cleared his throat. "I... the Whisperer, or Ronin, had gathered six men and had us meet in the guard's quarters. We climbed the wall and ran to the back of the mine. In there, we lost one of our six. He returned to the castle, maybe?"

"Probably the bloody spy," Madam Constance said without looking away from the table.

"Ronin went to scout out the entrance of the cave and was killed by an arrow. Someone definitely knew we would be there."

Lord Harbor listened, nodding. He picked up the vial and took a swig, setting it back down in front of him. A small amount remained.

Barloc continued. "With Ronin dead, we charged the scouts, losing two more. We killed them and found our last dead. It was just me and a man named Riedell."

Sir Vigor nodded. "He was one of my men. Big man. Smart."

With that said, the words grew heavier. "I, well, we were intercepted by two Howlers. We killed them both, but the blast from one of the guns shot right into Riedell's belly. He guided me on what to do next. He *was* a smart man.

"On his instruction, I went back to one of the scouts we'd killed, donned his armor, and joined the battle as one of the king's men. I killed two archers hiding off in the rocks and that's when I saw Lord Aziar."

Master Sapper finally spoke. "Little bastard saved my life. Aziar had me pinned, begging for someone to end me, but the hero here slipped his blade into their leader's back, and I had just enough time to cut down another soldier that had been called on to kill me."

Lord Harbor nodded. "You took an arrow up close." He indicated Barloc's shoulder.

Barloc nodded.

"Our own men shot you because you wore their colors. Foolishly smart. Ronin and Riedell. They'll be sorely missed. Ronin spotted soldiers and Riedell came up with ideas quicker than anyone I've ever seen."

A moment of silence passed through the group. They all looked down at the table until Lord Harbor reached for the vial and drained the remaining contents. "Well, on to business. I don't have long. I can smell the wound.... The keep falls into Madam Constance's hands."

Everyone nodded as if they'd known this all along.

"You will need to move fast. Gather our dead, even from the woods, and have a funeral for us all. Don't dig. No point. We burn our men and there are too many."

Barloc shuddered at the thought of so many bodies burning.

"You need to move soon. Most of those soldiers will return. A few may not, but the word will be spread, and a larger army will move. You can't sit here. We won this battle, and now we need to make the next move. We don't have the forces for another fight. The first order of business is we vote to make Barloc Maghild a Green Cloak. He's got my vote."

Barloc's eyes widened in surprise.

Everyone faced him again, nodding their accent.

Sapper spoke. "Aye, we have room for a hero."

Lord Harbor continued to nod. "Maybe it means nothing, but welcome, Barloc, if that's what you want."

Barloc nodded, thinking on where he stood not even thirty days ago. "I'll do my best."

"Very well," Lord Harbor drained the rest of his ale. "We currently have three bases throughout the kingdom. Madam Constance will travel north, Sir Vigor south, and Sapper west. You all know what to do. Small groups, blend in, expand the army. Dharah, you'll continue to deal with the spies however you see fit. It's probably better you don't tell anyone. Cease all written communication once you leave Drudgeburg, and finally, send all those you can trust back into slavery. *Only* those you trust."

Madam Constance. "I'm sorry, Harbor."

He laughed. "Sorry for what?"

"I wanted to sit together with you on that sunrise the morning we all break free."

Lord Harbor now cried. Not sobbing brays, but soft, honest tears. "We've come far, and it was worth it all. Just don't give up, and when you sit to watch this sunrise, just speak my name."

"What will I do?" Barloc asked.

"Have the funeral. Gather the plans, and see Madam Constance. She will guide you."

Barloc nodded, his eyes glued to her.

Master Dharah cleared his throat and leaned forward. He removed a parchment from his cloak. "I received word from Mindar. He has made it into Corvee as a slave driver. He won't be able to communicate anymore, but he's in. No word from Jargon, but Katiph promises he's in a good spot."

Barloc jolted forward. "Katiph? The Howler?"

Lord Harbor nodded. "Aye. He's one of ours, the bastard that he is."

Barloc shook his head. "Sorry, I just...." He thought of when Madam Constance had mentioned that Katiph was in on it all, but he still struggled to believe it.

"Aye," Sir Vigor said. "You *would* hate him, but I assure you he's ours."

Lord Harbor leaned against the table. "There is much more to this than you will ever know, Barloc. Not any one of us knows everything, and we have slaves working up the chains across the kingdom. They are to get as close to as many of the leaders and lords as possible, and even if it costs their lives, they'll attempt to dispatch them, but you already know this. Madam Constance has told you, even if it was against my will. It's been a bit harder getting our people to the king, but even then, we have numerous men and women hiding all over."

Barloc felt a sense of exasperation. He nodded, impressed.

Lord Harbor stood. "My advice to you all is to remember that it's no longer about you alone. You are now one of many, all fighting for the same freedom." He sighed. "I'll go die now in my bed. Constance. If you would join me. There are still a few private matters."

Madam Constance stood, stepped to Lord Harbor, and helped him to the door. Before he left, he spoke over his shoulder. "Keep the fire burning."

All the men circling the table spoke at once, "Keep the fire bright."

Chapter 28 – Farewell

Another funeral. Barloc stared at the pile of corpses mounted high in the center of Drudgeburg. He searched the many faces, attempting to find familiar ones. He'd help pull Riedell's body from the woods, but the face had blended with the rest. Same went for Ronin, Vicar Farlen, and the many fallen masters. The only person he clearly saw was Slaver Martin, whose belly hung out from the side of the pile like a tumor. Even the young Healer, Altha, who had helped him after the incident at the mines. *Too much death.*

A structure had been erected at the foot of the pile where Lord Harbor was to burn. The outer bailey remained full, but in a countable manner. Before the two previous funerals he'd seen, it would have been impossible to count attendance, but now, with so many dead, so many injured and in their bunks, and those who slipped away during battle, it became much easier.

Barloc sat alongside so many he didn't know, waiting for Madam Constance, Sir Vigor, Master Sapper, and Master Dharah to carry out Lord Harbor's corpse. A few conversations tittered around, but mostly the air filled with the taught silence of sorrow.

The corpse of a Howler sat close to the top of the pile, a gesture Barloc didn't care for. Madam Constance had insisted they collect any bodies found, including soldiers and Howlers. Before they'd gone out with the corpse carts, she'd addressed the mass of unfortunate collectors. "I'll not have all we worked for tainted by the gods because of our actions. These men, though our enemies, are also men of the gods we believe in, misguided as they may have been. While we must be strong and just, we also need to represent the value we place on the human life, or we risk falling into the same cannon as our enemies."

The doors to the keep banged open. Silence fell among the crowd, and a moment later, five Green Cloaks emerged from inner bailey with Lord Harbor hoisted upon their shoulders, Madam Constance at the lead. They slowly moved toward the pile of corpses. Sir Vigor had to walk with a hunch because of his height, but the rest moved with ease.

When they arrived, they placed Lord Harbor atop the wooden structure and fanned out on either side.

Madam Constance stepped forward, a rolled parchment in her hands. She spun in a circle, scanning the crowd around her. "I'm not as good with speeches as Lord Harbor was. He'd been a natural at warfare and motivating people, which is why we made it as far as we have." She unrolled the parchment, cleared her throat, and spoke as loud as she could, her voice carrying with ease. "Where we lost a great man, we didn't lose the cause. Lord Harbor risked everything to bring us together and build us up from the ground. Feeble attempts across the land have sprouted up only to be crushed by the king. The man before us made it possible for freedom to be a word we speak instead of dream."

A cheer broke with a few people that bled into many.

Madam Constance smiled. "This battle doesn't mean we've won. Look at the pile of bodies and you'll know this, but we are moving in the right direction. Together we'll fight for the freedoms we once had, but it will not be easy. It will not be kind, and many of us will die, but if we continue to fight, we'll make a difference." She referenced the parchment. "Once again, you have a choice. We move tonight, and we're splitting up. If you chose to join, then you're enlisting into our cause. If you attempt to leave after tonight, then you'll be treated as a traitor. Things change as of now. We can no longer stay here. It will become a death trap. We'll split up and spread out around the kingdom. We implore you to join, to help us bring back freedom into the world and stop King Sclavus. You'll have time to gather any items you wish to bring. We'll meet outside the gates before sun down. There you'll be divided. Those injured are welcome to join us by cart."

She turned back to the pile of bodies and Lord Harbor, and though she faced the opposing way, her voice carried with ease. "I'm sorry you can't join us on this journey, but thank you for laying down your life for us. Thank you to all who sacrificed their lives for us." She nodded at the Green Cloaks who grabbed up torches.

They pulled together for a moment, then spread out around the pile, lighting the kindling along the way. The flames burned slowly at first, but once they met the clothing covering the corpses, they spread faster.

Madam Constance faced the crowd again, tears shinning on her cheeks. "Once again, things change for us, but what we did here will echo across the kingdom. Sclavus will try to put a stop to us, but he has no idea what's coming for him. We'll meet outside the gate in one hour's time. Say your goodbyes, gather your things, and be prepared to travel. Gear up, for there are many dangers on the roads ahead.

"The Green Cloaks are to meet in the council chamber one final time before we depart." She lifted a fist into the air. "May their fires burn bright."

Though scattered, the audience a mixture of sadness, anger, confusion, and fear, said their words until the breath of fire overtook their feeble calls: "May their fires burn forever."

Chapter 29 – The Council Meeting

When Barloc entered the council room, his heart stopped and his good hand dropped to the hilt of his blade. Panic flooded his chest as he searched around him, startled to be looking into Katiph's eyes. *Katiph is one of them... one of us.*

Master Dharah ripped up a parchment from the pile on the end of the table and threw it into the fireplace.

Barloc moved to the end of the table where Lord Harbor had sat not long ago, bleeding and giving his final speech.

Everyone looked at him and then around, but no one spoke.

Barloc glared at Katiph.

Master Sapper laughed. "Stay yer blade and sit, Hero." He smiled.

Dharah laughed alongside Sapper and Katiph and a Green Cloak he'd not seen before.

Barloc shook his head, thinking of the day Katiph had purchased the slaves, and took a seat.

The door opened again as Sir Vigor and Madam Constance entered with two more Green Cloaks he'd seen but not met.

Madam Constance's eyes flicked between everyone in the room as she took her place at the end. "Sit, everyone." She stared at Barloc and then Katiph. "MJ-7... *Barloc* has become one of our newest Green Cloaks. He has the fight and the honor we need. He's done great things in the short time he's been here, and now he's part of the cause, so it's best we clear the air." Her voice filled the dark, small room. "Whatever hatred you hold for Katiph must be disregarded. He's been our ally. He's helped us from day one. He was an old friend of Sapper's before he was caught and enslaved."

Barloc's eyes widened and he rotated around. "Caught and enslaved? Pirate?"

Sapper shook his head.

Barloc nodded and stared at Katiph. "Howler?"

Sapper nodded.

Madam Constance broke into the conversation. "I didn't trust him *or* Sapper for a long time, but Sapper swore he could get a man on the inside. We thought he was trying to run or set us up, but Lord Harbor accepted Katiph and brought him onto the council. We had no choice but to vote him in. He's risked a great deal to help us."

Barloc waited until she finished. "We've had numerous issues with spies here. How do we know he isn't the one selling us out?"

Madam Constance nodded. "Because Sapper had the chance to run, and he didn't. Katiph had plenty of times he could have stopped us, but he didn't."

The cracking of the fire filled the room, a conversation of its own, until Sapper banged the hilt of his dagger on the table. "Enough of this. I've defended Katiph since I've been here. We've had to do some of the nastiest work for this operation. We've had to put on the role of the wolf to sell men and women back into slavery. We've had to hurt and kill people, some of those we loved, just to ensure our position. Ya want to see a hero? Well, sorry, boy, but not all heroes come in shining white armor." He pointed his dagger at Katiph, who watched in a careless manner. "This man has made more sacrifices than any I've met. We owe our entire operation to him, and I'll not have any more talk on the subject." He slammed his blade down, the tip stabbing into the old wood.

Heat flushed Barloc's cheeks. He glanced between them. "I'm really sorry."

Katiph finally sat forward, his voice as squeaky as the day they'd met outside the mines. "You're just a green little boy who hasn't seen the world. It's not your fault."

The words drew forth the memory of when his town was raided by Howlers and the little girl that had died beside him in the cart.

Madam Constance stood. "Remove all communications and parchments from your persons and place them on the table. Be certain there is no trace left on you, because when we leave here, we cannot afford for anyone to piece our story together."

Everyone in the room bustled around, including Katiph, throwing folded and rolled parchment onto the table. Master Dharah threw everything in the fire, and when Madam Constance returned to her seat, she spoke directly to Katiph.

"We move today. What news do you have for us?"

"Lord Aziar's men fell but returned promptly to the king. I'm expected to answer for the loss of their precious leader. I don't know how much longer I'll be able to help. I was charged with his guard party, but I wasn't about to lose my neck in the battle." He leaned back in his chair. "You want my advice? On my trip to Warshire, allow me to do a final sale. I think I can get them in somewhere good. I've got a wench on the inside who may be able to help me place one or two people within the castle walls, but after that, I'll need to vanish. I don't intend to show up for my meeting, so me being a contact is done."

Madam Constance nodded slowly, deep in thought. "Very well. What will you do next?"

Katiph shrugged. "I'm not going into slavery. I don't know that it's a good idea to continue being an outlaw. I've been dancing too close to the flame, and I feel like I've been revealed. I can vanish, go overseas, and find some common girl. Try to settle, or I can join your cause."

Madam Constance placed her hands under her chin in thought. "I want you to go to the castle. Sell the slave. Not two. You can sell one, but I want you to continue your work. Take the chance. We need a man in your position more than ever, so if you're willing, I feel you should fight to keep your cover."

Sapper snorted. "It's a death trap. Didn't ya hear him?"

Katiph lifted his hand for silence. He scanned the room as if understanding something. "Aye. I'll go. I'm not scared, and if I die, so be it. I'm tired of hurting people, but I can't deny what I'm good at." He took a deep breath and let it out. "Who will be coming with me this time?"

Everyone glanced around. Numerous chairs, crates, and barrels remained empty, a clear sign that their council had shrunk significantly.

Barloc counted at least fifteen empty seats. *He means us, and if she's going with one party, Sapper another, and Vigor another, then that doesn't leave very many to choose from.*

Everyone's eyes fell to the table, avoiding contact. No one raised a hand to volunteer.

Madam Constance's voice broke the silence, "Dharah. Why not you?"

"Surely I can help in another way." The other Green Cloaks nodded as if to say he'd stolen the words directly from his mouth.

Barloc scanned each face, ending on Madam Constance. "It sure does seem like it's going to fall on me."

Madam Constance shook her head. "No. Numerous reasons. It wouldn't be fair to give you freedom and on the same day send you back into chains, and you just don't have the passion behind the cause like we do."

Sapper laughed. "In other words, we don't trust ya to hold up yer end of the deal. We don't know anything about ya other than ya've got some fight."

Madam Constance shook her head. "No, we don't need to send any more right now. You work to secure your position, Katiph, and I'll worry about starting this later once we get settled."

Katiph now shook his head. "You're wasting a golden opportunity. I don't tend to trade close to Warshire, and I have a way in. Why would you pass that up?"

"It's not an option right—"

Barloc slammed his fist down, this time drawing everyone's attention. "I'm not a child, and I saved your life!" He glared at Master Sapper. "If anything, I would be the smartest choice here. Why waste the opportunity? I've been a slave for all my adult life, so trust me when I say I remember the role." His voice rose higher than he intended, calling everyone's attention. "I'll go. I've got more a place there than here, and now that I have something to fight for, it makes it all worth it."

Silence stole the room once more until Sapper nodded and clapped his hands together a few times. "Then it's settled. The hero's going. I don't think we need a huge explanation that yer job is to try and work yer way toward the leaders. Even if it means yer death, ya do all ya can to take out all ya can. Do ya agree to the terms?"

Madam Constance rose to her feet. "I'm in charge here."

Master Sapper matched her stance, mirroring her arms on the table. "Then why am I explaining what he's to do?" He pointed at Barloc but kept this eyes on her. "There's no room for love in this world. Not until King Sclavus is done."

They glared at one another until Madam Constance conceded. She sat back down.

Katiph smiled. "I do miss being an outlaw, hiding in and out of the mountains and forests, keeping out of the reach of the law, instead of working for them. Less exciting if you ask me. How am I to be a pirate if the law lets me sail my ships?"

Master Sapper returned to his seat. "Enough of this. That's very brave of ya, Barloc. Think about it while we finish the meeting. Ya don't have to, but it sounds like it would be the most effective way for ya to help."

Barloc nodded.

"Very well," Madam Constance said, her gaze lingering on Barloc. "From here, things change. We've lost a great many, but we can still make this work. We need to root out the spies. We can't risk traveling with them and have them damaging our plans, but I don't have a clue how."

Master Dharah spoke, "Leave them? We don't need all the extra weight. Maybe the king will believe we fell or disbanded, giving us a stronger chance to work the smaller pockets of the resistance."

Sir Vigor shook his head. "No. They just fought for freedom on our command. We can't leave them."

"Then what do you propose we do, Sir Vigor?" Madam Constance asked.

"I'm not sure, but that's not it. We need ranks to keep order. Harbor screwed it up by allowing the guards and slaves to separate. We could have kept the order and shifted the slaves to soldiers, but now we have Green Cloaks and free folk."

Master Dharah picked right up. "We can't go back and create these ranks. Not here. They will need to arrive into ranks... but not slaves. This needs to be a resistance now with proper ranks."

"That's it," Master Sapper said. "We'll travel in three groups." He counted the Green Cloaks, skipping past Barloc. "Two for each direction. When we arrive, we enlist ranks and we return to our structure at Drudgeburg, or something close."

Madam Constance nodded along. "It'll be hard. These locations aren't keeps like here but towns that have no or little security."

Barloc cleared his throat in order to clear the air. "You can't travel in all those groups. If you're attacked by Howlers," he cast a look to Katiph, "then you'll be too small and unorganized. You will need the numbers."

Katiph scoffed. "There are more dangers than Howlers out there, boy. King's men, other mercenaries and criminals, and vigilantes looking for the king's pardon, but he's right. You shouldn't travel like that, though there's no other way. You need to do your three groups and you need to move fast. Once there, then enlist people. Use the towns' defenses already in place. There must be something or they wouldn't still be towns. Peacekeepers. Anything. If you're even going to towns." He rolled his eyes. "Not that you would tell someone like me just what your plans were. Whatever the case, we need to move. You're already making a mistake traveling in the dark."

"We have no other choice." Madam Constance spoke, deep in thought, her voice sounding as it came from far away. "That settles it. We're to assemble the groups and move out. Do we have any other matters?"

"Aye," Sapper said. "What about the dungeons? We've still got Variegate down there."

Madam Constance's features fell grave. "You know what to do. Can you handle it?"

Master Sapper nodded. "It will be done."

"Anything else?"

No one spoke until Katiph pointed his dagger at Barloc. "You comin' or not?"

Barloc nodded slowly. "Yeah, I'll come. I'll do it."

Madam Constance stood. "Gentleman. From this this day on, it's no longer about the individual. We are fighting for the greater good of our people. This is no longer just your story, but we are one of many."

Everyone stood, including Barloc.

They began exiting the room, falling into conversation among one another.

Madam Constance stepped in Barloc's path. "Stay. I'd like to speak to you."

Chapter 30 – No Room for Love

Madam Constance sat on the edge of the table, the fire crackling behind her. "Why are you going?"

"It's not that serious. I'm only a slave when it comes down to it. If I can help stop this from happening to others, then it's worth it."

"I don't like the idea. There's something about you that breathes life into me."

Barloc stared at her, unsure of what to say, so he remained silent.

"It seems so silly to think about it with all this going on. What we just went through, and what we're about to do, but part of me wants you to come with me. Maybe we could see if anything came from this."

Barloc remained silent a moment longer. "I feel the same way. My mind continued to travel back to you while I was out there, scared for what had become of you, but when I saw you enter the room with Lord Harbor, I... my heart could have lived in my throat."

She pulled him into a tight embrace, their lips locking in a kiss.

Barloc's hands grasped the back of her cloak as they fumbled through their kiss. Warmth traveled into his belly, and when it seemed he couldn't take it anymore, he pulled away.

A tear spilled down her cheek. "Sapper's right, though. This world doesn't have room for love."

This abrupt change drained the warmth, replacing it with anxiety. "I can help you."

She shook her head. "I, too, thought of you while you were missing. I searched for you only to find that you'd gone with Ronin, and I feared that you would be a corpse burning in that pile. I was already distracted with these childish possibilities of love." She shook her head. "You need to go."

Barloc nodded. "You think I'll ever see you again?"

"Who knows. With my luck? No. You'll be dead the first night out there." She pulled him into another hug. "We need to leave."

He followed her to the door. She reached down to pull it open but stopped, turning back to him. "Don't waste your life. Play smart. It's a game that no one's ever really played before. Earlier I said that we are all now many parts of one story, that it's no longer about the individual."

He nodded.

"I hope to read your part one day."

Barloc smiled. "And yours for me."

She pulled the door open and they stepped into the daylight.

Chapter 31 – One of Many

Barloc stood beside Katiph, hidden in the tree line, not far from where Riedell and the two Howlers had their final showdown. A large mass of people gathered before the gates of Drudgeburg. A series of Green Cloaks sat mounted atop their horses, separating the groups, Madam Constance's long hair visible even from the distance.

Sir Vigor could have been a building on a horse, the way he towered over the others, and before long they split and rode away from the castle in their separate groups.

Katiph crossed his arms. "This is your last chance to turn back."

Barloc watched Madam Constance ride toward the crest of the hill where the king's men had barreled over not long ago, blood still wet in the dirt. She didn't know he watched her, but she looked around, even in the direction where he stood, as if searching for someone. Maybe him.

The desire to run out of the trees and slip into the group became overwhelming, but he remained stoic. *One of many,* he thought. At Drudgeburg, it was down to Lord Harbor's instructions, but now, separated through the world, with spies hidden across the kingdom, all working for the same goal of freedom, he truly became one of many. *The man standing beside me being one of the most interesting of them all.*

Katiph turned to him. "When we meet with the other Howlers, you're a slave. You're not a friend. I'm going to treat you horribly. I'll hit you and whip you and cut you and murder in front of you, and there's nothing you can do. I mean it. This is your last chance."

Barloc glared into his dark eyes. "No, I'm ready." He lifted his hands, the weight of the chains hanging from his wrists causing the sewn-up arrow hole in his chest to burn.

Katiph nodded. "Very well. Off we go."

Barloc followed, trying his best to keep the manacles around his ankles from tangling with the brush below. He stopped and glanced back at the castle one last time. He closed his eyes and took a deep breath, remembering each day he had at Drudgeburg, wondering if he would ever see his new friends again.

When he exhaled, he turned and followed Katiph into the woods and past where Riedell's corpse had sat propped against the tree.

"Move it, slave!" Katiph yelled over his shoulder.

The change in character verified how real everything had become.

Barloc walked behind him, his pace quickening, and in a fleeting thought, Drudgeburg and all its people slipped into the section of his mind where the memories of his family and youth lived. A section for dreams. *One of many.*

---THE END---

About the Author

Joseph Wade Zulauf III wears many hats while walking the streets of the writing world. He started with a focus on the short story, first winning the Marjorie Flack Award for Fiction. Then he became one of the editors for Daylight Dims, a horror anthology. He now works as an author at Evolved Publishing, where he created the chapter book series *The Balderdash Saga*.

For more information, or to connect with the author through social media, please visit his website at:

www.JWZulauf.com

Acknowledgements

Writing this book was a much different experience than when I wrote *The Balderdash Saga*. It's for an older audience, and the content is grittier and much more comprehensive. The characters are more complex, and... well, it's longer. It feels very rewarding to have arrived at this point, and now I must thank those who helped me get here. My family who is constantly on the receiving end of my divided time and attention. Evolved Publishing for all the constant assistance they offer, specifically Dave Lane (aka Lane Diamond). He has done so much for me over these past few years. My friend, Jason Adams, who helped me in every way he possibly could, and Deb Hartwell, my editor, who helped me shape this world, one stone at a time. Luke Spooner, my illustrator, who always breathes life into my work. You all helped bring a story to life that has been haunting my mind for years now.

What's Next?

J.W. Zulauf is currently hard at work on the second book in this *Kingdom in Chains* series of young adult fantasies. Please stay tuned to his website for updates and details: www.JWZulauf.com

More from J.W. Zulauf

THE BALDERDASH SAGA
Book 1: *The Underground Princess*
Book 2: *The Prince's Plight*
Book 3: *The Shaman's Salvation*

This series of lower grade fairytale adventures is perfect for kids 7-11 years old. Meet many friends, and a couple foes, on your visit to Balderdash. Whether you're searching for true love with Princess Scarlet, or fighting for honor with Roland, the pirate knight, there is something for every reader within these coffin tales.

~~~

Not all fairytales are about beautiful princesses and dashing princes. Some are about the corpses living below our very feet....

~~~

The Underground Princess:

Princess Scarlet is on a journey to find true love, but a malevolent force, Maleer, is in the process of dethroning her father, King Hurlock. Maleer intends to rule the underground kingdom of Balderdash, build an army, and break through the ground to invade the land of the living.

As Scarlet runs out of options to save those that matter most, she is forced to make decisions that will determine the fate of her entire kingdom.

~~~
~~~

The Prince's Plight:

After defeating Maleer, the people of Balderdash work to expand their kingdom by exploring the vast caverns in search of more graveyards. Although Hurlock and the shaman have adopted Kaylan, few in Balderdash trust the prince. Scarlet barely speaks to him, and Screech is the only one to show him affection. To escape the tension, Kaylan unofficially joins the Spelunkers, a group created by the shaman tasked with mapping the caverns.

On one of his excursions, Kaylan is startled to hear a woman's scream. After locating the source, he watches from the shadows as two men chase her down, swords drawn.

Kaylan realizes with horror that humans stand merely an hour's walk from Balderdash. He faces a critical decision. Should he run away to warn the rest of the underground kingdom about the human invaders in the caverns, or risk losing his life—and compromising the location of Balderdash—to save the woman?

~~~

The Shaman's Salvation:

The very existence of Balderdash is hanging by a thread. The kingdom is under attack by vicious creatures called Mana Beasts, and someone is after the shaman.

Will Balderdash fall because of the shaman's past actions? Will she lose it all, or will she sacrifice herself to save her people?
~~~

More from Evolved Publishing

CHILDREN'S PICTURE BOOKS

THE BIRD BRAIN BOOKS by Emlyn Chand:

Courtney Saves Christmas
Davey the Detective
Honey the Hero
Izzy the Inventor
Larry the Lonely
Polly Wants to be a Pirate
Poppy the Proud
Ricky the Runt
Ruby to the Rescue
Sammy Steals the Show
Tommy Goes Trick-or-Treating
Vicky Finds a Valentine

Silent Words by Chantal Fournier
Bella and the Blue Genie by Jonathan Gould
Maddie's Monsters by Jonathan Gould
Thomas and the Tiger-Turtle by Jonathan Gould

EMLYN AND THE GREMLIN by Steff F. Kneff:

Emlyn and the Gremlin
Emlyn and the Gremlin and the Barbeque Disaster
Emlyn and the Gremlin and the Mean Old Cat
Emlyn and the Gremlin and the Seaside Mishap
Emlyn and the Gremlin and the Teenage Babysitter

I'd Rather Be Riding My Bike by Eric Pinder

SULLY P. SNOOFERPOOT'S AMAZING INVENTIONS by Aaron Shaw Ph.D.:

Sully P. Snooferpoot's Amazing New Christmas Pot
Sully P. Snooferpoot's Amazing New Dayswitcher
Sully P. Snooferpoot's Amazing New Forcefield
Sully P. Snooferpoot's Amazing New Key
Sully P. Snooferpoot's Amazing New Shadow

Ninja and Bunny's Great Adventure by Kara S. Tyler

VALENTINA'S SPOOKY ADVENTURES
by Majanka Verstraete:

Valentina and the Haunted Mansion
Valentina and the Masked Mummy
Valentina and the Whackadoodle Witch

HISTORICAL FICTION

Fresh News Straight from Heaven by Gregg Sapp
SHINING LIGHT'S SAGA by Ruby Standing Deer:

Circles (Book 1)
Spirals (Book 2)
Stones (Book 3)

LOWER GRADE (Chapter Books)

THE PET SHOP SOCIETY by Emlyn Chand:

Maddie and the Purrfect Crime
Mike and the Dog-Gone Labradoodle
Tyler and the Blabber-Mouth Birds

TALES FROM UPON A. TIME by Falcon Storm:

Natalie the Not-So-Nasty
The Persnickety Princess

WEIRDVILLE by Majanka Verstraete:

Drowning in Fear
Fright Train
Grave Error
House of Horrors
The Clumsy Magician
The Doll Maker

THE BALDERDASH SAGA by J.W. Zulauf:

The Underground Princess (Book 1)
The Prince's Plight (Book 2)
The Shaman's Salvation (Book 3)

THE BALDERDASH SAGA SHORTS by J.W.Zulauf:

Hurlock the Warrior King
Roland the Pirate Knight
Scarlet the Kindhearted Princess

MEMOIR

And Then It Rained by Megan Morrison
Girl Enlightened by Megan Morrison

MIDDLE GRADE

FRENDYL KRUNE by Kira McFadden:
Frendyl Krune and the Blood of the Sun (Book 1)
Frendyl Krune and the Snake Across the Sea (Book 2)
Frendyl Krune and the Stone Princess (Book 3)
Frendyl Krune and the Nightmare in the North (Book 4)
NOAH ZARC by D. Robert Pease:
Mammoth Trouble (Book 1)
Cataclysm (Book 2)
Declaration (Book 3)
Omnibus (Special 3-in-1 Edition)

SCIENCE FICTION

THE PANHELION CHRONICLES by Marlin Desault:
Shroud of Eden (Book 1)
The Vanquished of Eden (Book 2)
THE CONSPIRATOR'S ODYSSEY by A.K. Kuykendall:
Imerium Heirs (Book 1)
THE SEEKERS by David Litwack:
The Children of Darkness (Book 1)
The Stuff of Stars (Book 2)
The Light of Reason (Book 3)
JAKKATTU by P.K. Tyler:
The Jakkattu Vector (Book 1)
The Jakkattu Insurrection (Book 2)
The Jakkattu Exodus (Book 3)
Two Moons of Sera by P.K. Tyler

SHORT STORY ANTHOLOGIES

FROM THE EDITORS AT EVOLVED PUBLISHING:
Evolution: Vol. 1 (A Short Story Collection)
Evolution: Vol. 2 (A Short Story Collection)

YOUNG ADULT

CHOSEN by Jeff Altabef & Erynn Altabef:

Wind Catcher (Book 1)
Brink of Dawn (Book 2)
Scorched Souls (Book 3)

RED DEATH by Jeff Altabef:

Red Death (Book 1)
The Ghost King (Book 2)

THE KIN CHRONICLES by Michael Dadich:

The Silver Sphere (Book 1)
The Sinister Kin (Book 2)

UPLOADED by James W. Hughes:

Uploaded (Book 1)
Viral (Book 2)

DIRT AND STARS by Kevin Killiany:

Down to Dirt (Book 1)
Living on Dirt (Book 2)

STORMBOURNE CHRONICLES by Karissa Laurel:

Heir of Thunder (Book 1)
Quest of Thunder (Book 2)

THE DARLA DECKER DIARIES by Jessica McHugh:

Darla Decker Hates to Wait (Book 1)
Darla Decker Takes the Cake (Book 2)
Darla Decker Shakes the State (Book 3)
Darla Decker Plays It Straight (Book 4)
Darla Decker Breaks the Case (Book 5)

JOEY COLA by D. Robert Pease:

Dream Warriors (Book 1)
Cleopatra Rising (Book 2)
Third Reality (Book 3)

Anyone? by Angela Scott

THE ZOMBIE WEST TRILOGY by Angela Scott:

Wanted: Dead or Undead (Book 1)
Survivor Roundup (Book 2)
Dead Plains (Book 3)
The Zombie West Trilogy – Special Omnibus Edition

WHITEWASHED by Adelaide Thorne:

The Trace (Book 1)
The Integer (Book 2)

CPSIA information can be obtained
at www.ICGtesting.com
Printed in the USA
FFOW02n1501140617
36712FF